"Let's go, move it!" Shaw shouted. *"Bannon, catch up with the others!"*

Bannon felt weird to be taking orders from Shaw, because yesterday Shaw had been taking orders from him. Bannon raised himself up on his hands and knees and pushed himself forward. The sound of the machine guns ahead became louder and seemed to be dead ahead. The First Squad made its way up the hill. Bannon was right in the middle, not far from Frankie La Barbara, who looked ridiculous with the big bandage on his nose. Farther down the hill they could hear Butsko shouting. Bannon pushed some branches away from his face and saw smoke and lightning up ahead, blowing against branches and leaves.

"There they are!" Bannon shouted.

Down and Dirty

by
John Mackie

A JOVE BOOK

Excepting basic historical events, places, and personages, this series of books is fictional, and anything that appears otherwise is coincidental and unintentional.

The principal characters are imaginary, although they might remind veterans of specific men whom they knew. The Twenty-third Infantry Regiment, in which the characters serve, is used fictitiously—it doesn't represent the real historical Twenty-third Infantry, which has distinguished itself in so many battles from the Civil War to Vietnam—but it could have been any American line regiment that fought and bled during World War II.

These novels are dedicated to the men who were there. May their deeds and gallantry never be forgotten.

DOWN AND DIRTY

A Jove Book / published by arrangement with
the author

PRINTING HISTORY
Jove edition / March 1984

ISBN: 0-515-07355-5

Jove books are published by The Berkley Publishing Group,
200 Madison Avenue, New York, N.Y. 10016. The words
"A JOVE BOOK" and the "J" with sunburst are trademarks
belonging to Jove Publications, Inc.

PRINTED IN THE UNITED STATES OF AMERICA

ONE . . .

"Japs!"

Bannon opened his eyes and sprang up inside the pup tent. He heard thrashing and flailing in the jungle. Guards shouted and shots were fired.

"Banzai!"

Bannon reached for his machete and pulled it from its sheath. Next to him Corporal Gomez cursed in Spanish and grabbed his M 1 rifle. Wearing only khaki shorts, Bannon pulled on his combat boots and tied the laces around quickly, then dived out of the tent. On his hands and knees he looked ahead and saw fighting in the moonlight at the edge of the clearing about fifty yards away.

"Let's go!" shouted Sergeant Butsko, running forward, holding his rifle and bayonet high in his right hand. *"Up and at 'em!"*

Bannon leaped to his feet, swung the machete over his head, and screamed like a wild animal as he followed Butsko. The night was hot and sticky, and birds shrieked high in the trees. All across the clearing, GIs burst out of their tents half naked, carrying rifles, shovels, and anything else they could lay their hands on.

"Banzai!" yelled a Jap coming out of the jungle.

"Get the bastards!" replied Butsko.

Bannon saw Japs fighting GIs at the edge of the clearing, overwhelming them and charging forward. A GI fell down ten yards in front of Bannon, and a Japanese soldier kicked the fallen GI in the face, jumped over him, and headed for Bannon.

Bannon gritted his teeth, planted his right foot firmly behind him, and raised the machete.

"Banzai!" hollered the Jap, holding his rifle and bloody bayonet in both hands, rushing toward Bannon.

The Jap was shorter than Bannon and much thinner, with a short beard covering his face and a soft cap on his head. The Jap shouted something and pushed his rifle and bayonet toward Bannon's heart. Bannon swung the machete down with all his strength, striking the Jap's left arm and chopping it in half. The Jap bellowed horribly, staring in disbelief at the stump of his arm, which gushed blood like a hose, and Bannon raised his machete again, bringing it down diagonally, catching the Jap on the neck and cutting through to his rib cage.

The force of the blow sent the Jap to his knees, and blood spattered Bannon's body and light-brown hair. He tugged the handle of the machete and pulled it loose as the Jap sagged to the side. Two Japanese soldiers with rifles and bayonets ran toward Bannon, who stood his ground, licking his lips nervously and holding the machete poised in the air.

The two Jap soldiers bumped shoulders as they rushed Bannon, and the one on the left lunged first with his rifle and bayonet. Bannon batted the bayonet out of the way with his left forearm and swung down with the machete, connecting with the top of the Jap's head, the blade of the machete sinking three inches into the Jap's brain. The other Jap thrust his rifle and bayonet forward, and Bannon couldn't work the machete loose from the first Jap's skull. He let go of the machete, pounced on the rifle of the attacking Jap, and kicked him in the balls.

The Jap screamed and stepped backward, locking his knees together and bending over in pain. Bannon grabbed his machete, pulled it out of the first Jap's skull, drew the machete back, and whacked the second Jap in the face, smashing apart his jawbone and nearly taking off the top of his head. The Jap fell in front of Bannon, and Bannon stepped over his dead body.

Soldiers fought all around him, and it was hard to tell who was friend and who was foe. They stabbed, slashed, and bashed each other, grunting and cursing, killing and moving on. Japanese officers shouted encouragement to their men, and Sergeant Butsko was in the thick of the fight, swinging his rifle and bayonet.

"Kill the fuckers!" he hollered.

Bannon saw Private Billie Jones struggling to kill a Jap facing him. Suddenly another Jap charged Billie Jones's back. Bannon leaped forward and raised the machete in the air. The Jap was ready to stab Billie Jones in the back, and Bannon brought the thick machete down on the Jap's left shoulder, slicing through to the bone. The Jap shrieked and turned to face Bannon, who was already on his backhand swing. His machete blade hit the Jap in the mouth and split apart bone and flesh until it came to a stop at the back of the Jap's head.

Bannon pulled the machete loose and spun around. He saw a Jap aiming a pistol at him. The Jap was too far away to hit with a swing of the machete, so Bannon threw the machete at the Jap to upset his aim and then dived after it.

The pistol fired, and Bannon heard the bullet whiz past his ear. He collided with the Jap and grabbed his wrist with both hands, elbowing the Jap in the chops. The Jap tried to knee Bannon in the balls, but Bannon turned his hip and caught the blow on his outer thigh. The Jap hit Bannon in the mouth with his free fist, but Bannon was tough and could take a good punch. Still holding the Jap's wrist in both his hands, he pivoted, twisted the Jap's arm, raised it in the air, and brought it down hard. The Jap's elbow landed on Bannon's shoulder and was bent out of shape. Bannon slugged him in the throat and the Jap fell on his ass, coughing, trying to get his breath.

Bannon picked up his machete and the Jap's pistol. He looked down at the Jap and swung the machete, cracking open the Jap's skull. He pulled the machete loose, looked up, and saw a whole wall of Japs moving toward him. Dropping to one knee, he aimed the pistol and fired, hitting a Jap in the chest. He moved the pistol a few inches to the right and fired again; another Jap went crashing to the ground. He took aim at the next Jap and shot him in the face. By then the fourth Jap was on top of him. Bannon fired when the Jap was less than five feet away and hit him in the gut. The Jap tripped and collapsed onto Bannon, the blood from his stomach oozing out onto Bannon's body.

Bannon pushed him off and stood up, the pistol in his right hand, the machete in his left. At that moment the battle seemed to converge on him, Japs and GIs struggling wildly, bumping against him, elbowing him, and one Jap broke through in front of Bannon, screaming and hooting, thrusting his rifle and bayonet toward Bannon, who held the pistol steady and pulled the trigger. The pistol bucked in his hand as it fired, and a dot the size of a marble appeared on the front of the Jap's khaki shirt. The Jap's eyes rolled up into his head and Bannon deflected the path of the bayonet with his machete. The Jap dropped to his feet; behind him came a Japanese officer carrying a samurai sword.

"Banzai!" shouted the officer.

"Fuck you," replied Bannon, and pulled the trigger.

Click!

The pistol was empty. Bannon threw it at the officer and it bounced off his head, but the officer kept coming, holding the handle of the samurai sword with both hands, the blade pointing straight up in the air. Bannon shifted the machete to his right hand and got ready. The Japanese officer raised his sword higher, his eyes glittering with murderous hate.

"Banzai!" he screamed.

He brought the sword down with all his strength, and Bannon raised his machete to block the blow. The sword struck the machete in midair and broke the machete's blade in half. Sparks flew into the air and Bannon lunged forward to avoid the downswing of the samurai sword. He bumped into the Japanese officer and their faces were only inches apart. He could see the Japanese officer's slanted eyes and sallow cheeks and smell his sour breath.

The Japanese officer stepped backward to get some sword-swinging room, and Bannon shot his hands into the air, grabbing the Jap's wrist with both hands, trying to kick the Jap in the balls. The Jap snaked a leg behind Bannon and pushed. Bannon tripped over the Jap's leg and fell to the ground, but

4

he held on to the Jap's wrist with both hands and dragged him down.

The Japanese officer fell on top of Bannon and karate-chopped him on the head with his free hand. Bannon saw stars for a moment, and the officer karate-chopped him again, but this time Bannon let go of the samurai sword and blocked the blow with his arm, punched the Jap in the mouth, and then grabbed his sword arm again and heaved, bucking like a bronco.

The Japanese officer was thrown off Bannon and landed on his back. Bannon bounded up and dropped with both his knees on the Jap's chest, knocking the wind out of him. He punched the Jap in the mouth, saw a rock lying on the ground a few inches from the Jap's head, picked it up, and slammed it against the Jap's forehead. The Japanese officer moaned and went limp.

Bannon snatched the samurai sword out of his hand, raised it in the air, and swung downward, lopping off the Jap's head. Fascinated, he watched the head roll away like a coconut. All around him, men still were locked in vicious hand-to-hand combat. A Japanese soldier ran toward him, carrying a rifle and bayonet. Bannon raised the samurai sword with both hands and brought it down with all his strength.

The sword sliced through the Jap's head, neck, and chest as if he were made of warm butter. Blood flew in all directions, and Bannon pulled out the sword as the Japanese soldier collapsed onto the ground. Bannon jumped over him, saw another Japanese soldier, swung the samurai sword from the side, and hit him in the ribs, the sword smashing through the Jap's chest and slicing open his lungs. The Jap toppled over and Bannon pulled out the sword, turned, and saw two more Japs coming toward him. He took a step backward, raised the sword high over his head, and slashed to the side. The blade chopped clean through the head of the Jap on Bannon's right and continued its path, burying itself in the shoulder of the next Jap, but by then it had lost much of its momentum.

Bannon pulled the sword loose as the Jap staggered beneath the sudden pain. Blood poured out of the Jap's shoulder, but he gamely tried to hold his rifle and bayonet steady so he could run Bannon through. He lunged and Bannon swung the sword, striking the Japanese soldier's rifle, sending sparks flying into

5

the air and knocking the rifle out of his hands.

The Jap stood defenseless, his shoulder bleeding, as Bannon raised the sword for the deathblow. The Jap turned and ran away, and Bannon went after him, swinging the sword down. He struck the Jap halfway between his left shoulder and his neck, and the sharp blade cracked apart the Jap's collarbone and ribs, ripping into his heart.

Blood gushed out and Bannon withdrew his sword, looking around at the grim hand-to-hand fighting everywhere.

"Hai!"

Bannon turned in the direction of the voice and saw a Japanese officer with a samurai sword poised high over his head, running toward him. A wave of fear swept over Bannon, because he knew the Japanese officer probably was an expert swordsman, whereas he himself was just fucking around.

"Yaaahhhhhh!" shouted the Japanese officer as he swung his sword down at Bannon's head.

Bannon raised his sword to block the blow, and the blades clanged together noisily, making a shower of sparks. The Jap pulled his sword back and swung it sideways at Bannon's ribs, but Bannon darted backward and the blade whistled through the air in front of him. The Jap jumped forward and raised his sword for another blow, and Bannon jumped backward again, looking toward the ground and hoping he'd see a pistol so he could shoot the Jap.

The Jap advanced again and swung his sword down diagonally. Bannon raised his sword and parried the blow, then cut down at the Jap's head, but the Jap was lightfooted and bounded out of the way.

Both men looked at each other, raising their swords high again. The Japanese officer appeared confident and knowledgeable about his swordsmanship, whereas Bannon was getting scared, but not scared enough to turn and run away.

The Jap swung and Bannon drew back, his sword still poised in the air. The Jap's blade swooshed within a few inches in front of Bannon's nose, and at that moment Bannon brought his own sword down. The Jap saw it coming, but there was nothing he could do. He was still in the middle of his own swing, off balance, his head unprotected.

Bannon's blade struck on the top of the Jap's skull and hacked it in two. Blood and brains flew everywhere, and Bannon felt some land on his face. He pulled the sword loose, slipped on a patch of mud, and fell to the ground. Rolling over, he looked up and saw a Japanese soldier in front of him, aiming a pistol down at him. Bannon felt naked and helpless and thought he'd come to the end of his road. He raised the sword in a feeble gesture to protect himself.

Blam!

The sword exploded in front of Bannon, and a bit of metal bore into his cheek. His sword hand stung from the shock, but otherwise he was okay. The Jap aimed the pistol again and Bannon rolled to the side, trying to become a difficult target.

Blam!

Bannon watched in astonishment as the Jap's knees buckled. Somebody had shot him! The Jap collapsed onto the ground and Bannon looked at the shattered samurai sword in his hand. It wasn't good for anything anymore, so he tossed it away and picked up a Ka-bar knife lying a few inches from the hand of a dead GI nearby. Then he jumped to his feet and saw a Japanese soldier with rifle and bayonet charging toward him.

"*Banzai!*" shouted the Jap soldier.

"*Banzai your ass!*"

The Jap soldier lunged with his rifle and bayonet, and Bannon went into motion. He whacked the bayonet to the side with a forearm block and buried the Ka-bar knife to the hilt in the Jap's belly. The Jap said "Ugh" and his eyes closed. Blood burbled out of his lips and he fell to the ground.

Bannon pulled his Ka-bar knife from the Jap's belly and looked around. The fight seemed to be thinning out, and bodies lay everywhere on the ground. Men still grappled and heaved against each other in the moonlight, but not as many as before. Out of the darkness and mist appeared a Japanese soldier carrying a rifle and bayonet. He wasn't running and his mouth hung open as he gulped down air. He was nearly as tall as Bannon, who was a six-footer, and he was as gaunt as a scarecrow.

He spotted Bannon and moved toward him slowly and deliberately. Bannon held the Ka-bar knife by its point, reared back his arm, and threw it. The knife flew through the air, heading straight for the Jap, who couldn't duck in time. The knife struck him on the chest, but it landed handle first and bounced off, falling to the ground.

The Jap grinned and advanced toward Bannon, who looked to the ground frantically to find something to fight with. Lying near his feet was an M 1 rifle without a bayonet on its end. Bannon scooped it up, aimed it from his waist, made sure the safety was off, worked the bolt, and pulled the trigger.

Click!

The M 1 was empty and Bannon's heart sank. The Jap soldier heard the click and advanced toward Bannon one cautious step at a time. All Bannon could do was turn the rifle around and grip the barrel so he could swing it like a baseball bat.

"C'mon, you slant-eyed cocksucker," Bannon said.

The Japanese soldier drew closer, holding his rifle and bayonet in both hands, and stopped in front of Bannon. Their eyes met and Bannon knew that one of them would be dead within the next minute.

"*Yoi!*" shouted the Jap, and thrust his rifle and bayonet toward Bannon's heart.

Bannon dodged to the side and the bayonet streaked past him. He swung the M 1 and the butt smashed into the Jap's head. Blood squirted out of the Jap's ears, nose, and mouth, and he was thrown violently toward the ground.

An order was shouted in Japanese, and Bannon looked up to see Japs turning back toward the jungle. They retreated, leaving behind heaps of bodies in the moonlight, twisted into grotesque postures of death. The GIs still alive dropped down on their stomachs and fired their rifles at the retreating Japs, shooting them in their backs, but the jungle was thick and soon swallowed up the Japs.

Bannon was breathing like a racehorse, and his muscles were strained by fatigue. He sat down heavily on the ground next to a dead American soldier wearing a complete jungle uniform and helmet; he must have been one of the guards who'd gotten it first. The soldier lay on his back and had a big gaping bayonet hole in his chest. Bannon pulled a bandolier of ammunition off the dead soldier's shoulder, took out a clip, and loaded it into his M 1 in case the Japs came back. Then he patted the soldier's shirt, found a pack of Luckies, and placed one of them between his lips. He probed through the dead soldier's pockets and found a Ronson lighter, which he pulled out, lighting the cigarette. He inhaled and felt the smoke stimulate his lungs and enliven his mind.

The jungle was carpeted with the bodies of the dead and wounded. Medics arrived, applying bandages and jamming morphine Syrettes into arms. Bannon was bleeding from a cut on his cheek and some nicks on his arms and he was splattered with Japanese blood. Insects buzzed around him and he thought he'd better go back to his tent and put some clothes on before they ate him up alive.

As he was summoning the strength to stand, he saw a huge hulk appear before him out of the darkness. "You okay?" asked Sergeant Butsko.

"Yeah."

"I want a report on the number of casualties in your squad."

"Right."

Butsko walked away. Bannon stood up, puffed his cigarette, and headed for his tent, glancing at the ground so he wouldn't step on anybody.

TWO . . .

At dawn Mayor General Alexander McCarrell Patch rolled out of bed. He was fifty-three years old, a West Point graduate, and commander of all American troops on Guadalcanal. He burped, lit a cigarette, and reached for his pants.

"Lieutenant Todd!" he shouted.

"Yes, sir!"

The door opened and young Lieutenant Todd entered, throwing a snappy salute.

"Good morning, sir!"

"Anything happen last night?" General Patch asked as he pulled on his pants.

"One of the battalions in the twenty-third Infantry Regiment was attacked by Japs, but it wasn't very serious. No Japs broke through. We didn't think the situation warranted waking you up."

"Bring me some black coffee, Todd."

"Yes, sir."

Lieutenant Todd dashed out of the room, and General Patch sat on the edge of his bed and pulled on his combat boots. It was January of 1943 and the Japs on Guadalcanal were licked, but they didn't seem to know it. The American soldiers and Marines had them on the retreat and were pressing them hard, but the Japs were fighting back savagely and making General

11

Patch's troops pay heavily for every foot of ground they got.

General Patch buttoned up his shirt and left his bedroom. He walked down the hall and entered his office, sitting behind the desk and looking at the map spread out on it. He located the Twenty-third Infantry Regiment, which had been attacked the night before. It was in the hilly jungle country west of the Matanikau River, not far from Ironbottom Sound.

There was a knock on his door.

"Come in!"

Lieutenant Todd entered, carrying a pot of coffee and a cup. "Shall I pour for you, sir?"

"Go ahead," said General Patch, still looking at the map.

Todd poured the coffee and placed the mug in front of General Patch. "The usual for breakfast, sir?"

"I think I'd like my eggs scrambled hard today."

"Yes, sir."

Lieutenant Todd turned and marched out of the office. General Patch sipped the hot coffee, and the steaming liquid cleared out his head. He looked at the position of his front line; it was several miles west of Henderson Field, the prime military objective on Guadalcanal. General Patch was afraid the Japs would land a large force on Lunga Point and retake Henderson Field before he could shift his troops back from the front lines west of the Matanikau. Henderson Field was being protected by only a token force of soldiers—the sick, lame, and lazy—while his first-class troops were in the field west of the Matanikau. Once again he wondered whether he should bring some of them back to protect Henderson Field—just in case—but if he did that, it would weaken his front line.

It was an agonizing problem, because if he guessed wrong it could mean death for many of his soldiers. He thought of how nice it must be to be a civilian, because if you guessed wrong you only inconvenienced yourself for a while, or maybe you would lose a lot of money, but what was money compared to the lives of young men?

General Patch lit a cigarette and smoked it while sipping his coffee. He was the commander on Guadalcanal and Tulagi and the buck stopped with him. He had to make the decision and he'd have to make it soon. After a while Lieutenant Todd brought him breakfast, and General Patch dined while continuing to consider the problem.

He finally decided that if the Japs tried to invade Henderson Field, their troopships almost would certainly be spotted by the American Navy and Air Corps long before they came close to Guadalcanal. That would give him plenty of warning, or so he hoped. He should be able to return his troops to Henderson Field in time to protect it if all went well.

But what if all didn't go well? What if Japanese troopships sneaked past the US Navy and Air Corps? What then?

The recon platoon was still traveling with George Company in the Second Battalion of the Twenty-third Infantry Regiment. The dead and wounded from the tussle of the previous night had been cleared away, and the men were breakfasting on K rations, consisting mainly of crackers and canned paste made from either meat or cheese. Everybody hated K rations even worse than C rations, but there was nothing else to eat.

Bannon, wearing a bandage on his cheek, chewed on a cracker and listened to Frankie La Barbara talk about the nurses on New Caledonia, where he had been a patient for a few weeks.

"There was this nurse called Grimsby, who was a skinny, nervous bitch," Frankie said, "and I knew what she needed: about eight inches of hot pepperoni. So one night I waited in a doorway while she was making rounds, and when she passed by I just grabbed. You shoulda seen the look on her face. I thought she'd shit a brick. She says, 'Whatta you think you're doing here, Private La Barbara?' and I told her, 'I'm gonna fuck the jelly out of your beans, Nurse Grimsby, that's what I'm doing here.'" Frankie laughed, his big shoulders heaving up and down.

"And then what happened?" asked Hotshot Stevenson, who had been a pool shark in civilian life.

"I pulled her into one of them rooms where doctors examine you and fucked her on the table."

"Just like that?"

"Well, she put up a little bit of a struggle at first, just to make it look like she wasn't easy, because women don't like

13

you to think they're easy. But they're all easy. They're all dying to get fucked. You just have to know how to go about it."

"I don't know about that, Frankie," said Homer Gladley, the big farmboy from Nebraska. "Sounds to me like you damn near *raped* her."

"That's what some women like. You'd be surprised. I used to have a girlfriend back in New York City who liked me to pretend that I was raping her. I used to get pretty rough with her at times, but the rougher I treated her, the better she liked it. You never know what women are really like until you fuck them, Homer. It's always the sweetest, nicest girls who become the worst sex degenerates once you get them going."

"Well, maybe that's the way girls are back in New York," Homer said, "but they're not like that back where I'm from. You've got too used to being around women who are psycho cases, Frankie."

"Oh, yeah?" Frankie replied. "Well, I'll make a deal with you. After the war's over, I'll come and visit you and I'll fuck a few of those women you're talking about who you say are so sane and normal. I'll find out what they're really like."

"Shit, they wouldn't let you touch them, Frankie."

"What makes you think so?"

"Because they're nice girls. They wouldn't let a guy like you get near them."

"Oh, no? You give me fifty dollars for every one of those girls back there that I fuck?"

"You give me fifty for every one you don't?"

Frankie extended his hand. "It's a deal."

Bannon watched them shake hands. He lit a cigarette and wondered if both of them would get through the war alive to follow up on their bet. The recon platoon had lost a lot of men already. Butsko, the platoon sergeant, had nearly been killed and had spent a long time in the hospital. So had Craig Delane, the rich guy from New York City, and Jimmy O'Rourke, the former movie stuntman from Hollywood. Corporal Sam Longtree, a genuine Apache Indian from Arizona, had been the platoon's point man until three weeks before, when he'd been

14

shot down. He, too, had been sent back to the hospital, and nobody knew if he was alive or dead.

When's it gonna happen to me? Bannon thought. *I'm long overdue.*

Bannon hadn't been seriously wounded since he came to Guadalcanal back in October. Every day he expected to get it, but he'd only suffered minor nicks and cuts. His worst, from a Japanese bayonet that pierced his side, hadn't even been enough for a trip back to the battalion aid station. The medic just bandaged him up and sent him back to the front.

"All right, you fucking guys!" Butsko shouted. "Strike those tents and get ready to move out!"

Bannon looked up at Butsko, who was built massively, like a gorilla. His shirt was off and his torso was covered with wide slabs of muscle. The thick black hair on his chest covered the scar of the shrapnel wound that had nearly killed him.

The men from the recon platoon grumbled and headed for their tents, pulling down the poles and unbuttoning the shelter halves. They rolled up the shelter halves with their blankets and tied them to their packs, checked their weapons, and then sat around again, smoking cigarettes, waiting for the order to move out.

"Hurry up and wait," said Frankie La Barbara. "This fucking Army is a pain in the ass. I'm getting so sick of this fucking Army, I'm about ready to explode. I wish I was back in that hospital on New Caledonia. I remember there was this little brunette—forget her name now—she was from Michigan or one of them other fucking states out there—don't remember which one—and anyway, one night we went swimming naked together in the bay. Any of you guys ever fuck a girl in the water? It's terrific, the best way to fuck, and she had a cunt like a little machine. If only I could get another nice little wound, nothing too serious, just enough to get me back there with all them nurses."

Private Morris Shilansky, the former bank robber from Boston, was getting tired of hearing Frankie talk about screwing nurses. It made him nervous and horny, and he had enough to worry about without being nervous and horny.

"Hey, Frankie," he said, "were there any nurses back there you didn't fuck?"

"Yeah, there was some that I didn't fuck. Why?"

"I think you been fucking your fist too much."

"What's that supposed to mean?"

"I'm sick and tired of listening to your mouth. Give it a rest for a while, willya?"

Frankie laid his rifle against his pack and stood up, hooking his thumbs in his belt. "You want me to shut up, you make me shut up."

"Okay," said Shilansky, taking off his helmet and getting up off the ground.

Shilansky walked toward Frankie, who stood with his thumbs in his belt and a sneer on his face. Bannon knew he should stop them, since he was their squad leader, but he was curious to see what would happen. Shilansky and Frankie were evenly matched in height and weight; they were both big boys with broad shoulders and tapered waists. Both had dark hair and swarthy complexions, but Shilansky had the nose of an eagle and thick lips, whereas Frankie's lips were thinner and his nose straight and handsomely formed.

When Shilansky got close to Frankie, both men raised their hands. Shilansky didn't stop; he just kept walking, and when he was within punching range he threw a straight right at Frankie's head, but Frankie ducked underneath it and shot a left to Shilansky's midsection, which Shilansky blocked with his forearm.

Both men stepped back a few paces, glaring at each other, as the recon platoon crowded around in a big circle, shouting advice and encouragement. Shilansky lunged in, feinted toward Frankie's gut with his left fist, then raised it up and smacked Frankie on the cheek. Frankie took the punch well and ducked to avoid Shilansky's right fist rocketing toward his nose, then slugged Shilansky in the gut, but Shilansky's arm rose in the nick of time and blocked it. Frankie danced back, dodged to the left, dodged to the right, and charged, shooting a left cross at Shilansky's head. Shilansky raised his guard to block the punch, and Frankie drove his right fist into Shilansky's stomach.

16

Shilansky said "Oof" and doubled over, and Frankie hit him with an uppercut that landed on Shilansky's chin, straightening Shilansky out and sending him flying backward. Frankie rushed after him, throwing punches from all directions, but Shilansky blocked most of them, got his wits together, saw an opening, and threw in a left jab that rocked Frankie's head back. Frankie was more surprised than hurt and lowered his hands; Shilansky hit him with a long overhand right.

The punched crashed on Frankie's face and Frankie's lights went out. Frankie dropped to his knees, and Shilansky was tempted to kick his head off, but he didn't want to fight dirty in front of all the guys, so he held himself back and waited for Frankie to get up.

"C'mon, you bigmouth cocksucker!" Shilansky said. "On your feet!"

Frankie cleared the cobwebs out of his head and dived at Shilansky, tackling him around the waist and bringing him down. The two soldiers rolled over and around on the jungle floor, punching each other, trying to gouge out each other's eyes and kick each other in the balls, while the rest of the recon platoon watched avidly and Hotshot Stevenson took bets.

"What the fuck's going on here?"

Everybody turned around at the sound of Butsko's bull-like voice and saw their big burly platoon sergeant pushing soldiers out of the way as he broke through the ring around Shilansky and Frankie La Barbara. He looked down at the two of them grunting and struggling on the ground, snorted angrily, and grabbed Shilansky by the back of his collar, pulled him off Frankie, and sent him flying through the air.

"You guys wanna fight?" Butsko snarled. "Fight with me!"

He gripped Frankie's shirt, pulled him to his feet, and punched him in the nose. Bone and cartilage cracked underneath his knuckles, and blood spurted into the air. Frankie went reeling backward and collapsed onto the ground, blood pouring out of his nose.

Shilansky got to his feet, holding out the palms of his hands. "Now, Sarge," he said, "I got no beef with you. Let's not get carried away."

"I got a beef with you, you fucking scumbag," Butsko

17

replied, rearing back his big fist and hurling it forward.

Pow!

His fist connected with Shilansky's face, and Shilansky's brain bounced around inside his skull. Out cold, Shilansky dropped to the ground.

Butsko raised his fists and spun around, looking into the eyes of his men. "Anybody else feel like a fight?" he asked.

Nobody said anything.

"Now get this straight, you fuck-ups," Butsko said, prowling around the center of the circle like a beast in a cage. "I'm tired of all the fights in this platoon. Next time there's a fight, everybody's who's fighting'll have to fight me next, all at once or one at a time; it don't matter a fuck either way to me. Got it?"

There was terrified silence all around him.

"I said got it?"

The men muttered that they got it. Some nodded their heads.

"I can't hear you!"

"We got it, Sarge!"

"That's better." Butsko wiped his mouth with the back of his hand and looked at Frankie La Barbara, who had drawn himself to a sitting position on the ground, touching his nose gingerly with his fingers.

"I think it's broken," he said.

"You're lucky that's all that's broken," Butsko replied.

Shilansky spit out a few teeth and a big gob of blood. Butsko looked around and spotted Bannon. "I wanna talk to you right now."

"Hup, Sarge."

Butsko walked away from the group and Bannon followed him. They stopped twenty yards away and Butsko took out a Chesterfield cigarette, lighting it up with his trusty old Zippo.

"Why didn't you stop that fight?" Butsko asked.

Bannon shrugged. "I thought I might as well let them kick the shit out of each other, since that's what they wanted to do."

"You're their squad leader. You should've stopped it the way I did. Since you don't want to act like a squad leader, you ain't a squad leader no more. And I'm taking away your stripes,

18

too, as of right now. You're a private again. Now get the fuck away from me before I do to you what I did to them."

Bannon was stunned. He'd worked so hard to get those three stripes, and now Butsko was taking them away. "Hey, Sarge, you can't do that without a court-martial!"

Butsko brought his face close to Bannon's. "Who says I can't?"

Bannon took a step backward and said weakly, "I dunno."

"You're goddamn right. Send Shaw over here. He's gonna be the new squad leader."

"Hup, Sarge."

Bannon double-timed toward Shaw, who was a former professional heavyweight boxer, and Butsko puffed his cigarette. *If I don't get some discipline in this platoon pretty soon, I'll bust everybody down to private E-nothing,* he thought.

The First Squad sat around the thick of the jungle while Butsko was talking with Shaw. Private Joel Blum, the recon platoon medic, was examining Frankie's nose.

"I think it's broken," Blum said.

"I know that," Frankie replied, "but will it heal straight?"

"I don't know."

"Well, what're you gonna do about it?"

"I'll bandage it up."

"But what if it heals crooked?"

"What if it does?"

Frankie jumped to his feet. "*What if it does?* Are you kidding? I don't wanna walk around with a crooked nose like that fucking Butsko! I don't wanna be an ugly son of a bitch like everybody else. Now, fix my fucking nose right now!"

"I can't fix your nose. I'm not a surgeon."

"Then send me back."

"I don't have the authority to send you back. Ask Butsko to send you back."

"He won't send me back."

"So whataya want from me?"

Blum painted Frankie's nose with Merthiolate. Frankie looked at Bannon. "Hey, Tex, you're a sergeant. You send me back."

"I ain't a sergeant anymore," replied Bannon.

Everybody looked at him.

"What the fuck happened?" Frankie asked.

"Butsko busted your nose and he busted me back to private."

"What!"

Bannon didn't answer. He took out a cigarette and lit it up.

"That son of a bitch," Frankie said.

Shilansky ran his tongue over his shattered gums. "And he busted up my mouth too."

Nutsy Gafooley, the former hobo, nodded. "He's been on the warpath ever since he got back from the hospital."

"That's because he didn't get no pussy back at the hospital," Frankie said. "I used to see him there sitting on the lawn, reading field manuals. He's a psycho case. He'd better never get in front of me if there's any shooting going on because I'll put a hole in his fucking head."

Shilansky snorted. "The bullet'd probably bounce right off. He's got a thick head."

"Nobody's tougher than a bullet," Frankie said.

Bannon looked at him. "Knock that shit off. If you shoot Butsko, I'll shoot you."

"What're you sticking up for him for? He just took away your stripes."

"He knows what he's doing out here better than any of us."

Frankie thought for a few moments. "That's true. Ouch!"

"Sorry," said Blum, who was applying a bandage to Frankie's broken nose.

"Here comes Shaw," said the Reverend Billie Jones, who had been a jackleg preacher in Georgia before the war.

Shaw was a tall heavyweight tipping the scales at 210 pounds. He'd had forty-six professional fights in civilian life, winning thirty-seven of them, with twenty-eight knockouts. He'd been ranked sixteen by *Ring* magazine and was trying to get a fight with a top-ten contender when he'd been drafted.

"All right, you guys," he said, "I'm the new squad leader. There will be no more bullshit or fucking around in this squad. You make trouble for me and you'll wish you were dead. Any questions?"

Nobody said anything.

"Okay, let's saddle up and move out."

The men hoisted their packs to their backs and formed a column of twos. Bannon was about halfway back and he realized it was nice to be an ordinary dogface soldier again, with no responsibilities and no decisions to make. Let Shaw have the worries. He'd soon find out that being a squad leader was no bed of roses.

The First Squad joined the other squads in the platoon and Butsko marched them to company headquarters, where they were issued hand grenades and bandoliers of ammunition. Then they sat around and smoked cigarettes, waiting for the order to move out.

It came at nine o'clock, and the Twenty-third Infantry Regiment moved into the jungle. They were deployed in a series of long columns, and men with machetes were in front hacking through the thick foliage. Everyone was vigilant, because the Japs were famous for their sudden sneaky ambushes.

The recon platoon was in front of the Second Battalion, and Corporal Gomez, the former pachuco from Los Angeles, was the point man in the recon platoon, thirty yards in front of the others, his narrow eyes darting around, searching for Japs, while his ears listened for Japanese footsteps and the rustle of underbrush.

Monkeys chattered high in the trees and birds screeched. Land crabs crawled along the jungle floor, along with wild pigs and crocodiles. The sun rose in the sky and Gomez perspired profusely, plastering his shirt to his skin. He became thirsty, took a swallow of water from his canteen, and kept going. He felt good being the point man for the platoon. For the first time in his life he was doing something important. Everybody was relying on him, and he didn't want to let anybody down. If he were back with the others, he'd let his mind wander and probably think of pretty Mexican senoritas with golden earrings and wide flowing skirts, but he disciplined his mind and made himself concentrate on the jungle, the sounds and sights, and the telltale movement that would indicate the presence of Japs.

The terrain consisted of thick jungle, scattered hills, and fields of kunai grass. After two hours of tough going, the battalion lost its cohesion as units swung to their left or right, trying to work around obstacles or take advantage of trails that suddenly presented themselves.

The advance became a series of small units moving in a westerly direction through the jungle, staying in touch through walkie-talkies. The sun became hotter and insects of every description buzzed around the men, biting them and raising huge welts on their skin. Shortly before noon Gomez came to a slight rise that indicated the beginning of a hill. He didn't know whether to go up it or around it, so he sat near the trunk of a tree and waited for the others to catch up.

A few minutes later the First Squad appeared through the jungle, and Gomez stood. Shaw, wearing his fatigue shirt unbuttoned to his navel and his sleeves torn off, walked toward Gomez.

"What you stop for?"

"Should we go up this hill or around it?"

Shaw thought for a few moments. "I don't know. We'd better wait for Butsko."

Shaw told the men to take a break. They collapsed onto the ground, sucking water from their canteens, then lighting cigarettes. All were exhausted and in rotten moods. They were mad at the Japs, mad at the Army, mad at everything. Several minutes later, Butsko arrived with the Second Squad.

"What's the holdup here?"

Shaw told him. Butsko looked up the hill. His recon platoon had become separated from George Company and he didn't feel like calling Captain Orr on the radio to find out what to do. Butsko liked to take charge and make his own decisions. He decided he'd better find out what was on top of the hill.

He told the second squad to take a break, then sat crosslegged on the ground and spread his map out on his lap. He placed his finger on the spot where they'd started in the morning and moved it across the map in the direction they'd traveled. His calculations led him to believe he was at the bottom of Hill 108, which was a solitary hill, not part of a system of hills. He thought he'd better take the platoon up the hill and see if anything was there.

The Third and Fourth squads arrived, and Butsko told them to take a break. Everyone puffed cigarettes and wished they were somewhere else. A few weeks earlier they'd been part of the force that had captured the Gifu Line, which was a Jap defensive position dug into a network of hills, and they'd developed a strong distaste for hills.

Butsko finished his cigarette, crushed it out against his boot, and fieldstripped it, scattering the shreds of tobacco to the ground. He balled up the small piece of cigarette paper, tossed it over his shoulder, and stood up, putting on his steel helmet.

"Okay, let's go!" he said. "First Squad on the point! Everybody else in a column of ducks! If we come under fire, fan out and get down! Move it out!"

The First Squad advanced up the hill in a column of twos, with Gomez far in front on the point, crouching low, holding his rifle in both hands, ready for anything. He raised his feet high in the air and brought them down carefully on the floor of the jungle, making as little noise as possible, just as they'd taught him in training at Fort Ord, California. The hill became steeper and Gomez bent forward. He pushed branches out of the way with the barrel of his M 1, but some snapped back at him and scratched his face anyway.

Pow!

A rifle was fired in front of him and the bullet slammed into a tree trunk two inches away. Gomez dropped to his stomach, rolled over, and came to a stop behind a tree.

"Japs!" he yelled.

Farther back, the recon platoon was hitting the dirt and spreading out. Butsko looked to his left and right to see if everything was going okay; he found nothing to criticize.

"Advance!" he shouted. *"Keep your heads down!"*

The recon platoon crawled up the hill and soon came under scattered small-arms fire. The GIs fired back and continued crawling slowly up the hill. Butsko had been through this before at the Gifu Line and knew what was happening. A thin screen of Japanese soldiers were in front of him and they'd retreat to their bunker or whatever they had up at the top of the hill. Sooner or later the GIs would come under machine-gun fire from the bunker and then their real problems would begin.

Frankie La Barbara carried one of the Browning automatic rifles in the platoon and was raking the jungle in front of him from left to right. Every fifth round was a tracer, and he could gauge the trajectory of his bullets by watching where they went.

The platoon had two BARs in each squad, and they put out a tremendous base of fire. The rest of the platoon advanced behind the fire, and every time a Jap took a potshot at an American, he was answered by a hail of BAR bullets. The Japs retreated up the hill, and the GIs went after them in smooth even waves, covering each other all the way, taking no crazy chances.

Frankie's BAR rested on two metal legs that extended down from the barrel, and the butt had a metal flap that permitted the rear of the weapon to rest securely on his shoulder. It had a handle midway up the barrel, so it could be carried like a suitcase, and it weighed about twice as much as an M 1 rifle.

The bolt slammed forward but didn't fire; the clip was empty. Frankie pulled the clip down and tossed it away, then reached into his cartridge belt and took out a fresh one, tapping it into the chamber.

"La Barbara, move that BAR forward!"

Frankie scanned the jungle in front of him, saw a boulder that would provide good cover, and jumped up, grabbing the BAR by its wooden handle. He ran in a low crouch and a Japanese bullet *zang*ed past his ear, making him flinch. Dropping lower, he scampered over the last ten yards, threw the BAR to the ground beside the boulder, then dropped onto his belly behind it, flicking up the rear sights and pulling the trigger. The BAR stuttered and danced on its skinny metal legs, and the red tracers made long arcing lines into the jungle ahead.

The recon platoon advanced steadily up the hill, and then, as it was nearing the crest, two Japanese machine guns opened fire on them. The recon platoon stopped cold; now the task was to find out exactly where the machine guns were. There might be one bunker up there or there might be a dozen of them, all mutually supportive like the ones in the Gifu Line.

"First Squad, move it out!" Butsko hollered. *"Squads Two, Three, and Four, give 'em cover!"*

"Let's go!" Shaw said.

The First Squad, which was on the far left flank of the platoon, moved up the hill while the other squads fired every-

24

thing they had toward the crest and drew most of the Japanese machine-gun fire. The First Squad crawled forward, not bothering to be quiet because the terrific racket around them masked their sounds.

"Let's go, move it!" Shaw shouted. *"Bannon, catch up with the others!"*

Bannon felt weird to be taking orders from Shaw, because yesterday Shaw had been taking orders from him. Bannon raised himself up on his hands and knees and pushed himself forward. The sound of the machine guns ahead became louder and seemed to be dead ahead. The First Squad made its way up the hill. Bannon was right in the middle, not far from Frankie La Barbara, who looked ridiculous with the big bandage on his nose. Farther down the hill they could hear Butsko shouting. Bannon pushed some branches away from his face and saw smoke and lightning up ahead, blowing against branches and leaves.

"There they are!" Bannon shouted.

The First Squad stopped just in time, because the Japs near the top of the hill spotted them and turned one of the machine guns on them, pinning them down. Bannon pressed his cheek against the moist jungle earth and smelled its stench. He remembered what he saw: the mouth of a cave with gun barrels pointing out of it.

"La Barbara!" yelled Shaw. *"O'Rourke! Get those BARs working!"*

Frankie raised his head to aim through his sights, and a Japanese machine-gun bullet smacked into the earth only a few inches away. He flinched, tried to raise his head again, and a bullet whistled past his ear. He lowered his head to the ground.

"La Barbara,—Whatsa matter with you?"

"You wanna fire this BAR, you can fire it!"

"I just gave you an order!"

"I just told you to go fuck yourself!"

Bannon couldn't help chuckling. It was nice not having to cope with Frankie La Barbara anymore. Shaw called Butsko over his walkie-talkie and told him that the Jap machine guns had been sighted. Butsko said he was on the way.

A terrific racket erupted down the hill, as the rest of the

rescon platoon charged the crest in waves. The Japanese machine gunners aimed their weapons to meet the threat, and Frankie and Jimmy O'Rourke were able to get their BARs going. The rest of the GIs in the First Squad fired their rifles, and soon one of the Jap machine guns swung around to give them a few bursts.

Bannon remembered that it was against a bunker like the one ahead that his good friend Sam Longtree, the Apache Indian, got shot. Longtree had tried to knock out the bunker all by himself and bitten off more than he could chew, but that Indian went insane in combat. All he wanted to do was kill Japs.

The rest of the platoon made their way up the hill, and the Japanese machine guns trained their fire on them again. Bannon wondered what the Japs in the cave were thinking, because surely they knew they were going to be wiped out before long. Why didn't they just surrender? Why did they fight to the death? The Japs were like inhuman creatures to Bannon. They didn't operate on the same wavelength he was on. They were all even crazier than Longtree.

The First Squad pumped lead into the mouth of the cave while the rest of the recon platoon charged up the hill. Finally Butsko got a clear look at the cave. The Japs had piled huge boulders in front of the entrance, and it would take a 155 howitzer to blast through them. He didn't have a 155 howitzer with him, so he'd have to burn them out.

"Gladley!"

"Yo!"

"Get that flame thrower ready!"

"Yo!"

"Everybody up the hill! Let's go!"

The recon platoon crawled forward squad by squad, covering each other's advance, firing steadily at the mouth of the cave. The First and Fourth squads closed in on the cave's sides, and the two Japanese machine guns swung from the side, frantically trying to stop the American advance.

The First Squad came within throwing range and tossed hand grenades toward the mouth of the cave. The Japs had arranged the boulders in front so that there was only a tiny opening, and the grenades bounced off the boulders and rolled down the hill, exploding ferociously.

"Stop the grenades!" Butsko yelled. *"Move in on the flanks!"*

The recon platoon split in half and approached the mouth of the cave from the sides. The Japanese machine gunners fired wildly, but the GIs had moved themselves out of range.

"Charge!"

The GIs jumped up and rushed the mouth of the cave from the sides. A Jap head and torso appeared in the opening; he was trying to get out with his rifle so he could get a clear shot at the GIs, but Hotshot Stevenson, the platoon sharpshooter, lined him up in his sights and pulled his trigger. The M 1 fired and the Jap caught a bullet in the center of his brain.

The other Japs in the cave pulled their dead comrade in as the recon platoon crowded around the sides of the opening. Butsko yanked a grenade from his lapel, pulled the pin, let the lever fly off, counted to two, and lobbed the grenade through the opening.

Screams issued from inside the cave, and seconds later the grenade detonated with a mighty roar. Smoke and flames shot out of the opening and the ground heaved beneath the GI's feet.

"Gladley!" shouted Butsko.

Gladley stepped toward the front of the cave and aimed the nozzle of his flamethrower toward the opening. He switched on the lever and fire shot out of the nozzle, sounding like a hurricane. The flames poured into the cave and Gladley held the nozzle steady. Terrible screaming could be heard from within, along with the crackling and spattering of human flesh as it roasted in the fire. A head covered with flames poked through the opening, and Butsko aimed his rifle at it, pulling the trigger.

Blam!

The head shattered into a dozen burning bits. The GIs dodged out of the way so that none of the fire would fall on them. Gladley maintained a steady stream of fire into the cave, and smoke poured out, smelling like a barbecue.

27

"That's enough," Butsko said.

Gladley turned off the lever and the column of flame shrank back to the nozzle.

"Gafooley!" said Butsko. "Get me a piece of wood to pry away those rocks with!"

"Hup, Sarge!"

"The rest of you keep your fucking eyes open."

Nutsy ran off into the jungle to get a piece of wood, and the GIs looked around at the jungle to make sure no Japs were sneaking up on them. Smoke billowed out of the hole and rose up toward the treetops. Everything became silent again, and soon the insects were chirping and birds called out to each other.

Nutsy returned with a thick branch from a tree. Butsko took it and wedged it between the boulders, heaving hard, separating them wide enough so he could get through.

"Bannon, Jones, Shilansky, come with me!"

Butsko held his M 1 ready and moved sideways between the boulders, entering the cave. Bannon was behind him, nearly gagging on the fetid smoke. On the floor of the cave were charred bodies torn apart by the hand-grenade blasts.

"Bannon, go back and see how far the cave goes!"

"Yo."

Bannon walked toward the rear of the cave and the light became dimmer. His foot touched something soft, and he looked down at the outline of another charred body. He also could perceive boxes and tin cans on the ground. Several steps later he came to the rear of the cave.

"This is the end of it!" Bannon shouted.

"Okay, let's get out of here!"

Bannon followed the others out of the cave and gulped down the fresh air outside.

"We might as well break for chow right here," Butsko said. "Squad leaders, post your guards."

THREE . . .

It rained that night, and in the poor visibility ten Japanese destroyers, carrying men and supplies, made their way through the American blockade of Guadalcanal, unloading near Cape Esperance.

Among the troops paddling to shore was Colonel Kumao Imoto, a staff officer under General Hitoshi Imamura, who commanded the army group that was fighting in the Solomon Islands and on New Guinea.

Colonel Imoto had helped draw up the evacuation plan for the Seventeenth Army on Guadalcanal and had been ordered to present the plan to General Harukichi Hyakutake, who commanded the Seventeenth Army. Colonel Imoto was short and dapper, wearing a freshly laundered and pressed uniform and highly polished knee-high boots; a thin mustache covered his upper lip.

The first thing he saw when he hit the beach was a bloated dead body, and he'd been a staff officer for so long that it shocked him. *Why doesn't somebody bury him?* he thought.

The landing party organized and began its long trek toward General Hyakutake's headquarters. The pouring rain drenched Colonel Imoto's uniform, and soon he looked like just another worn-out and bedraggled Japanese soldier on Guadalcanal, except that he was stouter, for staff officers in Rabaul ate better than frontline troops on Guadalcanal.

Around midnight Colonel Imoto came to General Hyaku-take's camp, a complex of shacks and tents near Tassafaronga Point. Rain poured down on him as he spoke with guards who told him where General Hyakutake's command post was. Imoto followed directions and soon came to a raggedy tent pitched at a bizarre angle, and inside he found Colonel Haruo Konuma and several other officers. The roof of the tent was leaking and the officers lay on beds made of coconut leaves. In a corner, Major Mitsuo Suginoo was shaving by candlelight. Suginoo recognized Imoto because they'd once served together in the same regiment.

"Well, well, well," said Suginoo, brandishing his razor, "look who's here."

Colonel Imoto squinted his eyes. "Is that you, Mitsuo?"

"It is indeed."

"What in the world are you doing?"

"I am preparing to die tomorrow."

"Are things as bad here as I've been told?"

"I'm sure they're even worse than you've been told," said Suginoo, cutting a swathe through the beard and shaving soap on his cheek. "A hundred Japanese soldiers are dying of star-vation on this island every day. There are reports of cannibalism in the field. Approximately one-third of our soldiers are so weak from hunger that they can no longer walk. We place them in holes with their rifles and they fight as best they can. Do you want to hear more?"

"No, thank you," said Colonel Imoto, horrified by what he had heard. "Where's General Hyakutake?"

"In a tent not far from here, but you'd better speak with General Miyazaki before you see General Hyakutake."

Colonel Konuma and Mayor Suginoo escorted Colonel Im-oto to a tent nearby that was the headquarters of General Shuichi Miyazaki, who was General Hyakutake's chief of staff. General Miyazaki was seated at his desk, drinking a cup of weak tea, when the three officers entered. Rain pelted the slanting roof of the tent, but none leaked through. Colonel Imoto saluted and reported.

"Have a seat, Colonel," General Miyazaki said. "What brings you to our lovely island?"

Imoto sat erectly on his chair. "I have brought General Imamura's order for the evacuation of Guadalcanal," he said.

General Miyazaki blinked, then glanced at Major Suginoo and Colonel Konuma. "Evacuation from Guadalcanal?"

"Yes, sir."

General Miyazaki groaned. "I don't believe it."

"It's true. I have the documents right here." Colonel Imoto took them from his briefcase and placed them on General Miyazaki's desk.

General Miyazaki examined the papers, his eyes drooping and the muscles in his face going slack. "So it's finally come to this," he said in a voice barely above a whisper. "What a tragedy."

The tent became silent except for the sound of rain on the canvas and wind thrashing the palm trees nearby. Colonel Imoto felt uncomfortable, like an intruder at a family gathering. General Miyazaki raised his eyes and looked at him.

"How can we evacuate Guadalcanal after losing so many men here?" General Miyazaki asked.

"The details of the evacuation are in the documents, sir."

"I know that, but I mean how can Headquarters let the island go after so much Japanese blood has been spilled here? Why cannot the effort be made to drive the Americans back into the sea?"

"Lack of equipment, men, and ships, sir. We are fighting on many fronts. It has been decided in Tokyo to consolidate our perimeter so that we can defend it more easily."

"But how can I order my men to run away with their tails between their legs after I've told them to fight to the death in their foxholes?"

"I don't know, sir."

General Miyazaki turned down the corners of his mouth. "After all we've been through here, it is unthinkable that we would retreat now. We do not mean to be disobedient, but we cannot carry out the order. We must fight on with furious intensity and die bravely, thus giving everyone an example of Japanese army tradition."

Colonel Imoto was flabbergasted by General Miyazaki's response, but before he could think of what to say, Colonel

31

Konuma spoke. "The evacuation order is ridiculous. It simply is not feasible to withdraw at this time. Our front is too entangled with the enemy, and if any of our men did manage to get on the ships, they'd end by drowning. It's impossible, so please return to Rabaul and leave us alone."

Colonel Imoto was beginning to think that he had walked into a nightmare. The rain, the tents, the rickety shacks—together with the bizarre behavior of the officers—were unsettling him. It seemed as if normal army discipline was breaking down on Guadalcanal. Gathering together his courage and will, he pointed to the orders on General Miyazaki's desk.

"Don't you realize," he said, "that those documents' constitute a legal order from the commander of the army group based on the wishes of the Emperor? Are you telling me that you refuse to obey the wishes of the Emperor?"

General Miyazaki looked at Colonel Konuma. They were confused and embarrassed.

"You say the Emperor is behind this?" General Miyazaki asked Colonel Imoto.

"Yes. The Emperor himself has made this decision."

"I see," said General Miyazaki. "In that case you are quite correct. This is not my decision to make. General Hyakutake will make the final decision. I will take you to him now."

General Miyazaki put on his steel helmet and raincoat, then led Colonel Imoto out of the tent and into the clearing. It was still raining and the sky was lighter because it was dawn behind the thick cloud layer. Everything looked wasted and desolate to Colonel Imoto, like the end of the world.

Finally they came to a tent pitched near the roots of a gigantic tree. General Miyazaki announced himself, and a high-pitched voice from within told him to enter. General Miyazaki threw the tent flap to one side, and Colonel Imoto saw the famous General Hyakutake sitting cross-legged on a blanket, his hands folded in his lap. A small black statue of the Buddha sat on an empty ammunition crate in front of him; evidently he'd been meditating. He was a slender, severe-looking man of fifty-five, and his eyes were as sorrowful as a dog's.

"This is Colonel Imoto," General Miyazaki said. "He has orders for you from Rabaul."

Colonel Imoto bowed and handed over the orders. General Hyakutake, still sitting cross-legged, read them, his eyes gradually widening. Then he laid the orders in his lap and sighed. "This is a most difficult order to receive," he said.

"I can appreciate that, sir."

"I cannot make up my mind right now. You'll have to give me some time."

Colonel Imoto was confused. "I'm afraid I don't understand, sir."

"What don't you understand, Colonel?"

"I don't understand what you have to make up your mind about."

"About whether to obey this order."

"But it is the wish of the Emperor."

"That's why I have to think about it."

General Miyazaki bowed. "We'll leave you to your thoughts, sir."

"Thank you."

General Miyazaki dragged Colonel Imoto out of the tent by his sleeve.

"This is a most peculiar place," Colonel Imoto said as the rain dropped from the leaves of the trees onto his hat. "I've never been in a situation before where Japanese officers decided which orders they'd obey and which they wouldn't."

General Miyazaki smiled faintly. "Welcome to Guadalcanal."

"Everybody up!" said Butsko. "Drop your cocks and grab your socks!"

Bannon opened his eyes inside the tiny pup tent he shared with Craig Delane. It still was dark and the rain was pouring down.

"I really can't take much more of this," said Delane, whose feet had slipped underneath the tent during the night and were resting in a puddle of mud.

"That's what you think," Bannon replied.

Outside they heard the clatter of the recon platoon waking up. Men cursed, knocked down tent poles, and checked their M 1s to make sure they were dry. Bannon reached for a cigarette and lit it up. Letting the cigarette dangle from the corner of his lips, he groped for his socks and pulled them on, smelling his armpits and the unwashed body of Craig Delane.

"I'd do anything for a nice hot shower," Craig Delane said.

"Don't talk about it," Bannon replied. "Don't even think about it."

"I really don't know what I was thinking about when I joined the Army," Delane grumbled.

"I don't want to hear it," Bannon told him. "I've heard it too many times already."

It was true: Delane couldn't stop talking about it. He came from one of the wealthiest and most socially prominent families in New York City, and his father could have paid somebody to have him declared 4-F, but Craig Delane enlisted in the Army infantry out of a weird sense of patriotism and the hope that pretty debutantes would admire him in a snappy uniform. He even turned down a commission because he wanted to be just another soldier, an ordinary GI Joe. *This is where idealism gets you*, Delane thought. *Up Shit Creek without a paddle*.

Bannon pulled on his socks; his toes hurt because he had a mild case of trench foot. His cheek was swollen where he'd been hit with the grenade fragment the day before, and his stomach growled with hunger. Delane farted and Bannon covered his nose with his shirt.

"Sorry," said Delane.

Bannon opened the tent flap to let some air in, but the rain came in too. It was a chilly, miserable morning and all his clothes were damp. He put them on, laced up his boots, grabbed his M 1 rifle, and crawled out of the tent, his mouth tasting foul, his teeth loose in his gums.

He stood up and looked around. Everything was gray and the ground was a slimy layer of mud. He remembered the sunny golden days on the ranch back in Texas, and it was like another world. *This fucking war is wearing me down*, he thought. *I'm not as strong as I used to be. I'll probably get shot any day now*.

He went to the latrine and took a shit while mosquitoes sucked blood out of his ass. Then he returned to his tent, where

34

he'd left his helmet out all night so it could catch rainwater. His helmet was full and he washed his hands in the cool water, rinsed out his mouth, splashed his face, and dried himself with his old moldy towel.

Next came breakfast; it was K rations again. The wood was too wet to make a fire, so he couldn't have hot coffee. But at least he could finish it off with a cigarette. He took out a Chesterfield and lit it up, sucking the smoke deep into his lungs as water dripped from leaves and branches onto him and a cloud of mosquitoes buzzed around him.

Bannon saw Shaw walk across the clearing toward Butsko's tent for Butsko's morning orientation meeting, and Bannon felt relieved that he didn't have to go through that shit anymore. It was nice not to have the responsibility and headaches. Let Shaw have it if he wanted it. Fuck 'em all.

Bannon knew they'd be moving out before long and thought he'd better check his M 1. He looked at it; the layer of oil he'd poured on the night before was covered with drops of water. He opened the bolt and looked down the barrel, and there was water in there too. He poured some oil on a patch and ran it through the barrel to get the water out and keep the metal from rusting. Wiping down the metal parts of the rifle with an old sock, he added another thick layer of oil.

Shaw came back and told the First Squad to break camp because they were moving out.

"Where we going this time?" asked Frankie La Barbara.

Shaw pointed west. "Thataway."

They struck tents, unbuttoned them, and rolled up the shelter halves with their blankets. Everything was soggy and wet, covered with mud and leaves.

"Delane," Bannon said, "I think I'm gonna get it today."

Delane shrugged and lit a cigarette. He didn't have the energy to disagree with Bannon because he was constipated and had a headache, and on top of that he wasn't sure that he had much longer to live either.

Butsko carried his full field pack, and his helmet was low over his eyes. He walked to the center of the clearing and shouted, *"Fall in!"*

The GIs hoisted their packs onto their shoulders and formed four squad ranks in front of Butsko, dressing right and covering down, standing at attention.

"Report!" said Butsko.

Jesus Christ, thought Bannon. *What does he think this is, a parade?*

Shaw saluted snappily. "First Squad all present and accounted for!"

Butsko saluted back. The other three squad leaders reported. Bannon figured Butsko was trying to get a little military discipline going in the recon platoon.

"At ease!" said Butsko.

The GIs moved their left feet out and clasped their hands behind their backs. Butsko looked them over, a scowl on his face. He, too, was unshaven, but his beard was thicker than theirs and grew higher on his cheekbones, which gave him a wild-animal appearance.

"All right," he said, "we're going Jap-hunting today. Pay attention, keep your eyes open, and I don't want any fuck-ups. If we run into any Japs, we'll take care of them ourselves unless there are a lot of them, and then we'll call for help. Any questions?"

Nobody said anything.

"Okay, now, I've been wandering around here this morning and I've been hearing a lot of pissing and moaning. You don't like the weather. You're sick of the chow. You wish you were home, sucking your mothers' titties. I'm getting sick of hearing it. You sound like a bunch of cunts. You make me sick. You'd better straighten out your backbones and wake the fuck up, because a dopey soldier soon becomes a dead soldier. Any questions?"

Nobody dared to open his mouth.

"All right, let's move it out. First Squad take the point."

Shaw led the First Squad in a single column into the jungle, and Gomez ran up ahead to be the eyes and ears of the platoon. The rest of the men followed, trudging into the jungle, soaked to their skins. Bannon remembered what Butsko said and tried to sharpen his senses, but it didn't work. He felt too rotten. The day was too awful. He had nothing to hope for. *Fuck it, let 'em kill me*, he thought.

The recon platoon made its way through the jungle on a narrow, winding trail. Rain fell, pinging on their helmets and dripping down their backs. Blisters formed on their wet feet and bugs ate them alive. The temperature rose and many of the men felt that they simply could not go on, but they did, placing one foot in front of the other, thinking about home and the wives or girl friends they'd left behind. All felt queasy in their stomachs from the constant diet of C rations and K rations. Frankie La Barbara thought of shooting himself in the leg so he could be sent back to the hospital on New Caledonia.

Branches scratched their faces and clawed at their clothes. Leeches dropped onto them from trees; the men didn't even feel them sucking their blood. They smoked cigarettes even though they knew cigarettes cut their wind, but they were young men and had vast reserves of energy. If they were twenty years older, they couldn't have kept up that pace for more than an hour.

At eleven o'clock in the morning they were still on the move and hadn't even taken a break yet. They were all exhausted, pissed of, and in pain. On the point, Gomez was in better shape than any of them, because he knew they all were relying on him. He willed himself to stay vigilant and strong and called on Jesus Christ to help him, for Gomez was religious in his own way and wore a gold cross around his neck with his dog tags, although he'd been a petty hoodlum in civilian life, rolling drunks and breaking into people's homes. He had even killed three men from rival gangs with his long, lethal switchblade.

The jungle thinned out in front of him and he came to the edge of a coconut plantation. The trees grew in neat rows and leaned lazily in all directions. The terrain was wide open compared to the jungle, and Gomez thought he'd better stop, because Butsko might want to go around the plantation rather than directly through it.

He leaned against a tree and looked up at the sky. The clouds were still dark and oily and the rain came down. *When is this rain going to stop?* he wondered. *I feel like I'm drowning in it.*

The First Squad appeared behind him and stopped. He waved

37

them forward and they advanced, seeing the plantation behind him.

"Jesus, looka there," said Frankie La Barbara. "I'm gonna get me one of them coconuts."

"Stay where you are!" Shaw said. "You don't go out there until you're told to go out there."

"Aw, stop breaking my hump, Shaw."

Shaw charged toward him. "What you say?"

Frankie didn't feel like getting into a hassle with Shaw, because Shaw's fighting prowess was well known, but he couldn't back down either. Shaw stopped in front of Frankie and brought his face to within six inches of Frankie's.

"I asked what you said!"

"I ain't said nothin'."

"I thought I heard one of your shitty fucking remarks. You got anything to say to me, you say it to my face, got it?"

"How can I do that, now that you got rank over me?"

"We can go off behind those bushes there and forget about the rank. I'll kick your fucking ass."

At that moment Butsko arrived with the Second Squad. "Now what's going on here?"

"Nothing I can't handle," Shaw said.

Butsko looked at Frankie La Barbara. "You up to your old tricks, scumhead?"

"Who, me?"

Butsko pointed at Frankie's bandaged nose. "You keep it up and one of these days I'm gonna put a bullet in your head. Get the picture?"

"Hup, Sarge."

Butsko took three steps toward the edge of the jungle and stopped, gazing from left to right at the coconut trees. It evidently was an enormous plantation, because there were coconut trees as far as he could see in all directions. He took out his map and Nutsy Gafooley held up his poncho to keep the rain off it. Butsko saw the plantation on the map and didn't know whether to go around it or through it. He decided he'd better call Captain Orr and ask what to do.

"Gimme the walkie-talkie," he said to Nutsy, who was his runner. "The rest of you guys take a break."

"Can we get some coconuts?" asked Frankie La Barbara.

"Yeah," said Butsko. "But be careful. There might be some Japs out there."

The men moved cautiously into the coconut grove and Butsko called Captain Orr on the radio, but he couldn't get through. The hilly terrain and thick jungle often blocked radio transmission. He'd been ordered to move in the direction that cut through the plantation and he thought he should just keep going. It would be easier than hacking through the jungle.

"Nutsy, get me one of them green cocounts."

"Hup, Sarge."

The men foraged for coconuts, hacking them open with their machetes, drinking the sweet milk, and scooping out the meat. The green coconuts were best because their meat was soft, almost like pudding, whereas the old coconut meat was as hard as wood. Before becoming soldiers, most of the men in the recon platoon never had seen a coconut in their lives. Now they ate one after another, and when their stomachs were filled, they sat underneath the trees and smoked cigarettes. The rain diminished to a light drizzle and the day became brighter. It looked like they'd have an easy time going through the plantation. Their morale improved.

Butsko stood up. "Okay, let's get going! Make diamond formations and keep your fucking eyes open!"

The recon platoon coalesced into four diamonds with squad leaders in the centers. The First Squad led the rest, with Gomez at the front of the formation and a BAR man on each extreme flank. The next three squads followed side by side, with Butsko in the middle of the Second Squad.

They advanced across the vast coconut grove, and mists rose eerily from the ground. The drizzle and fog made visibility poor, and the landscape reminded Bannon of a bad dream he'd once had. The GIs searched the trees and ground for signs of Japs but saw nothing. They expected Japs to start shooting at any moment, but that didn't happen either. In the distance they heard the beginning of an artillery barrage. The GIs felt wide open and vulnerable in the coconut grove.

Blam!

Everybody hit the dirt and looked around. The shot had

been fired from somewhere within their midst.

"Who the fuck did that?" Butsko demanded.

"I did!" replied Pfc. Cunningham in the Third Squad. "I saw something move in the tree over there!" he pointed.

Butsko looked up at the tree but didn't see anything suspicious.

"Hazleton!" Butsko said to the leader of the Third Squad. "Take somebody with you and see if anything's up there! And watch your step!"

Hazleton called out Cunningham's name and together they raised themselves from the ground, walking in a crouch toward the tree that Cunningham had fired at. When they got close they saw blood dripping down the trunk of a tree. High up on one of the branches lay a dead monkey.

"It's a monkey!" Hazleton shouted back.

Frankie La Barbara laughed.

"Shaddup, La Barbara!" Butsko said. "All right, let's move it out again!"

The men got up, brushed themselves off, and got into formation again. They resumed their trek through the coconut grove, still tense, looking in all directions.

Butsko was furious, but he didn't say anything. If there were any Japs around, they knew the recon platoon was in the vicinity, thanks to Cunningham's shot. But Cunningham couldn't help it. He had sharp eyes and that was good. If he could kill a monkey, he could kill a man.

Out on the point, Gomez peered ahead through the mist and drizzle. The rows of coconut trees seemed to go on forever. If there were any Japs ahead, they'd see him before they saw any of the others and they'd put a bullet through his head, so he wanted to be sure he spotted them first. He crouched low, narrowed his eyes, and scanned the treetops, the ground, and the trunks of trees from left to right, his finger on his trigger and the safety off, ready to plug anything that moved.

He became aware of a white mass behind the rows of coconut trees and blinked his eyes, because sometimes when he was looking too hard for something he saw things that weren't there. He stepped forward carefully, looking at the white mass, and then saw a roof and windows and the outline of a huge white mansion straight ahead. He stopped cold, unable to believe his eyes. It was like a mirage appearing suddenly out of the mist, and he'd never imagined such a lavish mansionlike edifice could exist on Guadalcanal. He'd never seen anything like it since he'd been on the island.

When he realized he wasn't hallucinating, he pointed toward the ground and then got down himself. The rest of the recon platoon dropped down too. Gomez turned around and placed his forefinger in front of his mouth, indicating that they should be quiet. Butsko crawled forward to see what the problem was, and as the big white mansion came into view, he too was amazed. He stared at it for a few moments; it looked deserted. Many of the windows were broken and the wall on one of the wings had a hole blown in it. Part of the roof on another wing was caved in, probably from a bomb. There were shell craters in the overgrown lawn surrounding the mansion. It had a wide veranda in front and long white columns holding up the roof, like photographs he'd seen in magazines of the great old mansions of the South.

"Stay here and keep your eye on the place," Butsko said. "There might be Japs inside, so don't make any funny moves."

"The joint looks empty to me," Gomez replied.

"Maybe and maybe not."

Butsko crawled back and called a meeting of his squad leaders. "There's a big white house over there," Butsko said. "It looks deserted, but maybe it ain't. We'll rush it from the front and rear. Squads One and Two will hit the front and Three and Four will hit the back. The signal to attack will be a shot from my gun. Set up your BARs so they can support the attack. Any questions?"

Nobody said anything.

"Get rolling," Butsko said.

The squad leaders crept away and moved their squads out. The first two squads formed a skirmish line in front of the mansion, lying on their stomachs, with the BAR men on the flanks. Butsko attached a grenade launcher to the barrel of his M 1 and affixed a hand grenade to it. Meanwhile the Third and Fourth squads worked around to the rear of the mansion. Not a sound came from the stately white structure. It reminded

Bannon of a wealthy old lady who'd fallen on hard times.

Butsko looked at his watch. He thought he'd give the Third and Fourth squads another five minutes. Then he glanced up at the mansion, scanning its facade, trying to find movement behind the windows. He wondered what kind of people had lived there before the war. Craig Delane told him once that Lever Brothers owned most of the coconut plantations on Guadalcanal. There was something in coconuts that they used for soap and stuff.

The five minutes were up. "Okay, let's hit it," Butsko said. "Move fast and shoot at anything that moves, but be sure you don't shoot any of our own people."

The GIs stood up. Butsko waved his arm forward. The long skirmish line moved through the coconut grove toward the mansion. They came to the edge of the grove and stepped out onto the wide lawn. The BAR men lay down with their weapons and the rest of the GIs moved forward.

"Double-time!" Butsko yelled.

The men ran forward, sweeping across the lawn to the front of the mansion. Butsko fired his rifle in the air, his signal to the Third and Fourth squads on the other side. Then suddenly the barrel of a machine gun appeared in one of the windows, but none of the GIs saw it until it started firing. The machine gun belched death at the charging skirmish line and shot down two GIs before the rest of them hit the dirt.

The BAR men saw the machine gun and directed streams of lead at it. Then another machine gun inside the house started firing, and the BARs split their fire between the two. Japanese soldiers with rifles appeared in the other windows, and Butsko realized his men were in a whole world of trouble. They couldn't go back and they couldn't stay where they were. They had to go forward.

His men returned the fire, but they were out in the open and the Japs were hidden behind windowsills. Still, the fusillades from the BARs and the GIs on the ground prevented the Japs from firing accurately. Butsko aimed his grenade launcher at the door of the mansion and pulled the trigger.

Ka-pow!

The grenade sailed into the air, flew over the wide veranda,

42

and landed in front of the door, where it exploded, splintering wood and leaving a big smoking hole where the door had been before.

"Charge!" shouted Butsko. *"Follow me!"*

The First and Second squads rushed the veranda as bullets whizzed all around them. Private Becker was hit in the shoulder, and Pfc. Doyle took a bullet in the gut. The GIs leaped up the stairs of the veranda, kicked wicker furniture out of their way, and ran toward the door.

Butsko was in front of all of them; he'd removed the grenade launcher from the end of his M 1 on the way in. As he neared the door he pulled a grenade from his lapel, yanked out the pin, and hurled it through the door. His men scrambled to the wall of the mansion and pressed their backs against it. They heard garbled Japanese spoken in a panic inside the mansion, and then the grenade blew, making the floor of the veranda tremble.

Butsko charged through the door and saw billows of smoke. He saw movement and fired his M 1 from the waist. GIs poured through the door behind him and spread out through the large living room, shooting the Japs who'd been shooting at them from behind the windowsills. Some Japs in the room fought back, but they were quickly outnumbered, and the rest fled through other doors. Butsko heard footsteps behind him and spun around. A door was kicked open and Sergeant Kelsey from the Third Squad charged into the room. Bannon saw something move behind a sofa and leaped over it, landing on the other side and seeing a Jap lying there, bleeding from the stomach and trying to aim a pistol at him. Bannon kicked the pistol out of his hand and stomped his face. He shot the Jap in the chest to make sure he wouldn't bother anyone again.

Butsko looked up at the ceiling and heard running footsteps. "This joint's fulla Japs. They're all over the fucking place. We'll split up again into two sections. The First and Second squads will take that side of the house—he pointed—and the Third and Fourth squads will take this side. Any questions?"

Nobody said anything.

"Move it out," Butsko said.

The platoon split up again and the men ran toward doors at

opposite ends of the living room, kicking dirty torn pieces of overstuffed furniture out of the way. Broken china and ripped curtains lay on the floor, and on the wall above the fireplace was a portrait of an eighteenth-century gentleman; it was riddled with bullet holes.

Bannon stuck his head around a doorway and *beeannnggg*— a bullet creased the top of his helmet, knocking him cold. He fell to the floor as Shaw lobbed a hand grenade around the corner. It exploded and a crystal chandelier in the middle of the living room came crashing to the floor. Private Blum, the medic, slapped Bannon's cheeks and Bannon opened his eyes.

Bannon saw GIs charge through the doorway. He picked up his helmet and looked at the crease down the middle. "Those fucking Japs," he said.

Bannon put his helmet on his head, grabbed his rifle, reeled groggily, and jumped over the threshold into the other room. GIs were firing their rifles in all directions, and the room echoed with the blasts from their rifles. Shaw ran across the room toward another doorway, pulled a grenade from his lapel, and pressed his back against the wall next to the doorjamb. He pulled the pin and tossed the grenade into the room; two seconds later it came flying back! Homer Gladley caught it in midair and threw it into the room again.

Barroooommmmmm!

The GIs charged through the door. Frankie La Barbara was the first one in the room, firing his BAR from the waist, raking the room from side to side and top to bottom with hot lead. The other GIs spilled into the room behind him. Japs were shouting in the corridor. A Japanese grenade came flying into the room and Shilansky caught it, throwing it out the window, where it exploded in midair and blew a hole in the wall of the mansion.

Bannon could see that the only way to stay alive was to move fast and keep the Japs on the run.

"Put some fire into that room!" he yelled.

The GIs fired into the doorway and Bannon took out a grenade, pulled the pin, let the lever fly away, waited two seconds, and hurled it into the corridor with all his strength.

He ducked out of the way and the grenade detonated, deafening everybody.

"Let's go!" Bannon said.

He charged through the doorway and saw a Jap on his knees on the floor. The Jap fired his rifle wildly, for he had a bullet in his stomach. Bannon shot him in the head and ran past him toward the stairs at the end of the corridor. He looked up the stairs and saw a grenade flying down at him.

"Hit it!"

The GIs dived to the floorboards and the grenade exploded, sending deadly shrapnel flying in all directions, tearing into the plaster of the walls. Bannon rose to one knee and heard an ominous metal clunk on the stairs—another grenade.

"Stay down!"

He flopped to the floor again, took out a hand grenade, and pulled the pin while holding the arming lever down. The Japanese grenade exploded on the stairs and the whole house trembled again. With the sound of the grenade still ringing in his ears, Bannon jumped up, let the lever on his hand grenade pop off, ran to the foot of the stairs, and threw the hand grenade up to the next landing.

Barrrooooommmm!

"Follow me!" Bannon yelled.

He ran up the stairs three at a time, holding his rifle ready to fire, and behind him, like a herd of cattle, came the rest of the men. Bannon reached the landing, saw a Jap face in a doorway, and fired wildly, but the Jap pulled back in time.

Behind Bannon was Shaw, who hurled a grenade into the room. The GIs dropped to the floor and hugged the walls.

Barrooooommmm!

Bannon charged into the room, which was filled with smoke, and a chunk of plaster fell down from the ceiling, shattering on his helmet. It startled him so much that he fired his rifle at nothing. Then Shaw came into the room, his rifle blazing, and next was Frankie La Barbara, spraying bullets everywhere.

The GIs piled into the room, firing in all directions, and when the smoke cleared they saw dead Japs lying everywhere, blown to bits by the hand grenade. Bannon heard movement down the hall and turned around. Homer Gladley heard it, too; he was standing closest to the door. He threw a hand grenade into the hallway. The grenade exploded thunderously, and Gladley led the charge out of the little room, firing down the hallway, which was lined with doors. Bannon saw a door closing, ran toward it, and threw his shoulder against it.

The door was knocked wide open and Bannon flew into the room. He saw a Jap wearing pants and no shirt, aiming a pistol at him. Bannon froze and then heard the rat-a-tat of a BAR. Three red holes appeared on the torso of the Jap, who went sprawling backward and crashed against a wall. Bannon looked behind him and saw Jimmy O'Rourke holding his smoking BAR in his hands.

"Cover me!" he said to O'Rourke.

Bannon flung open the door to a closet. A pile of clothes were on the floor. He shot a bullet into the pile, then kicked it, but it was only clothes. Spinning around, he looked at the bed, which was unmade; evidently the Jap with the pistol had been taking a nap. Across the room was another closet.

"Cover me!"

Bannon dashed across the room and opened the closet door. Inside were some Japanese uniforms with officers' insignia on the collars. A mirror was on the back of the door, and as Bannon looked at it, he saw a reflection of the bed: *Something was moving underneath it!*

He spun around and saw a small hand waving something white underneath the bed. Bannon and O'Rourke aimed their weapons at the hand and crouched down.

"Come on out of there!" Bannon said.

He heard a sob that could only come from a woman's throat, and then a long, slim arm appeared. After the arm came a dusky shoulder, followed by a head of long black hair. The head turned to show the face of a young native girl.

Jimmy O'Rourke nearly dropped his BAR. Bannon stared in amazement. The girl couldn't have been older than eighteen, and she might even have been thirteen, because you couldn't pinpoint the age of a native girl very well.

"No shoot!" she said.

"We no shoot," Bannon replied.

The girl crawled out from underneath the bed; she was stark naked. Bannon and Jimmy O'Rourke caught a glimpse of her breasts and bush before she pulled a sheet off the bed and covered herself with it. She was still crying.

"He want me do fickety-fick!" she said in a loud, hysterical voice. "I no want to but he hit me!"

"Bullshit," said O'Rourke. "She ain't got a mark on her. She's lying."

"I not lying!" she yelled. "I tell the truth!"

"Yeah, sure," said O'Rourke, who considered himself a clever guy. Nobody was going to put anything on him.

Bannon heard gunfire and grenade blasts down the hall. "I'll watch her," he said. "You'd better give the other guys a hand with your BAR."

"Why don't you give them a hand?"

"Because you got the BAR."

"I'll trade with you."

"I don't want that fucking thing."

"Well, neither do I."

"But it's yours. You were issued it, not me."

"Stop giving me orders," O'Rourke said, raising his chin in the air. "You're not the squad leader anymore."

Bannon looked him in the eye. "O'Rourke, after this is over I'm going to kick your fucking ass."

"I'd like to see you try it."

Both men glowered at each other, and the girl looked at them fearfully.

Bannon spat at the floor. "You're even dumber than I thought you were," he said to O'Rourke.

"Fuck you, cowboy."

"The others are gonna need that BAR out there."

"You just want me to go out there so you can be alone with the cunt here."

"Boy, am I gonna whip your ass."

"We'll see about that."

The sound of fighting diminished in the building. Butsko shouted orders in one of the wings. A hand grenade exploded in a far section of the building. Bannon looked at the girl. "What's your name?"

"Mary," she replied, trembling underneath the sheet wrapped around her. She looked at the dead body of the Japanese officer, walked over to him, and spat on his corpse. "He bad man," she said. "I glad he dead."

O'Rourke snorted and then said, "Yeah, sure."

"Shaddup, stupid," Bannon told him.

"Shaddup yourself, cowboy."

Bannon looked at the girl again. "How long you been here?"

"A few days."

"Where are you from?"

"A village that way." She pointed south. "The Japanese mens brought me here."

O'Rourke continued to look distrustful. "Anybody who'd believe that would believe anything."

Bannon turned to O'Rourke. "I thought I told you to shut up."

"Who cares what you say? You ain't shit around here anymore."

Bannon looked at the girl. "You got clothes here?"

"Over there." She pointed to her sarong, lying over a chair.

"Get dressed."

"Look the other way," she said.

"Shit," said O'Rourke. "I ain't turning my back on that broad."

Bannon pointed his M-1 at her. "Get dressed."

She walked smoothly and gracefully toward the chair, turned her back to them, and took off her sheet, and revealing her naked rear end.

"What an ass," O'Rourke said. "If I had an ass like that, I'd make a million dollars."

Bannon had to agree it was a great ass. She was a petite girl with nice curves and healthy legs. Her fanny was perfectly rounded, and Bannon felt an erection coming on. He flashed on his girl friend, Ginger, back in Texas, and felt a dull ache of longing. She put on her sarong, which was made of white cotton and had dark-blue flowers printed on it.

"Let's go," Bannon said.

They left the room and walked down the corridor. Men's voices could be heard, but no more shooting. Bleeding Japanese bodies lay on the floor, twisted into grotesque positions. They looked in a room and saw Blum treating a wound in the chest of Private Hilliard, who was only seventeen years old, the youngest man in the platoon. Hilliard had enlisted when he was sixteen. He was tall for his age.

Farther down the hall they found Butsko and the others in a room that had a radio on a bench and some dead Japs lying on the floor. Screeches and howls came from the loudspeaker as Pfc. Dunbar twisted the dials.

"I can't get through," said Dunbar.

"Maybe they broke it," Butsko said.

Suddenly the voice of a Japanese man came through the loudspeakers.

"Your mother's pussy!" said Dunbar into the mike.

"Nani?" said the Jap.

"Fuck you where you breathe!"

A clunk sound came from the loudspeaker and the connection was broken off. Butsko was aware that somebody had entered the room and turned around to see Bannon and O'Rourke with the native girl. Butsko stared for a few moments.

"Where she come from?"

"She was fucking a Jap officer," O'Rourke said. "I think we ought to shoot her."

Butsko looked at the girl, wondering what to do with her. Most natives on Guadalcanal hated the Japanese, but was she a traitor? Anyway, he had more important things to worry about. The Japs in the mansion probably had radioed back that they were under attack, and maybe Jap reinforcements were on the way. It would probably be a good idea to get out of that mansion, which was a great target for artillery. Maybe the best thing to do was advance through the plantation, set up a defense, and try to make contact with the rest of the battalion.

"Let's get out of here," Butsko said. "Bannon, you watch the girl."

"What about me?" O'Rourke asked.

Butsko gave him a backhand fist across the mouth, and O'Rourke's legs went wobbly.

"I just told you how it's going to be," Butsko said. *"Let's go!"*

49

Butsko stayed in the room as the others ran out into the corridor. He raised his rifle and slammed the butt into the radio, smashing it apart. He whacked the radio until it was nothing more than broken tubes, smashed wires, and a mangled chassis. Then he turned and left the room, following the others out of the mansion.

The GI's ran through the rooms, looking for food and sake, but there was nothing worth stealing. The Japs who'd been defending the mansion all looked skinny and undernourished as they lay sprawled dead on the floor. The GIs didn't take the Japs' weapons and ammunition because they had their own. They formed up on the front lawn of the mansion and Butsko told them to move west.

The drizzle had stopped, but the thick ominous dark clouds were still overhead. The GIs trudged through the coconut grove in a column of twos, with the First Squad in front and Corporal Gomez on the point. Bannon walked behind the First Squad with the girl.

"Why I have go with you?" the girl asked. "Why not I can go back to my village?"

Bannon pointed with his thumb back to Butsko. "Ask him."

The girl moved to go back to Butsko, but Bannon grabbed her shoulder. "Wait until we stop."

The girl made a face that indicated disagreement, but she kept on going. Bannon walked behind her, watching her fanny swing from side to side underneath her sarong. He knew she wasn't wearing anything underneath the sarong, and lust boiled up inside him. He wished he were alone with her so he could grab her. It had been so long since he had had a woman. He thought of holding her in his arms and screwing her for hours, doing all the weird things he liked to do in bed, gorging himself on her.

Meanwhile, on the point, Corporal Gomez thought he heard something. It was a faint hum that faded away and then came back again. He continued to walk, wondering if fatigue and hunger were making his ears play tricks on him, but after twenty more yards the hum became steady and didn't go away. Something was out there and he held up his hand.

The column stopped. Butsko ran forward to see what was

the matter, and on the way he became aware of the sound too. So did the other men. Butsko joined Gomez and listened.

"Sounds like a tank," Gomez said.

Butsko nodded grimly. He knew there might be more than one tank, and it probably would be accompanied by infantry. He wracked his brain for a plan of action. He didn't know how many Japs were coming and how many tanks. Maybe the best move would be to retreat and try to link up with the rest of the regiment, which shouldn't be too far away. He could report that a Japanese force was on the way and it could be dealt with by Colonel Stockton as he saw fit.

"Retreat!" he shouted. *"Hurry Up!"*

The recon platoon turned around and moved back toward the mansion. Gomez double-timed to take the point again, and they all retraced the path they'd made to the mansion. Behind them the sound of the tank became louder.

"Double-time!" Butsko shouted.

The men jogged back, their packs bouncing up and down on their backs. They came to the mansion sitting stolidly on the lawn, passed it, and plunged into the coconut grove behind. It sounded as if the tank were gaining on them.

Beeaaannnggggg!

A bullet whizzed past Gomez and hit Pfc. Propopescu in the chest. Pfc. Propopescu collapsed onto the ground and the rest of the recon platoon flopped onto their stomachs. The bullet had been fired from their front and was followed by a fusillade of bullets from the same direction.

Their retreat was cut off. Butsko thought quickly and decided their best cover would be in the mansion.

"Back to the building!" he yelled. *"Let's go!"*

The men got to their feet and ran hunched over toward the mansion. Bullets whistled all around them, slamming into trees, kicking up the dirt at their feet. They came to the mansion, vaulted up the steps, and poured through the door. Some dived through the windows facing the veranda, and Private Hitzig from Baltimore, Ohio, caught a bullet in his back. He fell on the steps of the veranda and broke his nose on a wooden plank, but he was dead and it didn't matter.

Inside the mansion the men didn't need anyone to give them

orders. They took positions by the windows and fired at the figures moving through the coconut grove.

Barrooooom! The mansion shook from an artillery shell, and a wall on its west wing was blown away. Plaster fell down from the ceiling in the main living room and filled the air with dust.

Barrooooom! Another shell hit the west wall and blew another massive chunk of it away. Butsko ran to the west wing and looked through the smoke and splintered wall. He saw a Japanese light tank at the edge of the coconut grove, and a second later a puff of smoke issued from its cannon as the vehicle rocked back on its treads.

"Get down!" Butsko shouted.

The shell whizzed through one of the openings in the wall and flew into the room, crashing into a far wall and exploding ferociously. Butsko was lifted off the floor, thrown ten feet, and landed on his ass. The ceiling collapsed on top of him and he was covered by plaster and splintered timbers. Smothering, choking on dust, he struggled frantically and burst out of the debris. Glancing through the opening in the wall, he saw the tank turning on its treads. Evidently it was heading for the front of the building.

Covered with white dust, Butsko looked like a ghost when he returned to the main living room. *"Gafooley!"*

"Yo!"

"Bring that bazooka over here!"

"Yo!"

Butsko ran to a front window, pushed Homer Gladley out of the way, and saw the tank rolling across the lawn near the edge of the coconut grove.

Beeeoooooowwww! A bullet ricocheted off the windowsill and made him duck. Behind him Nutsy Gafooley attached the halves of the bazooka together, pulled out the sighting mechanism, and handed the weapon to Butsko, who was crouching behind the window sill.

"Load me up!"

Nutsy opened the haversack and pulled out a bazooka rocket. He inserted it into the rear end of the bazooka, tied the wires around the terminal posts, and tapped Butsko's helmet.

Butsko gritted his teeth and set the sight for fifty yards. Then he raised his head and trained the crosshairs on the tank, which was turning around to face him.

Beeooowwww! Another bullet hit the ledge, making Butsko flinch, and he aimed again. The gun turret of the tank was swinging around toward him. He pulled the trigger of the bazooka and heard the faint whir of the magneto. The rocket shot forth and he ducked down. Moments later he heard an explosion. Raising his head, he saw a cloud of smoke and a shell crater beside the tank.

Barrrooooommmm! The tank fired its cannon again and a shell hit the wall of the main living room, blowing it to smithereens, filling the room with smoke. The men coughed and wiped dust from their eyes as Japanese bullets flew through the windows. Butsko raised his head again, aimed, and pulled the trigger, then ducked quickly. He heard the explosion and raised his head, hoping to see the wreckage of the tank, but it was still there, big and nasty; his aim had been wide again.

"Load me up!"

Nutsy Gafooley fitted a rocket into the tube again and tied up the wires. He tapped Butsko's helmet, and this time Butsko decided to aim to the right of the tank, because evidently the sighting mechanism had been knocked out of line.

Barooooooommmmmm! Another shell hit the wall, this time in front of Butsko. It exploded and Butsko felt himself being thrown back. He went sprawling across the floor, and a big splinter plunged into his left forearm. He landed on Nutsy Gafooley and a pile of debris covered them up. A group of GIs ran toward them to dig them out.

"Banzai!"

They heard footsteps on the veranda. Bannon knelt behind one of the windows and saw Japs rushing the door. One of them had a hand grenade poised to throw and Bannon shot him, knocking him backward. The grenade exploded on the floor of the veranda, tearing the Jap apart and a few Japs near him, but the rest kept charging.

Jimmy O'Rourke dropped down in the middle of the living-room floor, got set behind his BAR, and fired at the Japs as they converged on the door. The burst of fire hurled them back, but more kept coming. Two Japs vaulted through an unmanned window. Shaw was closest to them. He fired his M 1 from the waist and hit one in the stomach, but the other one landed, looked around, and ran at Shaw with his rifle and bayonet.

"Yaaaahhhh!" screamed the Jap, lunging at Shaw.

Shaw parried the thrust and slammed the Jap in the face with his rifle butt, knocking him backward. The Jap fell and Shaw shot him through the chest, then turned and was smacked in the face by a Japanese rifle butt. Shaw lost consciousness and dropped to his knees. The Jap pulled back his rifle and bayonet to run him through, and Bannon aimed at the Jap's head, pulling the trigger of his M 1. He was only a few feet from the Jap and couldn't miss. The bullet hit the Jap in the head and blew it apart like a rotten watermelon.

The other GIs in the room swarmed over the Japs who'd broken through and sliced them up with their bayonets. Then the GIs returned to their posts at the windows to fire at the Japs on the veranda and lawn. The Japs fell back before the fusillade.

Barrrooooooom! Another shell from the tank's cannon hit the wall, and this time it collapsed entirely. The stunned GIs looked up to see nothing between them and the Japs on the front lawn. Butsko threw a jagged length of two-by-four off him and got to his feet.

"Follow me!" he screamed.

The GIs ran out of the living room to the corridor on its right as Japanese machine guns filled the air with bullets. Private Kennealy was hit in the mouth and Corporal Farina caught a bullet in his groin, but the rest of them evacuated the room.

Butsko leaned against the wall in the corridor and looked down at the big splinter sticking into his arm like a spike. He grabbed it with his fist, took a deep breath, and yanked it out. Blood gushed after it. Private Blum was there to slap a bandage on.

"You okay, Sarge?"

Butsko ignored him. "Did anybody get the bazooka?"

Nutsy Gafooley raised it into the air. "Here it is, Sarge!"

"Bannon, take the bazooka and get that fucking tank!"

"Hup, Sarge!" Bannon looked at Gafooley. "Come with me!"

Bannon ran to the stairs and Nutsy Gafooley followed him, carrying the bazooka. Bannon wanted to shoot at the tank from an unexpected window and he'd have to be fast. A door burst open at the foot of the stairs and two Japs rushed in, one after another. Bannon and Gafooley were murky targets in the shadows and the Japs were outlined by the light. Bannon, on the run, shot the first one in the chest and the second in the gut.

"Somebody watch the back door!" Bannon shouted as he leaped up the stairs.

Gafooley followed him and they ran down the corridor, jumping over the bodies of dead Japs. They came to the room that had been occupied by the Jap officer and the native girl, and Bannon went inside. He crouched low and approached the window. Kneeling behind it, he took the bazooka from Gafooley and placed it on his shoulder. Gafooley loaded him up. Bannon got ready, then raised himself suddenly and looked out the window, seeing the tank below. Aiming quickly, he steadied the bazooka and pulled the trigger.

Swooooossshh! The rocket sped out of the tube, and the back blast blew apart the chair that was behind it. Bannon watched with a sinking heart as the bazooka shell landed to the left of the tank and exploded. He was surprised, because he'd had the crosshairs directly on the center of the tank's turret.

A Japanese bullet shattered the windowsill and Bannon ducked down. "We gotta go to another room!" he said. Duck-walking backward, he reached the door and ran down the corridor again with Gafooley a few steps behind him. They came to the radio room and went inside. Getting low, they made their way to the window.

"Load me up!"

Gafooley pushed in the rocket and Bannon reached the same conclusion that Butsko had earlier: The bazooka was firing too far to the left. Gafooley tapped his helmet and Bannon rose up, aimed to the right of the tank, and pulled the trigger. The rocket shot out and headed directly for the tank. Bannon's heart soared as the rocket hit the tank slightly below the turret and exploded. The turret was blown to bits and the tank rocked onto its side.

"I got it!" Bannon said.

He placed the bazooka on the floor and raised the rifle to his shoulder while Gafooley ran to the other window. They looked down and saw Japs rushing across the lawn to the veranda again. Bannon fired his M 1 and brought one of them down. He fired again and hit the Jap in the leg, spinning him around and sending him reeling. A Japanese machine gun opened fire and stitched across the windowsill. Bannon ducked down as the bullets flew into the room and slammed into the wall behind him.

Downstairs the Japs were rampaging through the mansion. They charged toward the cluster of rooms that the GIs were in, and the GIs fired everything they had at them. Butsko used his grenade launcher and shot it down the long corridors, preventing the Japs from getting too close. But a few Japs managed to get through the rear door and they charged up the stairs. Bannon and Gafooley heard them coming, and Bannon motioned toward the door of the bedroom. He and Gafooley pulled hand grenades from their lapels and yanked the pins. They turned the levers loose and hurled the grenades into the corridor.

The Japs screamed in alarm, and one of them tried to pick up a grenade, but it blew up as he was bending over and took off his head. The other grenade exploded before a Jap could get to it, and that was the end of the three Japs who'd made it through the door.

"Let's get out of here!" Bannon said.

They ran toward the stairs and heard a stampede of feet. Turning the corner, they saw five Japs coming toward them. Bannon reached to his lapel and pulled off his last grenade. He looked to Gafooley, but Gafooley didn't have any more grenades left. Bannon pulled the pin and hurled the grenade down the stairs. It took the Japs by surprise, and they all scrambled to catch it and throw it back, but they got in each other's way and the grenade exploded in their midst, pieces of hot shrapnel tearing them apart.

Bannon looked down the stairs and saw more Japs coming

through the door. He had no more grenades to throw; all he could do was run the other way.

"C'mon!" he said to Gafooley.

They dashed down the corridor, glancing into rooms looking for shelter, but there was nothing. The corridor turned right and they followed it around, seeing a window at its end and no stairs.

"What now?" said Gafooley.

Bannon poked his head out the window.

Beeaaannnnnggggg!

He withdrew quickly and looked around. There was a door; he didn't know where it led but it was their only chance.

"In here!"

They dashed into a room. It was a library. Books had been pulled off the shelves and lay strewn on the floor. A rat scurried out of Bannon's way as he tipped over the huge scratched oak table in the center of the room. He and Gafooley got behind it and loaded their M 1s with fresh clips. They heard a clatter of footsteps in the corridor, and Bannon took a deep breath. He imagined a Jap tossing a hand grenade into the room and shivered uncontrollably.

A Jap appeared in the doorway and Bannon pulled the trigger of his M 1. The Jap screamed and dropped to the floor. Another Jap showed his face and Gafooley fired, the bullet hitting the doorjamb, and the Jap ducked out of the way. A hand appeared and it tossed in a hand grenade. Bannon jumped up, caught it with one hand, and tossed it back.

Barrrooooommmmm!

The building shook violently and splinters of wood flew in all directions. When the smoke cleared there was a huge hole in the floor. Japs could be heard groaning on the other side of the door. Bannon and Gafooley waited, but they heard nothing.

"Do you think we killed them all?" Gafooley asked.

Bannon shrugged. They left the safety of the table and tiptoed to the door. Bannon peeked around the corner and saw three dead Japs and the hole in the floor. He looked down and could see the room below.

"Let's get out of here," Bannon said, jumping into the hole.

Wind whistled past him and he landed in a bathtub full of water. He crawled out of the bathtub and a moment later Gafooley landed with a mighty splash.

"Well, I needed a bath," Gafooley said, stepping out of the bathtub.

Bannon peered around the doorjamb and saw a bedroom with a canopied bed. He crossed the bedroom and heard footsteps in the hall. He and Gafooley dived under the bed and landed in a scattering of fresh ratshit.

Bannon looked toward the door and saw two sets of Japanese leggings. He heard Japs talking, and in the distance came the sound of rifles and machine guns firing. A grenade exploded and the floor trembled beneath them. The leggings disappeared from in front of the door. Bannon and Gafooley crawled out from beneath the bed and approached the door. They looked to their right and left and saw no one.

"What now?" asked Gafooley.

"We've got to get back to the others."

Bannon walked cautiously down the corridor toward the sound of the fighting. Gafooley followed a few steps back, looking into every room to make sure no Japs were lurking about. They came to a bend in the corridor and Bannon peeked around the corner. He saw a bunch of Japs; one of them happened to be looking back at him. The Jap pointed and shouted.

Bannon and Gafooley ran back in the direction they'd come from. Bannon turned through the first doorway and entered a little sitting room with paintings that had been used for target practice. He heard galloping footsteps behind him and knew the Japs were coming fast. Heading toward the window, he dived out of it and sailed through the air. The green lawn came up fast and he tucked in his head, letting his rifle go and tumbling over, breaking the shock of the landing. He picked up his rifle and saw Nutsy Gafooley coming down feet first. Nutsy descended in classic paratrooper style, touched his feet to the ground, bent his knees, and rolled to the side, absorbing the crunch smoothly. He didn't even drop his rifle.

Both men jumped to their feet.

"Let's get out of here!" Bannon said.

They ran toward the coconut trees, and the startled Japs

nearby opened fire. But there weren't many Japs outside now, and only a handful were at that end of the building. Bannon and Gafooley made a zigzagged dash for the trees and dove behind them, turning and firing at the Japs grouping on the lawn. The Japs dropped to their stomachs or scattered into the coconut grove. Bannon shot one in the ass and Gafooley managed to bring down two.

The sound of fierce fighting could still be heard from inside the house. Bannon was torn between the desire to go back and help the others and to run away while he still had the chance. He looked at the rear porch, wondering if he and Gafooley could get in that way.

"What're we waiting for?" Gafooley said.

Bannon didn't know what to do. Something told him to get the hell out of there, and something else said he couldn't leave his buddies behind.

"I'm going back inside," he said.

"Are you fucking crazy?"

"You don't have to come with me," Bannon said. "Go back and see if you can link up with the regiment. Tell them to get up here as quick as they can."

"I think you're nuts to go in there."

"Do as I say. When I move out, I'll draw all the fire. Then you can get away. Got it?"

Gafooley made a face. "This is the dumbest thing I ever heard of!"

Bannon held out his hand. "Good luck, buddy."

Gafooley refused to shake it. "You're out of your mind!"

Bannon slapped him on the shoulder. "Keep your head down and watch your ass."

"But . . ."

Bannon jumped to his feet and ran out of the coconut grove, holding his M 1 at high port arms, screaming like a madman to give himself courage. The few Japs outside in the vicinity fired at him, but Bannon was running like Jesse Owens at the 1936 Olympics, heading for the porch at the rear of the building. He leaped up the five stairs and saw a dead Jap lying in front of him, a Type 99 machine gun in his arms with a big curved clip rising out of its chamber. Bannon dropped his M

1 rifle as Japanese bullets ripped into the wooden planks of the porch. He slung the haversack of Japanese ammo clips over his shoulder, picked up the machine gun, slung the strap over his right shoulder, and held the big, bulky weapon in his arms. On his knees he swung around and fired a burst at the Japs running toward him across the lawn, making them scatter and drop down. Then he turned and charged into the back door of the mansion.

He flew through the door and saw three Japs at the end of a hall. They turned around and saw him; their jaws dropped open as he advanced toward them, held the machine gun tightly, and pulled the trigger. It bucked and stuttered in his hands, and the three Japs were riddled with hot bullets manufactured in their own country.

Bannon kicked them out of his way and kept going. He turned a corner and saw another hallway with a bunch of Japs inside. They heard him coming and looked back, but that was all they had time to do. Bannon opened fire and tore them to shreds, then noticed movement in a bedroom, swung around, and shot a Jap officer sitting on a bed, looking at a map. A noise came from the bathroom and Bannon turned in that direction. He saw a Jap with his pants down, sitting on the toilet, a panicked expression on his face, and Bannon gave him a burst in the gut. The Jap sank lower into the toilet, blood leaking from his torso. His head lolled to the side.

Bannon moved out into the hall again. He heard furious fighting not too far away. He ran through the winding corridor, ready to shoot at anything that moved, and came to the main living room in which he and the others had been fighting before. This time it was full of Japs, all with their backs to him, and Bannon pulled the trigger of the machine gun. It roared like a vicious beast and he swung it from left to right and back again, mowing down the Japs, who dropped their rifles and bent over backward, collapsing onto wrecked furniture and the floor.

Japs in the corridor on the far side of the living room turned around and Bannon plowed into them, firing his machine gun. They were too crowded together to do anything and were taken by surprise. Bannon kept his finger depressed on the trigger and massacred them, stomping on their bodies as he made his way toward the room where Butsko and the others were.

"It's me!" he yelled. "Don't shoot!"

He turned a bend in the corridor and saw a doorway piled high with furniture. In front of the doorway were Japs trying to break through. When they heard Bannon they turned around. Bannon pulled the trigger of his machine gun and held it steady.

Click!

The machine gun was empty.

Beeeooowwwww! A bullet ricocheted off the wall beside him. Bannon ducked into a doorway, ejected the empty clip, and jammed in a new one. He pulled the trigger even before he left the room, chopping up the doorjamb, and then stepped into the hall. The Japs in front of the barricade were down on their knees, aiming back at him, and *Blam*—a bullet hit him in the thigh, but he aimed steadily and swung the machine gun from side to side, spraying them with lead. Another Japanese bullet punctured his shirt and grazed his ribs like a red-hot poker, but that was the last bullet the Japs fired. They all slumped to the floor, leaking blood, and Bannon climbed up the barricade in front of the next room. Hands reached down and grabbed his shirt and arms. Shaw and Shilansky pulled him over the top and he stumbled down into the room.

Butsko stood in front of him, a bandage wrapped around his head. "What the hell are you doing here?"

"Hiya, Sarge," Bannon said weakly.

"You shoulda got away while you had the chance!"

"Nutsy's gone for help."

Bannon felt like he had a charley horse in his leg. Private Blum bent beside him and cut away his pant leg.

"The bullet went all the way through," Blum said. "You'd better lie down."

Bannon lay on the floor and looked around. The room had two windows, and GIs manned each one, firing at Japs outside. The room also had two doorways, piled high with furniture and junk, and behind these barricades the GIs tried to fight off the Japs.

On the floor were dead and wounded men. Only half the platoon was fighting back—about fifteen men.

"How is it?" Bannon asked Blum.

"If I can stop the bleeding, you'll be okay."

Blum poured on coagulant powder and sulfa to disinfect the wound. Then he wrapped on the bandages. Meanwhile the Japs attacked the room again, firing at the barricades and through the windows, but the GIs had good cover and were able to prevent the Japs from getting close enough to throw had grenades. The battle raged for five minutes, with bullets ricocheting all around the room.

"Shit!" said Frankie La Barbara. "I'm out of ammo."

"I just got one clip left," said Jimmy O'Rourke, who also had a BAR.

Japanese bullets slammed against the barricade and flew through the windows. The recon platoon had been doing a fair job of holding the Japs back, but now they were running out of ammunition and the Japs were becoming bolder. Butsko had only three clips of ammunition left, and he stuffed one of them into his M 1. He and the others would be wiped out if they stayed in the room. They'd have to either surrender or try to break away. Surrendering to the Japs was almost like committing suicide, so they'd have to make a run for it.

Bannon got up off the floor, picked up his Japanese light machine gun, and took a post by the window, firing at the Japs advancing on the lawn below. They had been edging fairly close to the window, but Bannon peppered them with bullets and made them pull back.

Butsko had one hand grenade left. "Okay," he said, "we'll have to make a run for it, because we can't hold out much longer here. Wounded men who are conscious will be carried along with us; they'll have to fight too. The rest will be left behind. Bannon, you lead the way because you've got the firepower. We'll fight our way into that living room, out the front door, down the steps, and into the woods. Any questions?"

"We'll never make it," said Frankie La Barbara.

"We can try. Anything else?"

"Can I say a prayer?" asked the Reverend Billie Jones.

"We ain't got time. Can you move okay on that leg, Bannon?"

"Yeah."

"Okay, everybody get ready."

Butsko took his last hand grenade, pulled the pin, and held the activating lever tightly. Crawling across the floor, he pushed his hand underneath the barricade, which was being splintered by Japanese bullets. The GIs at the windows ducked down and the Japs on the lawn charged.

Butsko let go of the lever, pulled back his arm, and dashed to the far side of the room, dropping to his belly on the floor with the others. Bannon lay in the middle of the room behind an overstuffed chair, his leg aching from his wound. He tried not to think about it.

Barrrrooooom!

The barricade blew apart in a brilliant, powerful flash, and Bannon was on his feet, running with a limp toward the doorway, firing the Japanese light machine gun in his hands. The corridor outside was full of Japs who'd gotten too close to the barricade and had been blown to Kingdom Come. Bannon ran down the corridor to the main living room. Japs appeared at the end of the corridor. Bannon held the machine gun tightly and pulled the trigger, and the corridor filled with the roar of the automatic weapon. The power of the bullets threw the Japs back, and the GIs followed Bannon down the corridor, the wounded riding piggyback on the unscathed.

Bannon was first in the big living room, which was full of Japs. He swung the machine gun from side to side and kept his finger on the trigger, his hands going numb from the constant vibration, and Japs were torn apart by the bullets, performing macabre pirouettes as they fell to the floor.

The room filled with GIs, firing at the Japs, and Bannon led them to the front door. He dashed out onto the veranda and a bullet whistled by his ear, slamming into the wall next to him. Bannon lowered his machine gun and fired from side to side as he ran along. Frankie La Barbara and Jimmy O'Rourke were behind him, shooting their BARs, sending out a hail of lead. Private Dole, who was wounded, rode on Homer Gladley's back and fired a Colt .45 with one hand. Craig Delane, out of bullets, scooped up an Arisaka rifle from the arms of a dead Japanese soldier and fired from the waist as he ran in a zigzag across the veranda. A Japanese light machine gun, like the one Bannon was carrying, chattered at the edge of the woods, and one of its bullets hit Shaw in the ankle, shattering bone. Shaw fell to the ground, and the Reverend Billie Jones picked him up and carried him toward the grove.

Bannon fired a burst at the Japanese light machine gunner and his assistant. One of his bullets ricocheted off the top of the gun and hit the gunner in the face. The assistant tried to take the position behind the gun, and Craig Delane shot him through the neck. Butsko ran toward the machine gun, picked it up, and threw the sack of ammunition over his shoulder.

Pow! A Japanese bullet hit him in the shoulder, knocking him onto his side. He got to one knee, spun around, and sprayed bullets at the Japs running across the lawn. Moving the barrel of the machine gun to the left, he sent a rain of death into the coconut grove, where other Japs were attacking.

Blood oozing down his arm, Butsko retreated toward the coconut grove. He took cover behind a tree, aimed the machine gun around the trunk, and blasted three Japs running across the lawn. Nearby, Bannon lay on his stomach, aimed his light machine gun, and pulled the trigger while moving his shoulder from side to side. Behind another tree, Craig Delane pumped bullets at the Japs coming through the coconut grove.

Clang!

The clip emptied and sprang into the air. Delane reached to his last bandolier of ammunition. It was empty.

"Out of ammo!" he said.

The Reverend Billie Jones tossed him a clip, which he fed into the top of his M 1. Delane fired at a Jap coming through the coconut grove, and the Jap dropped to the ground. A bullet ricocheted off the tree beside Delane's head, and splinters dug into his face, making little dots of blood appear.

The Japs closed in around the embattled GIs, who formed a circle in the coconut grove. The GIs fired their weapons frantically, and one by one they ran out of ammunition. Bannon pressed the last clip into his machine gun and saw Japs swarming through the coconut grove all around him. He couldn't move or fire fast enough; there were too many of them. A grenade came flying through the air and Jimmy O'Rourke stood up, swung his BAR like a baseball bat, and hit the grenade

64

back. It exploded in the coconut grove, knocking down a tree and killing a few Japs.

"Out of ammo!" said Homer Gladley.

Bannon fired the last burst from his light machine gun. "Out of ammo!"

Butsko knew that the end had come. "Fix bayonets!"

The GIs fastened their bayonets on their rifles. Bannon didn't have a rifle anymore, so he drew his bayonet and held it in his fist, waiting for the Japs to rush them. Morris Shilansky was the only one firing; then his empty clip clanged into the air.

The coconut grove became quiet. In the smoke and gloom they saw Japs moving among the trees, but there was nothing the GIs could do about it. None of them said anything. Adrenaline was pumping through their veins and they were ready to die.

"Sullender!" cried a Japanese voice from Bannon's front.

That took the GIs by surprise. They'd expected to be slaughtered and looked at each other, everyone wondering what the other was thinking.

"What do you say?" Butsko asked.

"What do *you* say?" Bannon replied.

"It's up to you guys. I'll do it any way you want."

"I think we should surrender," Delane said, blood leaking from the little holes in his face. "At least that way we'd have a chance."

"To do what?" Frankie asked. "Get tortured by the fucking Nips?"

Butsko had been on the Bataan Death March and a prisoner in a Jap POW camp on northern Luzon for several months. "You might be better dead than a Jap prisoner."

"We'll probably be dead either way," Bannon said, "but if we surrender, we might have more of a chance."

"Where there's life there's hope," the Reverend Billie Jones said.

"Oh, fuck you!" Frankie La Barbara said.

The voice of the Jap came to them through the grove. *"Sullender or die! We give you three minutes to think—no more!*

You cannot get away! You sullounded!"

Shilansky spat into the dust. "I don't know what to do. I'll do whatever you guys decide."

"Me too," said Homer Gladley.

"I agree with Bannon," said Shaw, whose boot was filled with blood. He gritted his teeth and made fists to keep the pain under control. "If we're alive, at least we've got a chance."

"C'mon," said Frankie La Barbara sarcastically, "the moment we stand up and throw away our guns, they'll mow us down."

"If we don't, they'll mow us down anyway."

Butsko would rather die fighting, but he believed Bannon had a point. He'd escaped from that Japanese prison camp in northern Luzon, and maybe they could escape from where they were going, but he wasn't sure that he could handle being a prisoner of the Japs again.

"It seems to me," he said, "that most of you guys want to give up and take your chances, right?"

The men grunted in assent, except for Frankie La Barbara.

"I don't want those stinking Japs to lay their hands on me!" Frankie said.

"There's nothing you can do to stop them now," Bannon told him. "It's all over."

"It ain't never over."

"Besides," Bannon continued, "help might be on the way right now. I sent Nutsy back to look for the regiment."

"Hey," said Frankie, "he might be on his way here with the whole regiment right now."

"Maybe," Bannon said.

"What's it gonna be?" Butsko asked. "Are we gonna surrender? Everybody who wants to surrender say *yo.*"

Everybody, including Frankie La Barbara, said "yo."

"Okay," Butsko said, "if that's the way you want it, that's they way we'll play it. You might as well have your last smokes now, because the Japs'll probably take your cigarettes away, and if any of you have anything you want to hide, this is the time to do it, but don't get caught. Those Japs out there aren't nice people."

Bannon's leg ached from the bullet hole. He wondered what

he had to hide and realized he didn't have anything. He took out a cigarette and lit it up, inhaling deeply, wondering when he'd ever be able to smoke another one.

Corporal Gomez was looking for someplace to hide his switchblade knife, which he'd brought with him all the way from the back alleys of Los Angeles. He took off his boot, dropped the switch on the bottom, and put his foot back in.

Frankie wanted to keep some cigarettes with him. "Hey, Blum, gimme some fucking tape."

Blum tossed him a roll and Frankie cut off a length, taping three cigarettes to the inside of his thigh, next to his testicles.

"Three minutes up!" shouted the Jap. *"Sullender or die!"*

"We surrender!" Butsko yelled back.

"Stand up and hold hands high! Leave weapons on ground!"

"You heard him," Butsko said.

The men in the recon platoon who could stand got up and held their hands in the air. The others lay on the ground and waited.

Japs moved toward them through the grove, holding their rifles ready, slipping from tree to tree. The Japanese officer shouted orders and the Japanese soldiers closed in. Bannon felt an unpleasant sensation of fear throughout his body as the Japanese soldiers moved closer. He was aware of all the atrocity stories, how the Japs tortured and killed the men on the Bataan Death March, chopped off the heads and legs of British soldiers they'd captured in Singapore, massacred tens of thousands of Chinese in Nanking, raping women, even killing babies. Bannon wondered if surrendering was such a good idea. Maybe it would have been better to die clean than be tortured to death. But it was too late for that now.

The Japs crept closer, pointing their rifles at the GIs, making sure they were unarmed. The officer appeared behind them, his samurai sword in his hand. He was dressed identically to the soldiers but wore brown knee-high boots instead of leggings and different insignia on his collar. He was nearly six feet tall, and Bannon was always surprised when he saw a tall Jap, because he'd been taught that they were tiny men. The Japanese soldiers fit the stereotype better; they were smaller, raggedy, filthy, and ferocious-looking.

"Move over there!" the Jap officer said to the GIs.

The GIs stepped away from their weapons and lined up several feet away. Shaw hopped on one leg with his arm around Homer Gladley's neck.

"Take off clothes and put in front of you!" the Japanese officer said. "Boots too!"

The GIs unhitched their packs and lay them on the ground. They took off their boots, cartridge belts, and clothes, laying everything in piles in front of them.

"Hurry!" said the Japanese officer.

The GIs finished undressing and stood up again as the insects descended on their naked bodies and sucked out blood. The Japanese officer shouted something and a few Japanese soldiers gave their weapons to their comrades and then moved forward to search the GIs. They ran their fingers through the GI's hair, prodded in their armpits and crotches, and made them bend over so they could see if anything was hidden up their assholes.

The Japanese soldier in front of Bannon sneered at him as he poked with his fingers. Working down Bannon's body, the Jap ripped the bandage off Bannon's leg with a sudden wrenching movement, and Bannon let out a howl of pain. The Jap probed the wound with his dirty fingers, examined the bandage, and then let it drop to the ground. He examined the bottoms of Bannon's feet, then moved to examine the next man, Corporal Gomez.

Bannon picked up the bandage and pressed it against his wound, which was aching so severely he could feel the pain in his bones. He wished now that he'd asked Blum to shoot him up with a morphine Syrette to stop the pain.

The Jap examining Frankie La Barbara found the bandage on his thigh and pulled it away, revealing three cigarettes but no wound. The Jap grinned and drew back his fist, and Frankie got ready. The Jap shot his fist forward and Frankie blocked the punch, hammering the Jap in the stomach. Keeling over in pain, the Jap dropped to his stomach as three Japs jumped on top of Frankie La Barbara, pummeling him to the ground.

Another Jap turned Gomez's boot upside down and the switchblade fell out. The Jap picked up the switchblade, looked at it quizzically, and tried to pull out the blade with his fingertips, but of course it wouldn't come out that way. He pressed the button, but the safety catch was on and the blade still wouldn't open. The Japanese officer shouted something and the soldier tossed the switchblade, which the officer dropped into his pocket. Then the soldier turned around and punched Gomez in the mouth. Gomez staggered back two steps but he didn't go down.

The Jap officer shouted, "Do not hide weapons! Anybody who hides weapons will be shot!"

The Japs continued their search of the GIs. Frankie got to his feet, his face bloody. He leaned against a tree because his head still wasn't clear. A Jap stopped in front of Butsko and looked into his eyes. Butsko's eyes didn't waver and he kept his backbone straight, because he'd already taken the worst that the Japs could dish out and he wasn't afraid of them.

The Jap searched him, poking and prodding, Butsko wanted to punch him in the mouth, but he stayed calm, holding his hands at his sides, his shoulder throbbing with pain. The Japs stepped back and joined the others searching through the GIs' packs, hooting with delight whenever they found food.

"Put your clothes on!" the Japanese officer said. "Do not try any escape, because we shoot you down like dogs!"

The GIs got dressed while the Japs confiscated their food. The Jap officer sat against the trunk of a tree and the Jap soldiers dumped the food at his feet. He looked at the cans and tried to read the markings. Then he said something in Japanese. His men divided up the cans and opened them while other Japs stood guard over the recon platoon.

Bannon watched blood ooze down his leg and drip to the ground. When the bandage had been pulled away, it also removed the scab that was forming over Bannon's wounds. Butsko noticed him.

"You okay?" Butsko asked.

"No talking!" shouted the Jap officer.

Blum turned around. "Can I treat that man's wound."

The Japanese officer said something to one of his men, who raised his rifle and hammered Blum in the head with his rifle butt. A wide gash opened on Blum's head and he fell unconscious to the ground.

Butsko gave them all a look that said *I told you so*. Frankie La Barbara sat up and touched his finger to his nose. It had been broken badly before, but now it was mashed all over his face.

The Japs ate hungrily and Bannon sized them up. They were skinny, their uniforms were raggedy, and many had holes in their shoes. None had shaven for a while. Behind them, in the coconut grove, were many more Japs. Everywhere he looked he saw Japs. He figured there must be at least two companies of them in the area. They were gathering their dead and wounded.

When the Japs finished eating, their officer gave them an order and they filled a sack with the extra food. Then the officer stood and stretched. He picked his teeth with a long pointy fingernail and looked at the GIs.

"Do not have such unhappy faces," he said. "Be glad we let you sullender. We would have killed you for what you have done, but we have a need for you, and that is why we let you sullender. On your feet!"

The GIs stood, and those who had difficulty were helped by their buddies.

"Walk that way!" said the officer, pointing to the mansion.

The men from the recon platoon moved south through the coconut grove, their shoulders hunched in defeat, as Japanese soldiers hurled taunts at them. One Jap threw a coconut shell, which hit Morris Shilansky in the head. Another Jap spat in Bannon's face. Japanese soldiers believed in fighting to the death and had contempt for anyone who would surrender. A Jap kicked Butsko in the ass, and Butsko wanted to turn around and tear his head off, but he just kept walking, his heart full of apprehension, wondering what would become of them.

FOUR . . .

In the late afternoon Colonel Imoto sat cross-legged in the tent that had been assigned him, writing in his diary. He was detailing his impressions of the Japanese Seventeenth Army on Guadalcanal, and it was even worse than he'd imagined. He'd been shown the bodies of Japanese soldiers who'd starved to death, and his escorts had taken him to a cave where a dead Japanese soldier lay with layers of meat sliced off his rump, evidence of the cannibalism he'd heard about. Imoto had been involved in the invasions of Hong Kong and Singapore and had seen the Imperial Army riding the crest of astounding victories, but never could he imagine that so soon would come a catastrophe of the proportions of Guadalcanal.

"Colonel Imoto, sir?" said a voice outside his tent.

"Yes."

"General Hyakutake would like to speak with you."

"I'll be right there."

Colonel Imoto thought he should put on a fresh shirt, but it wouldn't stay fresh long in the sweltering humidity. He buckled his samurai sword to his waist, put on his cap, and left his tent. Sargeant Kaburagi was waiting outside for him, and together they walked across the clearing. The rain had stopped, and small patches of blue sky could be seen in the cloud layer above. Occasionally the sun would come out for a

71

few minutes and then be swallowed up by the gloom again. Perhaps tomorrow the sun would shine and he could dry his clothes out.

They came to the command tent and Sargeant Kaburagi held open the flap. Colonel Imoto went inside, passed a few desks with officers behind them, and went back to the office of General Hyakutake, who sat behind his desk, his big ears making him look somewhat comical, but the expression on his face was deadly serious. General Miyazaki and Colonel Konuma sat on chairs in front of General Hyakutake's desk. Colonel Imoto marched to the front of the desk and saluted General Hyakutake.

"You asked to see me, sir?"

"Yes, Colonel Imoto. Have a seat, please."

Colonel Imoto sat on a chair and folded his hands in his lap.

"Colonel Imoto," General Hyakutake said solemnly, "I have decided to obey the order to evacuate Guadalcanal. But I must point out to you, and it won't be easy, and I can't say whether the evacuation will succeed as planned. At least I will do my best."

Colonel Imoto bowed slightly. "I'm sure General Imamura will be pleased to know that you intend to comply."

"I have been a soldier all my life and I cannot disobey an order that originated with the Emperor."

"I understand, sir."

"As I said, the evacuation will be most difficult. We must retreat slowly and fight every inch of the way, to make the Americans think nothing has changed. If we break and run, they'll slaughter us."

Colonel Imoto tucked his chin into his chest. "I doubt whether good Japanese soldiers will break and run, sir."

"Some have already," General Hyakutake said, "and a surprising number of our men have surrendered."

"No!"

"It's true. Lack of food distorted their perceptions and made them behave in a manner that would be unthinkable if they'd had normal nourishment. Of course, most of my men have fought on regardless of shortages and deprivation. I'd say that only a few hundred surrendered so ignominiously, but it is something to think about, isn't it?"

"It is indeed."

"We have some American prisoners also, of course. They surrender much more readily than we do, and lately we've been trying to capture as many as we can, because perhaps we can trade their men for ours at some point."

"An excellent idea, sir."

"And if not, it might be good for morale at home to march some of these captured Americans through the streets of our cities and towns, so our people can know that the Americans are not invincible."

"From what you've said, sir, I think it will be difficult enough evacuating your own men, never mind American prisoners."

"We'll see, but at any rate we'll have them if we need them."

"Yes, sir."

"I understand a regiment debarked with you last night?"

"That is correct, sir. It was the Sixty-sixth Infantry, commanded by Colonel Shibata, the son of General Shibata."

"Ah, yes, General Shibata. One of our finest generals. Too old for active duty now, of course."

"And Colonel Shibata's younger brother was a lieutenant who fought here and died."

"Really?" asked General Hyakutake. "I didn't know that."

General Miyazaki wrinkled his brow. "I don't seem to recall the name."

"Well," said Colonel Imoto, "he was only a lieutenant. I imagine he served in the field and evidently was killed in action. At any rate the colonel will probably want to avenge his young brother's death."

"No doubt," agreed General Hyakutake. "I imagine he'll be a real tiger, and that's just what we need here. An aggressive commander and fresh troops will help us hold back the Americans so that we can leave this accursed island. Have Colonel Shibata report to me first thing in the morning, will you?"

"Yes, sir."

"Good. And now what will you do, since you have delivered your message to me, Colonel Imoto? Will you return to Rabaul?"

"My orders are to stay with you here, sir, and accompany you back to Rabaul when you leave."

"Very good. Make yourself as comfortable as you can. I have a staff meeting here every morning at ten. I'll expect you to attend. That is all. You may leave."

"Yes, sir!"

Colonel Imoto stood, saluted, and marched out of the tent. In the clearing he put on his cap and looked up at the sky. The sun was covered by clouds again, but perhaps the next day would be sunny. He walked toward his tent, his spirits improved. He was glad that General Hyakutake would comply with the order to evacuate Guadalcanal, because it would have been very messy if he'd refused. Colonel Imoto would not have known what to do. He might even have had to commit harakiri.

Nutsy Gafooley was wandering through the jungles of Guadalcanal, looking for other GIs like himself, but couldn't find any. He didn't have a compass and wished now that he'd asked Bannon for his, but in the excitement of their parting he hadn't thought of asking.

When he left the plantation he'd heard the sounds of fierce fighting, but after a while it stopped. Nutsy believed the recon platoon must have been wiped out by the Japs and felt sick about it.

He stopped at a little glen shrouded with vines and branches to eat a can of C rations, then filled up his canteen at the stream, dropping two Halazone tablets inside to purify the water. He set out again, heading in an easterly direction, certain that he'd bump into GIs sooner or later. Whenever the sun came out he took his bearings and pressed on. Nutsy had been a hobo before he'd joined the Army and he knew how to get around in the woods. He hadn't slept with a roof over his head for three years before that first night he spent in an Army barrack at Fort Sill, Oklahoma.

In mid-afternoon he heard troops moving through the jungle,

and he hid to make sure of what side they were on. They turned out to be a Japanese patrol of five men, and Nutsy lay still behind some bushes, watching them pass. He waited until the Japs were gone and then he raised himself, creeping east again, looking and listening, wondering where in hell the American Army was hiding.

Later in the afternoon he heard another patrol and dived behind a bush. Peering through the leaves, he saw American GIs moving cautiously through the jungle.

"Hello, there!" Nutsy said.

The GIs scattered in all directions, dropping behind logs, hiding behind trees, looking about furtively.

"Hey, it's me—an American!"

"Show yourself and keep your hands up!"

Nutsy slung his rifle, raised his arms, and came out from behind the bush, forcing himself to smile in a friendly manner. The other GIs could see that he wasn't Japanese. They rose and approached him.

"What are you doing out here?" asked a second lieutenant.

"I'm in the recon platoon of the Twenty-third Regiment. We got trapped in a building back there"—Nutsy pointed— "and they sent me for help."

"A building? Out here?"

"Yes, sir. It was in the middle of a big coconut plantation."

The lieutenant took out his map, dropped to one knee, and looked for the coconut plantation. He found it, but there was no marking for a building. "Where was the building?" he asked.

Nutsy looked at the map and estimated its location. "Around here, I'd say." He touched his finger to the map.

"When did all this happen?"

"This morning."

"Do you think your people could have held out this long."

Nutsy shook his head. "I don't think so," he said in a low voice. "I think they got wiped out."

"I'll transmit the message to the Twenty-third Regiment," the lieutenant replied, "That's about all I can do."

The recon platoon survivors staggered over the jungle trail as their Japanese captors punched and kicked them, batted them with their rifle butts, and jabbed them with bayonets.

Shilansky carried young Private Hilliard on his back, and Shaw's arm was wrapped around Homer Gladley's shoulder. Bannon felt a terrible numbing pain every time he took a step on his bad leg, and Butsko couldn't move his left arm anymore because of the wound in his shoulder. Frankie La Barbara's nose was a mass of blood and torn cartilage, and Jimmy O'Rourke was bent over in pain from a deep cut underneath his ribs.

Private Blum, the medic, saw all the suffering around him, but there was nothing he could do. The Japs had taken his medicine bag away and hit him in the head with a rifle butt. Now he had a continuous headache and a feeling of general disorientation. He figured he probably had a concussion.

The Japanese soldiers taunted the GIs and spat in their faces. One of them walked alongside Bannon, staring hatefully at him. Bannon turned his head and stared back just as hatefully. The Jap punched him in the mouth, and Bannon was so weak he fell to the ground. A Japanese soldier shouted at him to get up, but Bannon couldn't move. The soldier raised his rifle and bayonet to kill Bannon, when Butsko stepped out of formation, pushed the Jap to the side, and bent over to pick Bannon up.

Another Japanese guard ran toward Butsko and bashed him in the head with his rifle butt. Butsko lost consciousness and fell on top of Bannon. The guard raised his rifle and was about to shoot, when the officer shouted an order and the Jap soldier lowered his rifle, a look of disappointment on his face.

"Get up!" yelled the officer. "If not, we shoot you!"

Bannon was conscious, but Butsko was out like a light as he lay on top of Bannon. "C'mon, Sarge," Bannon said. "Get up."

Butsko mumbled something. Private Blum broke formation, grabbed Butsko by his collar, and dragged him to his feet, wrapping one of Butsko's arms around his shoulder. Bannon pulled himself up from the ground, limped a few steps, took Butsko's other arm, and put it around his shoulder. Together Bannon and Blum helped Butsko along the trail.

The Japanese soldiers jeered at the GIs, kicking them in their asses, poking them with their bayonets. They vented all their frustrations against the GIs, and they had many frustrations because they were low on food, brutalized by their sergeants and officers, and continually forced to make suicide attacks.

One of the Japs, for no particular reason, kicked Frankie La Barbara in the shins, tripping him up. Frankie fell to the ground and something snapped in his mind. Getting up quickly, he rushed toward the soldier and tried to grab him by the throat. The soldier hit him in the face with his rifle butt, damaging Frankie's nose even more and knocking him cold. Frankie fell to the ground, and the Jap was going to step on his face when the Reverend Billie Jones bent down and scooped Frankie up.

The Reverend Billie Jones heaved Frankie over his shoulder and carried him along, although his knees were weak and he had a cracked rib. The Reverend Billie Jones hated the Japs all around him and thought they were demons from hell. He prayed for God to descend from heaven and wipe the Japs out, but God didn't come and one of the Japs stuck his bayonet in Billie Jones's ass about a half inch, just for the hell of it. Although Billie was weak and was carrying Frankie La Barbara, he jumped a foot in the air. *If I ever get through this,* he thought, *I'm gonna kill Japs with my bare hands. I'll squeeze their throats so hard their eyes will pop out. I'll kick them into dogshit. I'll skin the little yellow bastards alive.*

The recon platoon and their captors made their way through thick jungle and across fields of kunai grass. They climbed up and down hills, forded streams, and crossed gorges on swinging vine bridges constructed by natives. Finally, late in the day, they arrived at a camp nestled in a valley among wooded hills. Japanese soldiers weak from hunger crawled out of tents to watch them pass. Others, who appeared well-fed and sturdy, lined up along the path and jeered at the GIs. Bannon was struck in the face by a rock. Butsko was hit over the head by a length of wood. Frankie La Barbara, who was staggering toward the rear of the line, had a bucket of shit dumped over his head, and he went totally out of his mind.

He turned around and attacked the Jap who'd done the dirty deed, trying to kick him in the balls, but the Jap was fast and Frankie was slowed down by fatigue, hunger, and thirst. Fran-

77

kie missed his kick and then was hit in the head with a rifle butt. Staggering, he saw a dozen Japs jump on him, and he fell to the ground underneath their weight. They punched and kicked him until he was unconscious, and then Private Blum picked him up, slung him over his shoulder, and carried him along, although Frankie stank to high heaven.

In the middle of a clearing was a barbed-wire pen measuring around thirty feet square. A group of emaciated, filthy GIs were inside, blood caked on their faces and sores on their arms and hands. Some wore bloody, filthy bandages. The door to the pen was opened and the recon platoon marched in.

Bannon looked around. At each corner outside the pen was a little hut about six feet off the ground, and inside each hut were two Japanese guards. Two more Japanese guards manned the front gate. There was no shelter in the pen, only a hole that was the latrine.

The GIs dropped to the ground, hungry and thirsty, exhausted from their long trek across Guadalcanal. Bannon sat cross-legged on the ground and looked at the prisoners who were there already. They evidently received no food, no medical treatment, and plenty of beatings.

Bannon took a deep breath and realized he was in for the worst time of his life.

Colonel Saburo Shibata, the commander of the Sixty-sixth Infantry Regiment, heard the commotion as the American prisoners were marched into the camp. He stepped out of his tent and saw them being led toward the pen. Shibata had a wispy mustache and beard, which quivered with emotion as he watched the Americans enter the pen. It was possible that one of them fired the bullet that killed his brother, Kenichi.

His sword strapped to his side and his soft cap low over his eyes, he walked toward the pen. The gate was being closed and he saw the Americans sprawling on the ground in an unsoldierly manner. It was a disgrace to be killed by such rabble. Colonel Shibata felt sorry for his dead brother, who had been young and idealistic, but too frail for infantry warfare. His brother had flunked out of fighter-pilot school, and their father had obtained a commission in the army for him. Colonel Shibata figured his brother wouldn't last long in a pitched battle, and he was right. He was killed in his first action on Guadalcanal.

Colonel Shibata approached the pen and looked through the strands of barbed wire. He wanted to enter the pen and cut up the Americans with his sword, but he held himself still, his face expressionless. One of the Americans turned around and looked at him, and beams of pure hatred passed between them. The American had sandy hair and a bandage on his leg and seemed to be taunting Colonel Shibata. *If I ever get the chance, I'll kill you*, Colonel Shibata thought.

Bannon looked up at the Japanese officer and seethed with hatred. Unlike Colonel Shibata, Bannon made no effort to disguise his loathing. The officer's boots were polished, and Bannon figured he must have arrived recently on Guadalcanal. That meant the Japs were reinforcing their troops on the island. Perhaps they were planning a new offensive. *If I ever get out of here, I'll kill you*, Bannon thought.

Jimmy O'Rourke, with a big scab on his forehead, crawled toward Bannon, an ugly expression on his face. "Hey, Bannon," he said, "what happened to your girl friend?"

Bannon blinked. He'd completely forgotten about the native girl. Where the hell was she?

"I'll bet she betrayed us to the Japs," O'Rourke said. "I should have killed her while I had the chance."

Bannon didn't feel like arguing, and he thought O'Rourke might be right. Maybe it had been a mistake to let her live, but he didn't think so. He couldn't have stood by and let a woman be shot.

The Japanese officer turned and walked away. Bannon watched him go and then noticed an object flying toward his head. It was a rock thrown by a Japanese soldier, but Bannon couldn't duck in time. The rock hit him on the ear and drew blood.

O'Rourke chortled like an old buzzard. "Serves you right. If you hadn't let that girl go, we might not be here right now."

"You're a stupid asshole," Bannon told him. "You don't

have a brain in your fucking head."

"Oh, yeah? Well, I'm not the one who let that little traitor go."

"Knock it off!" said Butsko.

O'Rourke spat at the ground and crawled away. Bannon looked around and saw Frankie La Barbara lying motionless on the other side of the pen. Blum, the medic, knelt beside him, touching his face. Bannon got to his feet and limped across the compound, dropping down next to Blum.

"How is he?" Bannon asked.

"Out like a light."

"Is he hurt bad?"

"I don't think so."

Frankie smelled disgusting because of the bucket of shit that had been dumped on him. Bannon knew his wounds should be washed, but he had no water left in his canteen.

"Anybody got any water?" Bannon asked.

Nobody said anything. All of them had drunk theirs up, just like he had. Bannon stood again and approached one of the guards standing at the gate. "You speak English?"

The guard looked at Bannon malevolently, and Bannon didn't know whether he'd understood or not.

"Can we get a bucket of water in here?"

The Jap guard looked at the other guard and said something. The other guard smiled. The first guard motioned with his hand at Bannon, then unlocked the gate. He pulled it open and Bannon walked out of the pen. He thought the Japs were going to let him get a bucket of water.

Bam—a rifle butt hit him on the cheek and sent him sprawling to the ground. Dazed, he looked up and saw a shoe in front of his eyes. The shoe kicked him in the mouth and Bannon saw stars. The Japs got on either side of him and kicked him in the ribs, face, and groin. Bannon tried to defend himself, but he was weak and slow. One blow hit him on the forehead and knocked him out. The Japs kept kicking him for a while, then picked him up and threw him into the compound again, locking the door behind him.

Blum staggered over, dropped to his knees, and examined him. Butsko came over and collapsed nearby. Bannon's face was bloody, he had an ugly gash on his scalp, and he was limp as a rag.

"Anything broken?" Butsko asked.

"It's hard to say," Blum replied. "When he comes to, it'll be easier to find out."

Butsko gathered up his last reserves of energy so he could speak loudly. "Don't talk to the guards!" he shouted. "Just stay put and try to get some rest!"

Colonel William Stockton, the commander of the Twenty-third Infantry Regiment, was operating from a bivouac deep in the jungle. His telephones were wired in by his signal corpsmen, guards were posted everywhere, and hot chow was being prepared by his cooks from canned and dehydrated food.

Nutsy Gafooley approached Colonel Stockton's tent with great trepidation, because top brass scared the shit out of him. He had an inferiority complex to begin with, and top brass made it worse. The military system brainwashed GIs into thinking officers were better than they were, and it had worked with Nutsy.

He entered Colonel Stockton's big walled tent and saw Sergeant Major Ramsay seated behind a desk. "I'm Private Gafooley and I heard the colonel wants to talk with me."

"Go right in," Ramsay said.

Nutsy walked to the next tent flap, pushed it aside, and entered Colonel Stockton's office. Colonel Stockton sat behind his desk, puffing a pipe. He was lean, had silvery hair, and looked worried.

"Private Gafooley reporting, sir!"

"Have a seat."

Nutsy sat down and Colonel Stockton leaned forward, pushing his ashtray and package of Briggs pipe tobacco out of his way. "Tell me in your own words what happened out there, Gafooley."

Nutsy stuttered and muttered but managed to get out the story. He told how they'd come to the plantation, captured the mansion, and then were counterattacked by a large Japanese force supported by a tank. He described how they'd knocked out the tank, fought like bastards, and held off the Japs for an hour or so. Finally he told how Bannon had ordered him to try to get help. "The last thing I saw was Bannon fighting his way back into that house."

Colonel Stockton looked down at the map on his desk. The location of the plantation had already been radioed to him, and he realized that the recon platoon had got far in front of the main advance of the regiment.

"How many Japs were there?" Colonel Stockton asked.

"Two, maybe three, companies, but we killed a lot of them, sir."

"About how many would you say?"

"I'd say we wiped out nearly half of them."

Colonel Stockton puffed his pipe glumly. The recon platoon had been formed by him out of the toughest men in the regiment, and he felt responsible for what happened. His staff officers told him many times that he should have kept a tighter rein on Butsko, but he always declined to do so; he thought Butsko knew what he was doing. Butsko and the recon platoon had been in a lot of tough scrapes before, but never anything like this. They should never have tried to take that building without support.

"Was there any chance that they got away?" Colonel Stockton asked hopefully.

Nutsy shook his head. "I don't see how they coulda got away," he said in a low voice.

"*You* got away."

"I was lucky."

"Is there anything else important that you can tell me? Take a few minutes to think before you answer.

Nutsy recalled the battle for the big white house. In his mind he saw the fighting from room to room, the grenades flying around, the walls and ceilings collapsing as the tank fired its cannon. Then he flashed on the girl.

"We found a native girl, sir," Nutsy said.

"A native girl?" Colonel Stockton asked. "In the building?"

"Yes, sir. A Jap officer was fucking—ah, I mean, a Jap officer was in bed with her when we captured the place. She said the Japs had captured her, but some of the guys thought she was on their side."

"Hmmmm. Anything else?"

"Not that I can think of, sir."

"You sure?"

"I think so, sir."

"If you think of anything else, come back here and tell me. In the meantime, get yourself something to eat and find a place to sack out. Tell Sergeant Ramsay where you are in case I need you."

"Yes, sir."

Nutsy stood, saluted, did an about-face, and marched out of the office. Colonel Stockton's pipe went out and he placed it inside the ashtray. He wiped his face with his hands and then looked down at the map. *Well,* he thought, *they're almost certainly dead. Butsko bit off more than he could chew. Damn.*

Colonel Stockton thought he should send a few companies toward the mansion to see what was there, then questioned his own motives. If any other platoon had been involved in that mess, would he divert a few companies from his attack to check on them? He admitted to himself that he probably would. Evidently a heavy concentration of Japs was in that area and he couldn't just forget about it. But maybe one company would be enough. He'd order them to proceed carefully and stay out of trouble. If they found Japs, they should radio back for instructions.

He decided to send George Company, which was the company the recon platoon had been traveling with before they got separated from the rest of the regiment.

FIVE . . .

It was night in the POW compound and the men of the recon platoon slept fitfully. The sky had cleared and a half-moon shone in the sky over the tops of the trees. A bird screeched nearby and Bannon opened his eyes. He ached all over and his head rang as if bells were pealing inside his skull. He remembered being beaten by the Japanese guards and his heart sank when he realized he was not waking up within the safety of the American defense perimeter. He was a POW of the Japanese, who had never signed the Geneva Convention accords regarding the treatment of prisoners.

He looked around and saw the guards in their towers, hunched over, their rifles slung over their shoulders, silhouetted against the night sky. His kidneys hurt and he had to take a piss. Pushing himself to his feet, he stumbled across the compound to the latrine. Standing in front of it, he braced his feet and pissed into the hole. Glancing to the side, he saw the guard in the nearest tower facing him, looking at him through binoculars. *Take a good look, you bastard,* Bannon thought.

Blam!

Bannon jumped three inches off the ground. The guard leaned over at a ridiculous angle and fell out of his tower. Suddenly the woods erupted with rifles and machine-gun fire. The GIs in the compound snapped their heads up, thinking they

85

were in the middle of an attack, and they were. Bannon looked and saw figures swarming out of the jungle, running toward the POW compound. Another guard was shot out of his tower, and one of the guards near the front gate collapsed onto the ground.

Bannon stuffed his dick back into his pants and buttoned his fly. Figures charged toward the POW compound, and in the moonlight Bannon could see that they were natives wearing lavalava skirts and Army shirts. Four of them carried wire cutters in their hands, and they snapped through the barbed wire quickly while their comrades filled the night with the thunder of small-arms fire.

"Come on, hurry up!" shouted one of the natives.

The GIs ran with renewed energy toward the openings in the barbed-wire fence. Blum grabbed Frankie La Barbara's arm and dragged him along. Butsko helped Shaw, and Homer Gladley carried Hilliard in his arms like a baby. The natives fired rifles and submachine guns from a kneeling position at Japs coming out of their tents to see what was going on. The natives threw hand grenades and fired a bazooka, blowing up the larger tents. One of the rockets landed in front of the tent belonging to Colonel Shibata, knocking it down and covering it with earth. Colonel Shibata fought against the heavy canvas, expecting a dagger to break through at any moment and stab him to death.

Whistles were blown and Japs shouted orders. The GIs hobbled out of the prison compound and the natives grabbed them and helped them along. Some of the GIs in the compound were too sick and weak to move, and they were left behind. There was no time to fuck around.

The GIs and natives ran into the woods, and a thin screen of natives stayed behind at the edge of the clearing to hold off the Japs and let their comrades get away. Somebody thrust a submachine gun into Bannon's hand and he swung around, pulling the trigger and firing at Japs running toward the jungle. Two fell before the stream of bullets pouring out of his gun, and he felt a surge of joy and energy. The pain went away and he felt strong again.

Colonel Shibata finally made it out of his tent. "After them!" he screamed, waving his samurai sword in the air.

One of the natives took aim at him and pulled the trigger of his M 1 rifle. His aim was slightly off, but the bullet hit Colonel Shibata in the arm, spinning him around and throwing him to the ground. Japs ran around in confusion and disorder. They thought they were being attacked by a large American troop unit.

The natives retreated into the jungle. They knew the territory and led the Americans over the narrow paths, moving swiftly. The screen pulled back, turned around, and ran away. The Japs still didn't know what was going on. The entire rescue had taken less than ten minutes to bring off. An aide helped Colonel Shibata to his feet, and he, too, thought a major American attack was under way.

"Hold fast!" he shouted. *"There will be no retreat!"*

The Japs dropped to their bellies and formed a defense around the camp. They fired into the jungle and soon realized no one was firing back. Colonel Shibata, lying on the ground and holding his bleeding biceps, also became aware that the attack was over.

"Stop firing! Wait till they come back! Set up your machine guns! Where are the mortars?"

Someone came running toward Colonel Shibata, who raised his pistol. *"Don't shoot!"* yelled Lieutenant Isangi. *"It's me!"*

Colonel Shibata lowered his pistol and Lieutenant Isangi dropped to the ground. "The prisoners have been released, sir!"

"What!"

"Yes, sir! The barbed wire has been cut!"

Now Colonel Shibata knew what had happened. A raiding party had freed the prisoners. It wasn't a major attack after all.

"Lieutenant Isangi, send Company A after the attackers! They can't be far!"

"Yes, sir!"

Lieutenant Isangi sprang to his feet and ran off to organize Company A. Colonel Shibata stood and clasped his fist over his bleeding bicep. *"They've gone! The attack is over!"*

His men raised themselves from the ground, dazed by what had happened. All around them lay the dead and wounded bodies of their comrades. Colonel Shibata staggered toward the POW compound and saw the cut wires. Most of the prisoners were gone. He stared furiously at the prisoners who had not been able to run away and wanted to order all of them shot, but Imperial Headquarters claimed there was a need for them. Colonel Shibata couldn't imagine what for.

Sergeant Yuasa approached Colonel Shibata. "You've been wounded, sir! I'll get the medical corporal!"

Sergeant Yuasa turned and ran off. Colonel Shibata looked at the jungle and cursed. He'd been on Guadalcanal less than twenty-four hours and already he'd been humiliated by the Americans. He saw Company A run across the clearing and enter the jungle.

Company A got lost after twenty yards' penetration. They couldn't pick up the trail of the attackers in the darkness, and the jungle was a solid wall of vines and branches. The attackers hadn't used any of the main trails. The search was abandoned after an hour.

The long column moved silently over the narrow, twisting trails, and the natives helped carry the seriously wounded. Bannon walked without help, limping badly but feeling good. He didn't think he could last another day with the Japs, but now he was free. He felt elated and loved the natives in their lavalava skirts and Army shirts. They wore bandoliers of American ammunition crossed over their backs and chests and appeared to be a cheerful bunch.

They stopped for a break, and the natives gave the GI cigarettes to smoke. They offered water but had no food with them because they were traveling light. Finally they moved out again, and the moon shone brightly in the sky.

Near dawn they approached a cluster of huts in one of the thickest parts of the jungle. Weird statues towered twenty feet into the air, and men and women came out of the huts. One of the women looked familiar, and as Bannon drew closer, he recognized the native girl named Mary that they'd rescued at the mansion. She was standing next to a bearded old man supporting himself with the aid of a cane.

"Welcome to my village," said the old man.

Butsko, battered and weary, staggered toward the old man. "Are you in charge here?"

"I am."

"My name's Butsko. Thank you for saving us."

The old man looked at the girl. "Thank my daughter. She's the one who told us you'd been taken prisoner."

Butsko looked at her. "Thank you."

"You saved me from the Japanese. I only did what was right."

Bannon moved next to Jimmy O'Rourke and gave him an elbow in the ribs. "And you wanted to shoot her," Bannon whispered.

"How was I supposed to know?" O'Rourke asked.

Butsko looked at the old man. "How did you find us?"

"My men followed your trail back to the Japanese camp. It was not difficult."

"Thank you again."

"You must be hungry. We have food. Come."

The old man led them to a clearing among the huts. Women brought crates of C rations, and the cans were passed around. The natives opened the cans and the GIs ate hungrily. Cups of coconut milk were given to the GIs, who drank the cool, sweet liquid down.

"Do you have a radio here?" Butsko asked the old man.

"It is broken."

"I'd like to get word to our army about the Japanese camp."

"We will send a messenger after you have eaten."

Butsko grunted and ate his can of franks and beans. He drank coconut milk and looked at the girl, who was sitting silently beside her father, casting shy glances at Bannon. *What's going on here?* Butsko thought.

The old man explained in halting, strangely accented English that he was chief of the little tribe and they hated the Japanese, because the Japanese were cruel to them, beating up the men, raping the women, stealing everything in sight. "When they first came we were glad to see them, because we thought they would grant us our independence, but then we found out that they were worse than anything we had known before. Their propaganda officers told us we would be their brothers in the Southeast Asia Co-Prosperity Sphere, but their soldiers treated us like slaves, so we have rebelled against them. The Australians and your army have helped us with arms and supplies, and we in turn have helped you. We hope you will give us our independence after the Japanese are driven away."

"I don't know anything about that," Butsko said. "I am only a sergeant and I take orders like everybody else."

After the meal the soldiers went down to a nearby stream and took baths. The men who were severely wounded were washed by native women, and their dirty uniforms were exchanged for lavalava skirts. Private Blum dressed their wounds with medical supplies the natives had obtained from the US Army. Butsko went to the chief's's hut to write out his message for Colonel Stockton.

The GIs trudged back to the camp, where huts had been prepared for them, straw mats on the ground. The men lay down and soon fell into deep slumber.

SIX . . .

Bannon was awakened by the laughter of children. He opened his eyes and saw sunlight streaming through openings in the straw walls of the hut he was in, making a golden glow inside the hut. At first he didn't know where he was, but then it all came back: the fight at the big white house, their capture by the Japanese, and the rescue.

Frankie La Barbara rolled over and groaned, his face bandaged. "Somebody shut them fucking kids up," he snarled.

Bannon patted him on the shoulder. "Take it easy, buddy. They're our hosts."

"I'll kick their little fucking asses!"

Butsko opened his eyes. "What's going on in here!"

Shaw rolled over. "Shaddup, Frankie, willya? You always got your big yap open."

"I'll shut up when those kids shut up."

They heard more laughter and giggling outside the tent, and then all at once they realized the voices weren't just children's. There were women out there! Frankie crawled over the other GIs to the door, which was covered by a hanging rectangle of bamboo and straw. He pushed it out of the way and saw a gaggle of children and young girls playing behind piles of freshly laundered uniforms and socks.

"Cunt!" said Frankie.

"Where?" asked Corporal Gomez, diving toward the door.

Gomez was followed by Homer Gladley, Morris Shilansky, Tommy Shaw, and Jimmy O'Rourke. Butsko reached for the pack of cigarettes the chief had given him the night before. He put one in his mouth, lit it up, and threw the pack to Bannon.

"Wow, looka that one!" Frankie said, pointing to a native girl.

"I wonder if it's okay to fuck them," said Shilansky.

Butsko turned to them, spitting tobacco crumbs out of his mouth. *"Keep your hands off them, you bunch of scumbags!"*

"How come, Sarge?" asked Frankie La Barbara.

"Because they just saved our asses and I don't want no trouble!"

"But, Sarge, they're so friendly."

"I just gave you an order! You'll treat them girls like your kid sisters—or else!"

"Aw, Sarge."

The men frowned and grumbled as they gawked at the beautiful young native girls. The girls wore sarongs and had flowers in their long black hair. They clapped their hands and played with the children. Some held up GI uniforms, indicating that they were clean and dry.

"Can we go out to get our uniforms, Sarge?" Homer Gladley asked.

"Yeah, but keep your hands off the broads."

The GIs crawled out of the tent, stood, and approached the piles of uniforms while leering at the girls. They searched through the piles for their clothes while the girls giggled and the children gazed at them with awe.

In the tent Butsko and Bannon were smoking cigarettes and taking it easy. They'd go out and get their own uniforms after the others were finished. It was peaceful and comfortable in the tent, and the sound of voices outside was charming. The Japs had taken their watches; Butsko estimated from the angle of the sun that it was the middle of the afternoon.

"I been thinking," Butsko said. "I like the way you handled yourself yesterday, and I'm gonna give you the First Squad back. You're a buck sergeant again."

Bannon nodded. "Good enough."

"I figure we'll stay here for a couple of days, because some of the men aren't well enough to move yet. Then we'll head back to our lines. We'll be okay here, provided the animals keep their hands off the girls."

"That's gonna be a problem, Sarge. Some of those girls look awfully willing."

"I will cut off the dick of any man who screws one of those girls."

"You tell the men that and I'm sure it'll stop them."

The men came back into the tent with their uniforms.

"They did a great job," said Morris Shilansky. "I ain't had a pair of clean socks since I can't remember when."

Gomez held up his underwear. "Gee, clean shorts. I don't think I can handle it."

The men took off their lavalavas and put on their uniforms.

"Listen to me, you guys," Butsko said, "and listen close. I told you that I don't want you messing with those girls, and I meant it. If any of you screws any of them poor little innocent girls, I will personally cut your fucking dick off!"

Frankie La Barbara made a face and rolled up his eyes. *"Cut my fucking dick off?"*

"You heard me!"

"I ain't never heard anything like that in my life!"

"You heard it now. And there's one more thing. Private Bannon is now Sergeant Bannon again, and he's the squad leader of the First Squad like before."

Everybody looked at Bannon. He winked at them. "Hiya, guys. Remember me?"

"Jesus Christ," Frankie said, "what next?"

Bannon puffed his cigarette. "I think I'm gonna get my uniform. Out of my way, shitheads."

Bannon pushed them aside and crawled to the door of the hut. He pushed it out of the way and stood up in the shade, wearing only his lavalava. A bunch of kids and girls were goofing around a few feet away. Mary, the one they'd rescued from the Japanese, was kneeling before a pile of clothes.

"These yours," she said.

"Oh," he replied, bending down to pick up the clothes.

She pulled them away suddenly and smiled coyly. "I wash them myself."

"Thank you very much. That was very nice of you."

"You welcome."

She smiled dazzlingly. Her skin was smooth and coffee-colored, and the fragrance surrounding her was like tropical flowers. *She's flirting with me*, Bannon thought. *She doesn't know it, but she's playing with fire.*

He reached for his clothes again, and she snatched them away before his fingers could reach them, clasping them to her bosom. The children and other women laughed at Bannon and clapped their hands gleefully.

"Why won't you give me my clothes?" he asked her.

"If you want, come and get."

She stood and took three steps backward, pinching her legs together like a mischievous little child. He rose and reached for the clothes again. She jumped back like a little rabbit. He advanced and reached out his hand. She shook her head and retreated.

"What do I have to do to get my clothes?" he asked.

"Come take them."

She was playing a game with him, he saw that now. *Okay, I'll play games if that's what she wants.* He turned to walk back to the hut, then lunged at his clothes. She screeched and hopped back, then smiled nervously, because she knew he would try to outsmart her. He rushed her and she screamed again, running away.

Bannon chased her, limping on his left leg, and she dashed through the village, dodging around huts, waiting for him to get close and then running away again, laughing like a child. The little children followed, giggling and having a wonderful time. Adult men and women looked up from what they were doing and smiled indulgently. Bannon pursued the girl around the village twice; then she cut out into the woods.

Bannon saw her long black hair flowing behind her and the white soles of her feet as she kicked up her heels. She ducked behind a bush and he went after her, but she wasn't there when he reached the spot. He heard a whistle and looked up. She was leaning beside a tree, waving his clothes from side to side.

He charged toward her and she turned and dashed off, ducking underneath the branches of a tree, laughing gaily, leaping over a boulder, her sarong riding up her long, slim legs. Bannon pursued her but knew he could never catch her. The jungle was her home, and she knew this particular part of it well. She could hide six feet away and he'd never know she was there. So he'd have to get tricky himself. He spotted a bush and dived underneath it, then crouched and made himself still.

She flitted about nearby in the jungle, laughing merrily. Then, a few minutes later, she stopped. She was aware that he wasn't following her anymore. He could imagine the bewildered expression her face.

"Here I am!" she said, trying to attract him again.

He didn't make a sound.

"I'm over here!"

Again he didn't respond.

The jungle was silent. She was wondering what to do. He rattled a branch in the bush he was hiding behind.

"Is that you?" she asked.

He didn't reply.

"Are you all right?"

He felt cruel, teasing her that way, but kept his mouth shut and shook the branch again. He heard her moving closer. Peering through the brush, he saw her come into view, her face very serious, carrying his uniform in her arms.

"Where are you, GI?" she asked.

He wiggled the branch ever so slightly, and her head snapped toward it, eyes focusing.

"Are you there?"

He remained absolutely still, watching her through the branches. She tiptoed closer, cocking her head from side to side, trying to see around the bush, hoping to pick up more sounds with her little ears. She approached the side of the bush, paused, then turned the corner to move behind it.

He sprang up and grabbed her slender wrists, and she screamed like a frightened animal, her body stiffening, her eyes bulging out of her head in horror.

"Gotcha!" he said.

She relaxed and looked angry, but could not repress the smile creeping onto her face. "You very sneaky," she said.

"You're damn right," Bannon replied.

She handed over his clothes.

"Thank you."

"You welcome."

He tucked the clothes under his arm. "Well, I guess we might as well get back to the village."

"Why so much hurry?" she asked, looking demure, giving her eyelashes one slight flutter.

"I'm in no hurry," he said.

"Then let us sit and talk for a while."

"Okay."

She dropped gracefully to the ground and sat with her legs tucked underneath her. Bannon didn't know how to sit, because he was wearing the short lavalava skirt with no underwear. He decided to lie on his side and hold up his head with his hand.

She reached into her bodice and took out a half-pack of Chesterfield cigarettes. "I have brought these for you."

"You think of everything."

"I wash your clothes too."

"You did?"

She nodded solemnly.

Bannon took the cigarettes and the little pack of matches tucked into the cellophane. "You are very good to me and I appreciate it. You are a very nice girl."

"You save my life," she said. "I do anything for you."

Bannon could think of a few things that he'd like her to do, but he didn't want Butsko to cut his dick off, so he didn't mention them, lighting a cigarette instead.

"You are married?" she asked.

"No. Are you?"

She shook her head. "You have a girl friend back in your country?"

"Sort of."

"What is *sort of*?"

Bannon blew smoke into the air. "I guess you could say that I have a girlfriend."

"You love her very much?"

"I don't know."

"If you not know, you not love her much."

Bannon shrugged. "Maybe." He puffed his cigarette. "What about you? Do you have a boyfriend?"

Her eyes twinkled. "Many."

"I can believe that. You're very pretty."

She pushed air at him with her hands. "You GIs full of baloney."

"It's the truth."

"Ha!"

He inhaled the cigarette and looked her over, and a scrumptious little morsel she was to his eyes. Her breasts were small, her legs the color of honey. Her eyes looked right through him to his naked soul, and her shy, coy manner was bringing out the beast in him.

"What is it like where you are from?" she asked.

He looked around at the jungle. "Oh, a lot different from here. We don't have so many trees and there's not so much wetness. Mostly we have grass for miles and miles, as far as the eye can see, and we have herds of cattle that eat the grass. The sun is hot like here, but it's a dry heat, and people say it's very good for you." Bannon described Texas and, in doing so, evoked it for himself. He remembered golden vistas, mountains and canyons, rodeos, and honky-tonk Saturday nights. She could sense him going away from her, drifting back to that land so far away, a land she could only dimly understand.

"What did you do there?" she asked.

"I was a cowboy."

"A what kind of boy?"

"I worked with the cattle, moving them around, stuff like that. I rode a horse a lot."

"Why they not call you a horseboy?"

Bannon shrugged. He'd never thought about that before.

"Tell me about your girl friend?"

"There's really not much to tell. She's a few years older than you, a little taller, and she's got red hair."

"Red hair!"

"Well, it's not really red. It's more of a brown color."

"It must look very funny."

"Not really."

"You think she is pretty?"

"Yes."

The girl frowned. "You think she is prettier than me?"

Bannon had been around women enough to know that a man could not answer questions like that. If you give the woman the answer she wants to hear, she'll say you're lying, and if you give her the opposite answer, she'll scratch your eyes out.

"You're very pretty," he told her, hoping to evade the question.

"Prettier than your girl friend with the funny red hair?"

"I haven't seen her for so long that I forget what she looks like."

She pouted. "I don't believe you. You think I'm ugly."

"That's not true."

"Yes, it is."

"No, it's not."

"You are a bad man."

"Why am I a bad man?"

"Because you not tell truth."

"But I did tell you the truth."

"No, you didn't."

"What makes you think I didn't?"

She narrowed her eyes at him. "Because you not act as if I pretty."

"What do you expect me to do."

"Well," she said huffily, "if you not know what to do, you even worse than I thought. I leave now. Good-bye."

She moved to get up, but Bannon grabbed her wrist.

"Hey, don't be mad," he said.

She tried to break loose, but his grip was like iron. "Let me go!"

"I thought you said I saved your life and you'd do anything for me."

"That was before!"

She tried to punch him in the mouth with her free hand, and he caught her wrist in midair. His forward lunge caused him to fall on top of her.

"Be nice now," he said.

"I hate you!"

She squirmed underneath him, trying to get loose, and he could feel her strong, lithe body beneath the thin cotton of her sarong. All he wore was a thin cotton lavalava skirt, and he was getting turned on. She could feel him getting turned on, and she struggled harder.

"You a dirty man!" she said.

Bannon hadn't had a woman since he had left Australia, and he was only twenty-three years old, with more hormones than he knew what to do with. Her sarong slid up her thighs, and his lavalava slid up his. Their legs rubbed against each other, and he could feel her little cupcake pressed against his raging erection.

"Pig!" she said.

"Now, now. Calm down."

He was bigger and stronger than she, and he held her wrists tightly, gazing down into her limpid eyes. She realized the futility of her struggle and went limp underneath him, looking up into his eyes.

"You're so pretty," he said.

"Ha!"

"It's true. You are."

A wicked expression came over her face. "Prettier than your girl friend?"

"Yes," Bannon replied, because Ginger was long ago and far away.

"You sure?"

"I'm sure."

"You not lie?"

"I not lie."

She closed her eyes, her chest still heaving with the exertion of her struggle. He lowered his face and kissed her lips; they tasted like exotic tropical fruit. She moaned softly and he let her wrists go, running the palms of his hand over her silken hair and bringing them to rest on her shoulders, squeezing them as her tongue slid through his lips. He licked her tongue, and the fire of passion burned hotter inside him. An artery in his throat throbbed like a tom-tom, and a loud rushing sound was in his ears. She wrapped her arms around his shoulders and hugged him tightly to her, kissing him passionately, and they bruised each other's lips, scraping teeth.

They squirmed against each other, clawing at each other's garments. He tugged the top of her sarong and the material fell away, revealing her breasts. They weren't as small as he'd thought; the tight top of the sarong only had made them appear that way, because it flattened them down, but they were nice handfuls, like grapefruits. He cupped her right one in his hand, the first tit he'd felt in nearly six months, and nearly swooned. He lowered his head and pressed his lips against the nipple, sucking it into his mouth, running his tongue across it, making it hard and pointy. She dug her fingers into his hair and pulled him tightly against her breast. Her breast puffed like a marshmellow around his lips and nose, and he opened his mouth wider to take more of it in.

It was delicious and he nearly came in his lavalava. While sucking her right tit, he pushed more of her sarong away and dropped the palm of his hand on her left tit, running his thumb over the nipple, making it hard too. She kissed his scalp and chewed his hair, undulating her hips, pushing his lavalava down.

He loosened her sarong and pulled it off while she unwrapped his lavalava, throwing it underneath a bush. Naked now, their bodies came together. Bannon held her tightly and felt as though he'd been drenched with fire. She was so soft, so smooth, so wonderfully alien to him, and she was biting his chin so hard he thought she might draw blood, but he didn't care.

He reached down between her legs; she already was soaking wet. The sensation was familiar, because he'd had a substantial amount of sex in his life, and yet foreign, because you can never get enough of pretty girls. He slid fingers through the slippery crevice, the magic spot he thought about, dreamed about, and craved all the time.

She grabbed his cock and squeezed it so hard some juice oozed out. Bannon's balls were at a rolling boil, and he felt ecstasy radiating out of his groin. She was frail and small and he was afraid of hurting her but couldn't control himself.

He pushed her down onto her back and she spread her legs.

100

Her bush was covered with moisture and gleamed like diamonds. He held his cock in his right hand and lunged forward. She touched her fingers to its head and guided it in. Bannon thought his head would explode as it sank in all the way. Her little lamb chop quivered with delight, and Bannon had an orgasm on the spot.

But he was a young man, and young men have orgasms all the time. He didn't need to rest, he didn't have to go to the bathroom, and he didn't feel like smoking a cigarette. All he wanted to do was fuck himself silly, and that's exactly what he proceeded to do. He drew his steaming, dripping member out of her furnace, paused for a moment, and plunged it back in. She raised her knees in the air and sucked air through her clenched teeth because she thought she might die of pleasure.

He pulled out and pushed in and then pumped her steadily, while she wagged her hips from side to side and whispered words he didn't understand into his ear. He ran his hands down her swaying body and cupped her ass in his hands; it was a round, firm, muscular ass—not hard like his own ass, but with a marvelous resilience and texture.

He held her steadily and worked her like an expert, although he wasn't thinking much about what he was doing; it all came naturally. She rubbed her nipples against his hairy chest, placed her hands behind his head, and pressed his mouth against hers. He slipped his tongue into her mouth and she sucked it in a pulsating rhythm in time with the motion of his pile-driving ass.

Birds whistled in the trees and monkeys looked down at them and cackled. Insects buzzed around them and sucked their blood, but they didn't give a damn. She wrapped her legs around his waist and wrestled him hard, and he pushed deeply into her, pulled out slowly, and pushed in again. He moved his hips in a spiral motion, corkscrewing in and out, a trick he'd learned in a whorehouse in El Paso.

Suddenly Bannon remembered Butsko, and his pecker shriveled a bit, but the girl was so beautiful and her body so fine, he didn't care if Butsko did chop his dick off, because this would be worth it; life could offer nothing more.

Then she moved in a strange way—he couldn't figure out

exactly how—but it changed the angle of her vagina and brought a delicious friction to bear against the head of his cock, the most sensitive part of his body. Bannon's tongue stuck out and his eyes goggled. He thought he was going to die, because no one could possibly survive such wonderful sensations. They were so powerful that he could no longer move. She had him in some kind of weird leg-lock and she was doing all the moving.

"Give me your milk," she whispered passionately into his ear, and then bit his earlobe.

Bannon couldn't move or get away. She had him where she wanted him and his soul was jelly in her hands. He could feel her drawing the orgasm out of him, and never in his life had a woman put him under her control so thoroughly. She played him like a violin, and his balls exploded, the hot silky substance shooting out of him like fire.

Bannon felt as if somebody had plugged him into the Boulder Dam turbines. His ears tingled and his eyes protruded out of his skull as his body went into convulsions. Rapture jolted every cell in his body, even down to his toes. His cock felt like it was six feet long, throbbing deliciously, gushing like a fire hose.

She whimpered and squealed and bit his shoulder as her own fireworks went off. Bannon wrapped his arms around her clumsily and held her tightly because he was afraid she would get away. The experience was bending his mind to the point where he'd thought he'd get so far out he'd never come back again, so he held on and buried his face in her neck, drooling like a child, his eyes rolling up into his head.

Finally neither of them could move anymore, and they collapsed against each other. She lay with her legs flat on the ground, spread out her arms, and tried to breathe. Bannon could feel her breasts rising and falling underneath him. He wondered how such a little person could have as much strength and endurance as she. He gulped down air and thought he'd faint, raising his head a few inches in the air and turning away from her so his flow of air would be unobstructed. When his head was clear, he rolled off her and fell on his back beneath the bush. He patted the ground all around him with his hands until he found the cigarettes and matches, then lit one up and looked to the treetops, where a family of monkeys was looking down at him.

"You are all right?" she asked, still breathing heavily.

"I think so," he replied.

"I thought I killed you."

"I thought you killed me too."

She rolled over and lay her face on his chest. "I love you," she said. "Why don't we get married?"

"It's okay with me," Bannon replied, for he was still in the bright glow of sexual love.

"Okay. I talk to my father when we get back."

Bannon puffed the cigarette and thought of what life would be like with her on Guadalcanal after the war. They'd eat bananas, coconuts, and fish, and fuck in the sun all day. To hell with Texas. To hell with Ginger Gregg. She'd probably forgotten about him long ago anyway, and besides, she couldn't fuck as good as this island girl.

"I love you from the moment I first see you," she murmured into his chest.

"No kidding?"

"I look at you and you were like a god, I swear it. And you save my life like a god. I not belong to me anymore, and I not belong to my father. I belong to you."

"You saved my life too," Bannon said. "I belong to you as much as you belong to me."

"We belong to each other," she said.

Bannon puffed his cigarette and massaged her neck as she purred against his chest. He hadn't been this happy since his last night with Ginger Gregg.

She stirred and kissed his nipples lightly, going from one to the other and then back again. Moaning softly, as if she were eating something delicious, she pressed her lips against his chest, working down his belly. His pecker twitched to life and he hoped she was going to go all the way down. She held his pelvis in her hands, poking her tongue into his belly button, and then moved lower, licking his lower abdomen, making Bannon's toes curl.

Her cheek scraped against his pubic hair as she went down

and took the head of his rigid cock between her lips. Bannon dug his fingernails into the dirt and hoped she'd mangle it firmly with her mouth, but she was gentle at first, manipulating it lightly with her lips and tongue, tantalizing him. Bannon closed his eyes and smiled, all thoughts of the war far away. Her mouth played with his pecker for a while, then she opened wide and lowered her head, forcing his pecker deep into her throat. She tightened her lips around him and sucked hard.

Bannon thought he was going to come on the spot. He opened his eyes to slits and looked at the beautiful island girl sucking him off. He placed his hand on the back of her head as she moved up and down, sucking furiously, massaging his dick with her tongue. Bannon worked his pelvis to keep time with her. She held his cock in her hand to steady it and glided her mouth up and down. Bannon groaned, his tongue hanging out, and he gripped her head more firmly.

He'd come twice already, so he was able to hold back now. Her head bobbed up and down and she shuddered, making little animal sounds, becoming so excited that she even bit him a few times, but it was a good pain. Bannon drifted off into a sexual reverie. He thought of having sex with her in a hundred ways, in all the positions, on beds and in bathtubs, even high up in the branches of trees. He wanted to devour her, swallow her down, and make her a part of him forever.

He came like a demolition charge with a long fuse. His orgasm fizzled and sizzled, sending sparks through the tissues of his skin, and then the flame touched his main charge and he exploded. His cream shot into her mouth, and she swallowed furiously but couldn't contain it all. It dribbled down her chin and still she kept sucking, draining him dry. Spasms racked his body, and the head of his cock tingled maddeningly. He bucked like a wild bronco and she held on like a rodeo rider, never letting that big fat thing fall out of her mouth. It squirted again and again, and then nothing would come out, but she continued to work. He thought she would suck up his balls, guts and heart, but he didn't care. It was pure delirium.

Gradually her motion diminished and he went flat on the ground. His cock softened and she let it fall from her mouth. Exhausted, she crawled up his body, kissed his lips, wiggled her fanny, and stuffed his cock inside her. He felt her, warm and wet, and didn't think he could do much for her, but she kept wiggling and soon he was hard again. She rocked and twisted, and Bannon placed his hands on her ass, enjoying its warmth and smmothness. They were both tired, so this time they made love languorously, with lots of moans and sighs and soft little kisses.

SEVEN . . .

The sun shone brightly in the sky, but its golden rays didn't reach the jungle encampment of General Hyakutake's headquarters. The thick leaves and tangled vines of the dense jungle area blocked out the sun and made the encampment dank and gloomy. Colone Saburo Shibata marched across the clearing, his left hand resting on the handle of his samurai sword, a scowl on his face. He was still pissed off about the escape of the American prisoners the night before, and the wound in his shoulder bothered him. The medical corporal had removed the bullet and bandaged the wound. He'd applied no painkilling drugs or antiseptics, because medical care in the Japanese army was primitive compared to the US Army.

Colonel Shibata entered one of the headquarters tents and was ushered into a cramped area that had a map table in its center. Surrounding the table were General Miyazaki, Colonel Imoto, and Major Suginoo. The air smelled like stale, rotting canvas, and a kerosene lamp illuminated the map. Colonel Shibata drew himself to attention and saluted General Miyazaki.

"Colonel Shibata reporting, sir!"

"At ease, Colonel," General Miyazaki replied, smiling faintly. "I hear you had a little trouble last night."

"Yes, sir. Some American prisoners got away with the help of natives, as far as we can tell."

"You were wounded, I see."

"It's nothing, sir."

"Good." General Miyazaki looked down at the map. "Natives have been bedeviling us ever since we came to this godforsaken island. They have not responded to our offers of friendship and brotherhood, preferring instead to remain lackeys of British and American imperialism. Well, so be it. They will pay for their stupidity." General Miyazaki pointed to Cape Esperance on the map. "We're retreating to here, where the ships will pick us up so that we can leave Guadalcanal." General Miyazaki looked at Colonel Shibata. "Your battalion will act as a block, slowing down the Americans and making them think our intentions are to defend Guadalcanal to the death and not abandon the island. You will move your men to the front today and relieve troops fighting here, in the vicinity of the Bonegi River. Then you will slowly give up ground, making the Americans pay for every inch of it, and withdraw to Cape Esperance, where you too will be evacuated. Do you have any questions, Colonel Shibata?"

Colonel Shibata looked down at the map, glowing in the flickering light from the kerosene lamp. "How many American troops are there on Guadalcanal?"

"We estimate thirty thousand, maybe more."

"How can my battalion hope to hold back thirty thousand men?"

"You won't be fighting them in an open field, Colonel. The terrain here is extremely difficult, consisting of thick jungle, swamps and mountains. Fighting usually breaks down to small-unit activity. The Americans are scattered all over the island, but you will concentrate your battalion near the coast to protect our withdrawal from Cape Esperance. The Americans don't know that we're withdrawing. When they run into your fresh troops, they'll probably think we're mounting a counterattack. They'll dig in instead of pressing forward. They'll be confused. And all of us will get away. Do you understand?"

"Yes, sir."

"Good." General Miyazaki looked at Major Suginoo. "Get the bottle of sake."

"Yes, sir."

General Miyazaki smiled at Colonel Shibata. "We shall drink a toast to the health of the Emperor before you leave."

"Very good, sir."

Colonel Shibata watched Major Suginoo pour sake into little tin cups. Colonel Shibata was not pleased with his assignment because it was a rearguard action, a dirty, inglorious job. He would have liked to have a part in a major attack, not an ignominious retreat. But still, orders were orders. He would do his best, and perhaps he could find some natives to punish for what had happened the previous night.

The little tin cups half full of sake were passed around, and General Miyazaki raised his in the air. "To the Emperor!" he shouted.

"To the Emperor!" cried the others in the tiny tent.

For Nutsy Gafooley it was like the recurrence of a bad dream. He was in the coconut plantation again, leading George Company toward the mansion. George Company was deployed in a series of diamond formations, with Captain Orr at its center, as it made its way through the rows of trees. Nutsy, up front with the point man, Pfc. Edwin Garfield, remembered how the recon platoon had been fired upon by the Japs and how they'd attacked the big white mansion, which should be straight ahead. Nutsy was afraid they'd have another big fight with the Japs, and he didn't think he could go through it again.

Toward noon Pfc. Garfield stopped suddenly. "There it is!"

Nutsy peered through the coconut grove and saw the whiteness in the distance. "I see it too."

Garfield waved his hand, and Captain Orr came running forward with his new executive officer, Lieutenant Holt.

"What is it?" Orr asked.

Garfield pointed. "There's the house, sir."

Captain Orr and Lieutenant Holt looked ahead. Captain Orr was old for his rank, because he'd been an enlisted man in the Army for nearly twenty years before becoming commissioned as an officer shortly after Pearl Harbor. Lieutenant Holt was fresh out of the University of Utah and Officer Candidate School.

"There she is," Captain Orr said. "Send a squad up to that house to see if anybody's home."

"Yes, sir."

"Take Nutsy with you. He's been here before."

"Yes, sir."

Nutsy felt tense as he walked off with Lieutenant Holt. He didn't want to get near that mansion; it was a place of horror for him. He'd come too close to getting killed and seen too many of his buddies lying dead on the floor.

Lieutenant Holt hadn't been with George Company very long, but he knew that Sergeant Kaczmarczyk was a good man. He approached Kaczmarczyk and told him to take his squad forward to check out the house.

Kaczmarczyk was short and husky, with close-cropped blond hair and tattoos of girls, daggers, skulls, and regimental crests up and down both his arms. On the back of his left hand it said *Death Before Dishonor,* and his top two front teeth had been knocked out by a Japanese rifle butt, which made him look fearsome.

"Okay, let's go, boys," he muttered.

His men stood and adjusted their packs on their backs. He looked at Nutsy.

"Stay close to me."

Kaczmarczyk inclined in his head toward the mansion, and they set out in that direction, spreading into a skirmish line and keeping their heads low. Nutsy remembered what had happened the day before, when the Japs had turned loose their machine guns as soon as the recon platoon got close. He crouched closer to the ground than the others and was ready to hit the dirt at the first hostile sound.

They moved closer to the mansion and stopped at the edge of the lawn. Kaczmarczyk looked at the big building in amazement, because he'd never seen anything like it on Guadalcanal.

"Gafooley," he said, "come with me. The rest of you cover us."

Nutsy's blood turned to ice. The last thing he wanted to do was walk across that lawn. He looked at the windows and expected Jap machine guns to suddenly appear and spit lead.

Kaczmarczyk stepped onto the lawn and Nutsy followed him. Kaczmarczyk's knees were bent and his shoulders hunched, because he, too, expected a sudden shot. He carried his carbine in both hands with one finger on the trigger. His eyes swept back and forth across the windows, looking for the telltale movement that would betray the presence of Japs. Nutsy remembered how he and the recon platoon had charged the mansion across that very lawn and how it had been quiet like that before all hell broke loose.

They drew closer to the mansion, and Nutsy saw bodies lying on the front porch. The breeze picked up and he could smell rotting flesh. At the foot of the stairs Kaczmarczyk stopped and looked up at the building, checking the windows again.

"C'mon," he said.

They climbed the steps and walked across the porch. Nutsy looked at the dead, bloated bodies of Private Perloff and Pfc. Gilleland. Flies swarmed around their bodies and clusters of maggots ate their flesh. There were no Japanese bodies around.

They approached the front entrance of the mansion; a big jagged hole was where the door used to be. Kaczmarczyk pressed his back against the door and looked inside, seeing wreckage and more dead bodies. The building was completely silent. Kaczmarczyk motioned with his head and entered the main living room, followed by Gafooley, who saw more of his buddies lying around and rotting. The stench was powerful and Nutsy felt the bile rise in his throat.

Kaczmarczyk took a dirty handkerchief out of his back pocket and held it over his nose. Nutsy covered his face and his hand, but the stink came through. There was Private Reid lying at the foot of the fireplace with maggots all over his face.

"Jesus," said Kaczmarczyk, "it looks like a slaughterhouse in here."

"It was," agreed Nutsy.

Kaczmarczyk walked down a corridor toward the room where the recon platoon had made its last stand. He climbed over the wreckage in front of the door. Just then he heard a rustling, thrashing sound. Something moved in a corner of the room, and Kaczmarczyk held his carbine in both hands, flicked off the safety, and pulled the trigger.

The carbine was in its automatic mode and fired like a submachine gun at a big black shadow moving toward the window. It was a buzzard, and the bullets ripped through his feathers. The buzzard collapsed on the windowsill, a piece of flesh in its mouth.

The mansion was silent again. Kaczmarczyk realized that if buzzards were in the house, there probably weren't any live Japs around. The stink was getting to him. Many bodies were mutilated beyond recognition by explosions.

"Let's get out of here," he said.

They ran down the corridor, across the living room, and out the door. The rest of George Company was assembled at the edge of the woods and watched them flee across the front porch and leap down the steps. Kaczmarczyk and Nutsy dashed across the lawn and entered the woods.

"What's wrong?" said Captain Orr.

"Building's full of dead GIs," Kaczmarczyk said. "Stinks like hell. I don't think there are any Japs in there."

Captain Orr motioned for his radio operator to come closer and called Colonel Stockton but couldn't get through. Looking around, he saw some hills in the distance. The tops of hills were usually the best places from which to transmit messages. He decided to head in that direction, but first he'd better do something about the building. The Japs might occupy it again, so maybe it would be best to burn just the damn thing down.

"Lieutenant Holt!"

"Yes, sir?"

"Take some men and torch that building."

"Yes, sir."

Lieutenant Holt gathered together some men and they walked across the lawn toward the building. Nutsy dropped to his knees beside a tree and threw up his breakfast. The smell and horror of seeing his dead buddies had been too much for him. He felt a hand on his shoulder.

"Are you all right, son?" asked Captain Orr.

"I'm okay, sir," said Nutsy, reaching for his canteen and looking up at Captain Orr.

Captain Orr's face was scarred with acne, and his eyes were tiny and steel-blue. "You sure?"

"Yes, sir."

Captain Orr walked away, and Nutsy took a swig of water, swishing it around in his mouth and swallowing it. He wondered whether the entire recon platoon had been wiped out or if some had gotten away. It was hard to tell, since so many bodies had been blown to bits. He couldn't imagine Butsko being dead. Butsko had always seemed invincible to him. They were probably all dead. Nutsy didn't think he could deal with it.

He looked up and saw smoke billowing out of the windows of the mansion. The men from George Company were inside, setting fire to the stuffing from furniture and piles of splintered wood. It was a hot, sunny day, unusual for the month of January, which was the wettest month of the year on Guadalcanal; the mansion, made of old wood, wouldn't last long.

The GIs ran out of the building and across the lawn, reporting to Lieutenant Holt, who told Captain Orr that fires were raging throughout the first floor of the building.

"Let's stick around to make sure," Captain Orr said.

They knelt at the edge of the lawn and watched huge tongues of flame lick the windows. Curls of smoke rose from the roof, and sheets of flame could be seen through the opening where the front door had been. Nutsy was right; the dry old wood was going fast. The inside became an inferno, and flames crept up the outer walls. There was a huge booming sound and sparks flew out the windows as one of the floors collapsed. The GIs could feel the heat against their faces and had to move back.

"Let's get out of here!" said Captain Orr.

George Company formed into a column of twos, and Lieutenant Holt led them in the direction of the hills nearby. Nutsy looked back and saw swirling flames envelope the old mansion, which had become a funeral pyre for his dead friends in the recon platoon.

EIGHT . . .

Bannon lay on the grass and the native girl still was on top of him, nuzzling his neck while he smoked a cigarette. Now that the sex was over, Bannon was getting scared. He'd been in the forest for a long time with the girl, and Butsko would figure out that he'd screwed her. Bannon was afraid that Butsko could cut off his dick just like he said he would, and the thought of it sent a tremor through his body.

"What's wrong?" the girl asked.

"Nothing."

"You are cold?"

"I'm not cold."

"You are having bad dreams, I think."

"Yeah, that's it."

"I know what you think now," she said sadly.

"What?"

"Never mind."

"Come on, tell me."

"I bet you think maybe you not want to marry me like you said before when your thing was hard."

"No, no," Bannon said. "That's not it."

"Then what is it?"

"It's kinda complicated."

"You think I am a dumb girl? You think I will not understand?"

"No, it's not that."

"Then what is it?"

"Well," Bannon said, "it's like this. You know who Sergeant Butsko is?"

"You mean the big ugly one with arms like this?" She held the palm of her hand near her upper arm to indicate Butsko's nineteen-inch biceps.

"That's the one."

"Well, he said that if any of us does dooby-do with one of you girls, he'll cut our things off."

Her jaw dropped open. "No!"

"Yes."

"Why he say that?"

"Because he don't want no trouble."

"What trouble could happen?"

"Some of the guys in the platoon don't have all their marbles."

"Their what?"

"They're a little crazy. They might do something wrong, like rape somebody."

"Oh." The native girl pinched her lips together. "You think one of those men would do something like that?"

"I'm surprised it hasn't happened yet."

"Oh, my goodness sake!"

"Yeah, they're a bad bunch."

"Well," she said, "I tell him to not cut off your thing. He have to kill me first!" Her brow became furrowed. "You think he'd kill me?"

"No. Butsko's very polite to women, usually."

Her face brightened. "We gonna get married anyways!"

"Right."

"Let's go back and tell my father."

"You don't think he'll mind?"

"No, because he always say it time I get married."

"To an American soldier?"

"My father love American soldiers. He be very happy to have you as his son."

They picked up their clothes and got dressed. The girl wrapped herself in her sarong and Bannon put on his clean uniform, which felt strange next to his skin. It was the first time he had worn a freshly laundered uniform in over a month. But he'd left his boots behind in the tent, so he had to follow her barefoot as they returned to the huts.

With every step Bannon felt increasing fear and misgiving. He knew that once Butsko got mad, he wouldn't listen to reason. He'd just attack and cut off Bannon's dick. There would be no time for explanations. Bannon glanced at his watch; he'd been in the woods nearly three hours and was extremely hungry. Butsko would know by now that he'd run away with the native girl. A shiver passed up Bannon's spine as he thought of Butsko waiting for him, big and ugly, with a machete in his hand.

They approached the huts. Bannon shuffled his feet, but the girl held his hand and pulled him along. Through an opening in the bushes Bannon saw Frankie La Barbara sitting underneath a tree, smoking a cigarette and talking with two little kids, laughing and joking. The kids turned around suddenly at the approach of Bannon and the girl, and Frankie stood up. He spotted Bannon and the girl coming through the woods and walked toward them.

"You'd better find someplace to hide," Frankie told Bannon. "Butsko's gonna kill you when he gets his hands on you."

Bannon thought he'd play dumb. "What I do?"

Frankie glanced at the girl. "You know what you done, and Butsko knows too. You been boffin' this little girl after he toldja not to."

Meanwhile, unknown to all of them, another little village kid had been bribed by Butsko to tell him when Bannon and the girl showed up. This little kid was on his way to Butsko's hut while Bannon and Frankie were talking.

"What am I supposed to do?" Bannon asked. "Go fucking AWOL?"

"I think that might be a good idea for you right now," Frankie said.

The girl stepped forward and put her foot down. "He not going anywhere! We getting married!"

Frankie raised his eyebrows. "Huh?"

"That's right," Bannon said. "We're getting married."

"Are you fucking kidding me!"

"No."

Frankie winked at Bannon to indicate he knew that Bannon wasn't really going to marry the girl.

"No," said Bannon, "I'm really gonna do it."

Frankie looked the girl up and down. "Maybe it's not such a bad idea."

Suddenly the jungle was rent with a sound that was like a wild bull elephant on the rampage, only there were no wild bull elephants on Guadalcanal. The door in front of Butsko's hut was thrown to the side, and Butsko stood there in his clean uniform, his machete in his hand, lightning bolts shooting out of his eyes.

"Where is he?" Butsko screamed.

Bannon turned pale. "I'm getting the fuck out of here!"

He turned to run, but was barefooted and stubbed his toe on a rock. Shouting in pain, he tripped and fell to the ground, rolling over and holding his big toe in both his hands. The girl knelt beside him, spit on his toe, and rubbed it with her fingers.

"Ouch!" screamed Bannon.

Butsko heard everything and came charging into the jungle, holding his machete high in the air. Frankie La Barbara ran for his life, and Bannon was so scared, he thought his heart would stop beating.

"If he kill you," the girl said, "he have to kill me first."

Butsko burst into the little clearing and looked down at Bannon on the ground. "So there you are, you fucking hound!" said Butsko.

Bannon held up the palm of his hand. "Now, Sarge..."

Butsko flashed his machete through the air. "You know what I'm gonna do to you!"

"But listen..."

"Listen my fucking ass!"

The girl threw herself between them. "Leave him alone!"

Butsko snarled and shifted his weight from foot to foot as he tested the blade of his machete with his finger. "Out of my way!"

"No!"

"I said out of my way!"

"No!"

Butsko was so angry, he wanted to tear apart the jungle. If there was anything he couldn't tolerate, it was insubordination. But the girl stood between him and Bannon, and he didn't want to hurt the girl.

"You're even lower than I thought," Butsko said to Bannon, "and I always knew you were pretty low! How could you take advantage of a kid like this!"

Bannon opened his mouth to speak, but his throat was so constricted with fear that nothing came out. He coughed, cleared his throat, and said weakly, "We're getting married."

"That's right," said the girl, "we getting married."

Butsko wrinkled his nose. "You're getting married?"

"That's right," Bannon replied, trying to smile.

"It true," the girl added.

Butsko's face twisted grotesquely and he looked as though he might turn green. *"How could you tell such a rotten fuckin' lie to this kid?"*

"It's not a lie, Sarge," Bannon said. "I'm gonna marry her. I'm in love."

"In love!"

"That's right. And you can be the best man if you wanna."

"Best man!"

A crowd was gathering, and the natives appeared very worried, because Butsko was obviously on a homicidal rampage. Many didn't speak English well and didn't know what they were talking about. Butsko looked like he was going to chop up the chief's daughter and the soldier with his bright, shining machete.

"You little fuck," Butsko said, trembling with anger, "you're a private again as of right now!"

"Why can't you make up your mind, Sarge?"

"I'll fucking kill you!"

Butsko charged Bannon and the girl, holding his machete high in the air. At that moment the little old chief showed up with his retinue of armed guards.

"What is wrong, my friends?" the chief asked.

Butsko stuttered and got tongue-tied, because he didn't know how to tell the chief that Bannon had been off in the woods, fucking his daughter.

The girl stood up. "Father," she said, fluttering her eyelashes, "I am getting married to this man."

The old chief blinked. "You are?"

"Yes, Father."

The old chief looked at his daughter and then at Bannon. A smile creased his face, because his daughter was sixteen and it was time she got married. "Very fine," he said, "very fine."

The girl rushed forward and kissed her father. Bannon still lay on the ground, looking at the machete in Butsko's hand. Butsko lowered the machete and let it hang at his side. Little children jumped on Bannon, slapping and kissing him. Frankie La Barbara had watched everything from his hiding place behind a tree and scratched his head in mystification. The girl turned, took Bannon's hand, helped him up, and led him to her father.

"Father," she said, "this is the man I marry. His name Bannon."

Her father spoke better English than she did and was more skilled in the ways of foreigners. "How do you do," the old chief said. "Welcome to the family." He shook Bannon's hand.

"I love your daughter, sir," Bannon said, looking at Butsko out of the corner of his eye, just in case Butsko made a sudden lunge. "I'll try to make her happy."

The old chief looked up at the sky. "It is a good day for a wedding. I had been wondering why this was such a good day, and now I know. The gods are smiling on you and my daughter." He clapped his hands twice. "The wedding will take place this afternoon."

Everybody applauded except Bustko and the other men from the recon platoon, who were bewildered by this sudden turn of events. The girl walked up to Bannon and smiled shyly.

"I not see you again until we're married."

"Anything you say," Bannon replied.

Butsko finally found his voice. "Hey, listen, we're pulling out of here first thing in the morning, marriage or no marriage!"

The chief nodded. "I understand, because the war goes on, but one day when the war goes away my son will come back to his village."

Frankie La Barbara covered his mouth with his hand. "Sure he will," he muttered.

"The preparations for the marriage will begin now!" the chief declared. "The marriage will take place in the middle of the afternoon and will be followed by a feast." The chief looked at Butsko. "You are the bridegroom's sergeant, which means you are like his father. It is up to you to make sure no harm comes to him before the wedding."

Butsko nodded numbly.

The chief pounded his staff twice in the ground for emphasis, then turned and walked away, followed by his retinue of armed guards. The girl was surrounded by the young maidens of the village, who led her in another direction, followed by a swarm of children. The men from the recon platoon were left alone in the jungle beside the village. Frankie dropped down to the ground and held his stomach as he cackled and laughed madly.

"Bannon's gettin' married!" he said "What a fuckin' joke!"

Butsko looked at Bannon and pointed his machete at him. "You're gonna go through with this, you little fuck, or else!"

"Don't worry about it, Sarge," Bannon said. "I wanna go through with it. I love the girl."

Butsko spat at the ground. "You don't even know what love is, you fuckin' jerk-off."

George Company made it to the top of a hill shortly after high noon, and Captain Orr told them all to take a cigarette break. Pfc. Nordell, his runner, tried to raise regimental headquarters on the radio and finally got through. He told the radio operator on the other end that Captain Orr would like to speak with Colonel Stockton. The radio operator replied that Colonel Stockton was in the field, but Major Cobb was available.

Nordell handed the headset to Captain Orr, and a few seconds later the voice of Major Cobb, the regiment's operations officer, came over the airwaves.

"What is it, Orr?"

"I just wanted to report we found that plantation house unoccupied except for casualties from the recon platoon. We couldn't make an accurate count because a lot of them were destroyed by grenades. We set fire to the building and tried to contact headquarters but couldn't get through, so we climbed to the top of Hill Eighty-three, where we are now, so we could transmit. What should I do?"

"Stay where you are and keep your eyes open. If you see anything, report it. If you have any trouble, get the hell out of there. The regiment will probably catch up to you around this time tomorrow. Any questions?"

"No, sir."

"Over and out."

Captain Orr handed the headset to Pfc. Nordell and turned to Lieutenant Holt. "Post lookouts and have the men dig in. We're gonna be here for a while."

Lieutenant Holt saluted. "Yes, sir."

A stream ran by the little native village, and the men from the recon platoon were bathing in it. The chief had sent them a small bar of soap that he'd received with his supplies, and the GIs passed it around, sudsing up and frolicking in the water. The food and rest had caused their strength to return, and even the wounded were able to lie on the bank of the stream and wash themselves.

Craig Delane, the recon platoon intellectual, was amazed by Bannon's decision to marry the native girl, because he knew all about Bannon's girl friend Ginger Gregg back in Texas. How could a man shift the direction of his love so suddenly? Delane took life seriously, and he knew that he could never do such a thing.

"Hey, Bannon," Delane said, "are you going to tell Ginger about this?"

Bannon shrugged as he rubbed the bar of soap into his armpit. "I dunno. I ain't really thought about it."

Frankie La Barbara guffawed. "What's he gonna tell her for? What she don't know won't hurt her."

"But aren't you supposed to marry Ginger?" Delane asked.

"Yup," said Bannon.

"Well, you can't marry both of them, can you?"

"I dunno."

Butsko was nearby, the hair on his head, chest, and shoulders covered with soap suds. "He don't wanna know. He don't wanna think about it because he's a fuck-up. He's thinkin' with his dick instead of his head."

"Naw," said Bannon, "it's not that."

"Bullshit."

"I'm gonna marry that girl, that's all I know," Bannon said. "Why the fuck not?"

Butsko pinched his nose between his thumb and finger and lowered his head beneath the water. When he came up, all the soap suds were gone. Shaw dived underwater, swam a short distance, and surfaced. Shilansky covered his little finger with soap and inserted it into his ear, trying to clean all the wax out.

"Tell me something," Delane asked Bannon, "how can you fall in love with somebody you don't even know? I mean, she doesn't even speak much English!"

"I can't explain it," Bannon said, splashing water on his face, "but I love her."

"What he's trying to say," Frankie La Barbara declared, "is that he loves to fuck her."

Bannon became annoyed. "It's not just that."

"Is she a good fuck, Bannon?"

"Shaddup, Frankie."

"Why is everybody always telling me to shut up?"

"Because you talk too fucking much."

"Bannon," said Delane, who was really trying to understand, "how can you fall in love with somebody you don't even know?"

"I know her," Bannon replied.

"Not very well."

"As well as I need to know her."

"But you haven't lived with her. You don't know what she's like."

"My father never lived with my mother before they got married, and they got along okay."

"But they must have known each other for a while."

"You can be around somebody your whole life and still not really know them."

"I don't know," Delane said, shaking his head. "I'm confused."

"Don't worry about it," Bannon told him. "Everything's gonna be okay."

"Sure," said Frankie La Barbara. "What the fuck does he care? We're leaving tomorrow morning and he'll never see her again."

"I'll come back someday," Bannon said.

"Sure you will."

"What about Ginger?" Delane asked.

"I don't know," Bannon replied, "but it'll all work out somehow."

Butsko groaned. "'It'll all work out somehow,'" he said, mimicking Bannon. "What a fucking asshole you turned out to be."

"I know what I'm doing," Bannon said, a note of anger in his voice, "and if anybody here doesn't like it, he can go take a flying fuck at the moon."

Colonel Stockton returned to his headquarters at three o'clock in the afternoon, and the first thing he did was go to the tent of Major Cobb to find out what had happened while he was away.

"Ten-*hut!*" shouted an officer when Colonel Stockton entered the operations tent.

"At ease!" said Colonel Stockton. He looked at the officers circling the map table; they had been moving around pieces of wood that indicated the companies in the regiment. "Anything happen while I was gone?"

Major Cobb stepped forward. "Bad news, sir. It looks like the recon platoon was wiped out."

A chasm opened up suddenly inside Colonel Stockton, but he stood erectly and didn't let anything show. "What do you mean?"

"Captain Orr found them in that old plantation house. They'd been dead for quite a while."

"None got away?"

"Captain Orr said he didn't know. Some of the bodies were

blown apart by grenades and shell bursts and nobody could say who was who."

"Anything else?"

Major Cobb pointed to the map and told of the movement of the regiment west across Guadalcanal. "I've told Captain Orr to dig in where he is and that we'd probably catch up with him tomorrow."

"Very well. Carry on."

"Ten-*hut!*"

Colonel Stockton turned and walked out of the tent, crossing the jungle clearing to his own tent. He nodded to Sergeant Major Ramsay at the front desk, then went into his office and sat down heavily behind the desk.

He'd been hoping that somehow the recon platoon had gotten away, but now he knew there was little to hope for. The recon platoon had been at the wrong place at the wrong time and had gotten it.

He sighed and reached for his pipe, feeling depressed and sick to his stomach. He didn't want to do any work, but his companies were on the attack and he couldn't slack off now. Filling his pipe with tobacco, he turned down the corners of his mouth and shook his head. Then he reached for the communiqué on top of the pile.

Bannon sat alone under a banana tree, smoking a cigarette. He was bathed and shaved, dressed in his clean uniform, and waiting for somebody to tell him what to do. Occasionally children would approach him, point their fingers, and giggle. He could see activity in the center of the village, girls and old ladies dashing from hut to hut. In another hut some men were chanting. It was pretty weird.

A few feet away the other survivors from the recon platoon lay around, nursing their wounds. They smoked cigarettes, played poker with dog-eared cards, and talked about women and good times. The Reverend Billie Jones read his Bible.

"This ain't gonna be a Christian wedding," he mumbled. "It's gonna be a pagan wedding, and a pagan wedding ain't a real wedding."

"Aw, go fuck yourself," Frankie said, holding a pair of kings and a pair of fives in his hand, wondering how much he should bet on them. None of them had money, and they were using pebbles as poker chips.

"Yeah, what does it matter?" asked Shaw. "It's just a fuckin' ceremony. Don't mean nothin'."

"What do you mean, it don't mean nothin'?" asked Billie Jones. "There's always a third partner in every wedding, and that's God."

Frankie La Barbara snorted derisively. "I don't think God's ever come to Guadalcanal."

"Fuck God," said Jimmy O'Rourke. "I don't believe in all that shit. if He comes down and stands in front of me, then I'll believe in Him."

"Someday He might," Billie Jones said.

"Bullshit."

A group of little children with flowers wrapped around their waists and hanging from their necks approached in a procession, and everybody looked at them. They were trying to be solemn, but smiles and giggles came through. They walked up to Bannon.

"You come now," one of them said.

Bannon put out his cigarette and stood up.

The children turned to the other GIs. "You too."

"You mean we gotta break up the poker game?" Frankie La Barbara asked incredulously.

"You heard the kid," Butsko growled. "Let's go to the wedding."

Everybody scooped out what he'd put into the pot, and Frankie put the deck of cards in his shirt pocket. They stood and the kids lined them up, with Bannon in front. Children formed a column in front of Bannon and walked toward the center of the village.

The GIs followed them, and Butsko was feeling guilty about the way he'd been treating Bannon. He realized that Bannon was just a kid essentially, and if he wanted to get married, let him get married. Who was to say he knew more about love than Bannon? His own marriage was a catastrophe and none of his love affairs had ever worked out. Bannon might be dead tomorrow, so why not let him get married?

Butsko wanted to make everything right between him and Bannon before the ceremony, so he pushed his way forward through the GIs until he was at Bannon's side.

"Hey, kid," Butsko said. "I'm sorry about everything. I hope your marriage works out, and if you don't want to marry her, you can still get out of it. I won't cut your dick off."

"I wanna go through with it," Bannon said. "It's time I got married. You wanna be my best man, Sarge?"

"Sure, kid. I'll be your best man."

The procession passed thatched huts, and eyes looked at them from the shadows inside. Finally the children stopped in front of a hut and moved out of the way so there was nothing between the hut and Bannon.

Then, around the corner, they saw another procession coming, this one of young girls, with Mary, Bannon's bride-to-be, in the center, walking with her head held down, flowers in her hair. Bannon was getting nervous, because he was becoming aware of the seriousness of the affair. This was a real marriage and he'd never been through anything like it before.

Bannon and the GIs were to the left of the hut in front of them, and the girls were to the right. A big space was between them, and into this space marched the elders of the tribe, led by the chief himself. They were very solemn, and when they stopped they stood stiffly.

Now what? Frankie La Barbara thought, scratching himself and working his shoulders, shifting his weight from foot to foot. He remembered when he'd married Francesca at the Church of Saint Gennaro on Mulberry Street in New York City; it hadn't been anything like this. The organ had been playing and all his relatives had been there, including a few uncles who were in the mob. *Come to think of it,* Frankie said to himself, *maybe it wasn't so much different from this.*

The door of the hut in front of them moved to the side, and a man came out wearing a grass skirt. A tall hat made of feathers sat on his head, and a strand of animal teeth hung from his neck. His body was tattooed and his beard was long and gray.

127

He wore gold rings through his ears and nose.

Butsko jabbed Bannon with his elbow. "This looks like the preacher," he muttered.

The priest raised his hand and beckoned to Mary and Bannon. Butsko pushed Bannon, who walked forward toward the priest, as did the girl. Bannon and the girl stopped in front of the priest, and the girl took Bannon's hand. They glanced at each other, and Bannon could see that the girl was very serious.

The priest chanted in a strange language. He waved his hands around and did a little dance. Bending over, he picked up some dirt and passed it from one of his hands to the other while continuing his chant. Raising his voice, he sprinkled some of the dirt on the heads of the couple in front of him, then dropped the rest on the ground and danced in circles on it.

The priest gesticulated with his hands and seemed to be telling a story in his hoarse, monotonous voice. He made a few motions that Bannon considered obscene, then danced around them three times. Finally he stood in front of them and clapped his hands together once.

The natives crowded around Bannon and the girl, jumping up and down, offering congratulations, and Bannon knew that the ceremony was over. The old chief shook his hand.

"May your marriage be happy and last forever," he said.

Bannon wanted to kiss his bride, but there were too many people between them.

"Aren't we supposed to give each other rings or something?" he asked the chief.

"You give each other yourselves," the chief said.

The GIs lined up to shake Bannon's hand.

"Give her one for me," Frankie La Barbara said to Bannon with a lewd wink.

"If you ever need any help, you know who to call," said Morris Shilansky.

"I'm glad to see you're finally settling down," said Homer Gladley.

"God bless the both of you," said the Reverend Billie Jones.

The GIs made their way through the throngs to kiss the bride, and everybody was cheering and laughing.

A gaggle of children got behind Bannon and pushed him toward Mary as more children pushed her toward him. They came together and kissed; she felt so slender and soft in his arms, something like paradise. Everybody retreated from them. The priest made a pronouncement in his language.

"We must go now," the girl said to Bannon.

"Go where?"

"I will show you."

She took his hand and led him away down the long row of huts. Everybody was silent. Bannon realized they were going someplace where they would be alone. *Well, I'm married now,* he thought, *and it's time for me to do my husbandly duties.*

NINE . . .

Late in the afternoon the Sixty-sixth Regiment began its relief
of troops on the Japanese front. Colonel Shibata ordered his
men to dig in a few hundred yards behind the lead elements
of General Hyakutake's Seventeenth Army, and those elements
retreated through his lines, leaving his regiment to face the
advancing Americans alone.

Colonel Shibata toured the area with his staff and saw emaciated Japanese soldiers crawl out of holes, looking more like
rats than men. Some couldn't walk and had to be carried away,
and others were so close to death there was some discussion
about burying them forthwith, but Colonel Shibata ordered that
they be carried away too.

The big guns were left behind, and Colonel Shibata's soldiers manned them. They'd brought crates of their own
ammunition on their backs, which weren't enough for a sustained artillery barrage, but if used properly and sparingly they
could do a lot of damage. Colonel Shibata designated where
he wanted pillboxes and bunkers. He ordered all the trails and
roads covered with concentrations of troops and thinned out
his men through the jungle, which would be difficult for the
Americans to pass through quickly. His line stretched in an arc
from Ironbottom Sound inland to a range of mountains, and
as the Americans pressed him, he'd fall back gradually to Cape
Esperance.

Colonel Shibata was shown a cave where the corpse of a Japanese soldier had been carved up like a pig. Other soldiers had evidently been feeding off this one, and Colonel Shibata was horrified. He left the cave quickly and continued to deploy his regiment.

The image of the carved-up soldier haunted him for the rest of the afternoon. To him it symbolized the complete breakdown of the Japanese army on Guadalcanal. General Hyakutake should have ordered mass hara-kiri before he'd let the situation deteriorate so badly that Japanese soldiers were eating each other for dinner. It was a violation of everything Colonel Shibata believed as an officer in the Imperial Army.

As the sun sank toward the horizon, Colonel Shibata climbed to the top of a mountain on the extreme right flank of his line and looked east toward the part of the island held by the Americans. In the fading light he could see only wide stretches of jungle and fields of grass, but he knew the Americans were down there, moving toward him. There were many more of the Americans than there were of his own men, and he knew full well that the Sixty-sixth Regiment might not be able to evacuate Guadalcanal.

Perhaps the decision had been made in Imperial General Headquarters to sacrifice the Sixty-sixth Regiment in order to save the remainder of General Hyakutake's Seventeenth Army. If so, it was all right with Colonel Shibata. A soldier's duty was to die for his country.

Colonel Shibata descended the mountain and walked across his front line to his headquarters while dirty, bedraggled Japanese soldiers streamed through his lines on their way to Cape Esperance. They staggered under the weight of their packs and equipment, their skin sallow, their heads like skulls.

Colonel Shibata entered his tent. His aide, Private Suzuki, had laid out his tatami mat and arranged his clothing in a neat pile. On top of the pile was a photograph of the Emperor, and Major Shibata picked it up.

It showed the Emperor on his day of enthronement seventeen years earlier. The Emperor stood stiffly wearing heavy silk robes embroidered with paulownia blossoms, second in sanctity only to the chrysanthemum; the robes were similar to the those of a high Shinto priest. The Emperor carried a priest's scepter in his hand and wore the tall, swooping hat of a priest.

"Ah, sir," said Colonel Shibata, looking at the picture, "I swear before you that I and my regiment will never fail you, for we were placed on earth to do your will."

Colonel Stockton sat at his desk and in the fading light of day read a letter from his brother, who owned a huge lumber business in the state of Maine. His brother, whose name was Harold, discussed life on the home front, the ration books for food and gas, the war-bond drives, the collections for scrap metal, rags, and paper. Colonel Stockton wished there was some news about his wife, who'd left him for a young captain and had last been seen in Paris before the Germans occupied that city. Colonel Stockton often wondered what had become of her, and sometimes he wished the Germans had shot her, while other times he missed her and hoped she was all right.

"May I come in, sir?" said Major Cobb from the other side of his tent flap.

"Sure, Frank."

Major Cobb, stout and round-shouldered and wearing wire-rimmed glasses, entered the office, a sheet of paper in his hand. "We've just received a radio transmission from Captain Orr, sir. He says there's a lot of Jap activity directly in front of him."

"Does he give coordinates?"

"I'll show you."

Major Cobb walked behind the desk and pointed at the map. "Here, here, and around here."

"Hmmm. General Patch has been expecting a last all-out offensive from the Japs, and maybe this is it. I'd better notify him personally right away, and you alert the battalion commanders."

"Yes, sir."

The phone on Colonel Stockton's desk rang and he picked it up. "Yes?"

It was Sergeant Major Ramsay on the other end. "Sir, a

133

native is here with news about the recon platoon."

Colonel Stockton was staggered. News about the recon platoon?

"Send him right in!"

The flap was pushed aside and a native appeared, wearing a lavalava skirt and an Army shirt with bandoliers of ammunition crisscrossed on his chest. Accompanying him was Lieutenant Dorsey from Baker Company. Lieutenant Dorsey approached the desk and saluted.

"Sir, we found this native in our company area approximately an hour ago. He asked to speak with you personally."

Colonel Stockton smiled and nodded to the native. "I'm Colonel Stockton. I understand you have word about my reconnaissance platoon?"

The native marched to the desk and saluted British-style, with the palm of his hand facing the colonel. "I am Corporal Kavasubu, sir. I have a message for you from Sergeant Butsko."

"He's alive?"

"Oh, yes, sir. He alive." Corporal Kavasubu handed over the message that Butsko had written.

Colonel Stockton took it eagerly, laid it on his desk, and read it. Major Cobb leaned over his shoulder and read it too. Butsko wrote tersely about the fight at the mansion, the capture, and the escape. He listed the names of the men still alive; there were only twelve. He said he'd try to work his way back to the American lines as soon as his wounded could travel and asked for further instructions.

Colonel Stockton looked up at Corporal Kavasubu. "Can you read a map?"

"Yes, sir."

"Can you show me where your village is?"

"Yes, sir."

Corporal Kavasubu walked behind the desk, looked at the map, and pointed to a spot of dense jungle. "Here."

Colonel Stockton looked at the spot and realized it was to the south of the Japanese activity reported by Captain Orr. He wrote a note ordering Butsko to take his men to Hill Eighty-three, where Captain Orr was, and wait for the rest of the regiment to arrive. He cautioned Butsko about getting near the Japanese troop build-up.

"Can you give this message to Sergeant Butsko?" Colonel Stockton asked.

"Yes, sir."

"Can you get there by morning?"

"Good. You might as well leave now, because you have a long way to go."

"Yes sir."

Corporal Kavasubu saluted, turned, and left the office. Colonel Stockton looked at Major Cobb. "Radio Captain Orr and tell him to be on the lookout for Butsko and his men."

"Yes, sir."

Major Cobb walked quickly out of the office, and Colonel Stockton looked down at the map, making a red circle around the village where Butsko and the recon platoon were holed up. *So the son of a bitch made it,* Colonel Stockton thought, reaching for his pipe. *An old war horse like Butsko doesn't die so easy.*

Corporal Peter Kavasubu slipped into no-man's-land shortly after dark. Barefoot, he made his way through the dense jungle, stopping suddenly whenever he heard unusual sounds and stepping out again when he felt assured there was no danger.

He climbed hills and crossed swamps infested with crocodiles. He passed silently through vast fields of kunai grass, never bothering to check his compass, because he was born and raised on Guadalcanal and knew it well. Clouds appeared in the sky, obscuring the moon and stars, and around midnight a light drizzle fell, hissing against the leaves and vines. Kavasubu gradually became soaked to the skin, but he was accustomed to that too.

At two in the morning he stopped to rest underneath a taro tree with leaves as wide as an elephant's ears. He ate some K rations and drank water from his canteen. Closing his eyes, he breathed deeply, thinking of how peaceful the island had been before the Japanese came. He looked forward to the day the Japanese left. Then he could return to his life of hunting and gathering food, and if he ever needed money, he could work on one of the coconut plantations. He would miss the American soldiers, because they were playful fellows and very generous with food and cigarettes. Only their officers were serious, like the Americans who used to manage the plantations in the old days. Peter Kavasubu didn't like their officers so much and noticed that American soldiers didn't particularly care for them either.

He stood, checked his equipment, and moved out again. He knew he was drawing close to the Japanese positions the American colonel had told him about and would have to be extra careful. He paused every several minutes to listen for ominous sounds, then moved into the bush again, crouching low to the ground, smelling the familiar odor of rotting vegetation and animals that had been killed by other animals.

He came to a coconut grove at the base of a hill. It was a wild grove, not part of any plantation, and the trees weren't growing in straight lines, but they were spaced farther apart than ordinary jungle trees and he wondered whether he should go around it for purposes of safety.

He decided that would take too much time, and he couldn't discern any danger ahead. He'd go directly through the grove, hopping from tree to tree, because he wanted to deliver his message as quickly as he could.

The rain was falling harder as Peter Kavasubu passed through the coconut grove. His eyes scanned the ground so he wouldn't trip over any fallen coconuts. A wild dog howled somewhere in the distance and sent a shiver up Peter Kavasubu's spine, because there were many things in the jungle that he didn't understand and that frightened him. He believed that spirits lived in the trees and that the animals had their own gods. You had to behave honorably and not let any of the hidden beings get mad at you. Although Peter had been baptized by the Christian missionaries who'd come to the islands, he still retained his old superstitions. He knew that Jesus Christ would understand.

He stopped behind a coconut tree bent over so far that it looked like it would crack in two. Listening to the jungle, a big drop of water fell on his nose and he wiped it away. He couldn't see the moon and didn't have a watch, but estimated that it was around two o'clock in the morning. Time to get going if he wanted to reach the village by dawn. He stepped out from behind the tree.

Blam!

The bullet hit him in the face and his lights went out instantly. He was dead before he hit the ground and lay still. Figures appeared in the grove ahead of him. They were Japanese soldiers, well fed and in uniforms not yet torn to shreds, a patrol from Colonel Shibata's regiment. They approached cautiously in waves, covering each other, looking in all directions. Finally they came to the dead body of Peter Kavasubu. A private bent down and rolled him onto his back.

"A native," he said.

"Search him," said the sergeant.

The private went through Peter Kavasubu's pockets, finding some American coins, a handkerchief, the tooth of a crocodile, and the message from Colonel Stockton. He unfolded the message and handed it to the sergeant.

"It's written in American," the sergeant said.

"Doesn't look very official," said another soldier.

"You never can tell," the sergeant replied. "We'd better take it back to headquarters. Get his weapon and ammunition."

The soldiers took Peter Kavasubu's M l and his bandoliers of ammunition. The sergeant waved his hand and the Japanese soldiers walked away, leaving Joseph Kavasubu bleeding on the floor of the coconut grove. It didn't take long for the bluebottle flies to find him and begin feeding on his corpse.

Bannon and Mary lay in each other's arms as rain pitter-pattered on the thatched roof of their hut. They'd finally finished doing what young married couples do on their wedding nights, and Bannon was smoking a cigarette before going to sleep.

"I bet you friends think you crazy for marrying me," the girl said sleepily, lying on top of Bannon.

Bannon nodded. "They sure do."

She laughed softly. "Americans are so strange. They not understand love."

"Well, marriage is usually a big thing back in the States."

"A big thing here too! What you think?"

"I know, but back where I'm from, people usually wait a long time before they get married."

"What for?"

"So they can get to know each other better."

"You find that out after you get married."

"But Americans like to be sure."

"You mean Americans not sure when they in love?"

"I guess not."

"Are you sure of me?"

"Yes."

She kissed his chest. "You very different from other Americans. I see that right away."

"What did you see?"

"I cannot explain, but I see. What did *you* see?"

"I dunno. I guess it was something I felt more than saw."

"Yes, that the way it is. It something you feel in your heart. What about your girl friend in America?"

"What about her?"

"You love her too?"

"No," Bannon lied, because he wasn't sure of how he felt about Ginger just then. She was so far away, and he hadn't heard from her for so long.

"Someday I like to go to America with you, okay?"

"Sure," said Bannon, although he didn't know how he could bring a dark-skinned girl like her back to Texas. Maybe he could say she was Mexican. A lot of cowboys married Mexicans, but she didn't have a Mexican accent. Maybe he could teach one to her, but how could he do that? He decided not to think about it. He wasn't sure he'd be alive at that time the next day, so why worry about Texas?

Colonel Shibata felt a hand on his shoulder and opened his eyes. He heard rain pelting the roof of his tent.

"Wake up, sir," said Lieutenant Isangi.

Colonel Shibata sat up. "What is it?"

"One of our patrols killed an armed native and found this message on him." Lieutenant Isangi held out the piece of paper.

Colonel Shibata looked at the English writing, which he didn't understand. "What does it say?"

Lieutenant Isangi had been a military attaché in London for two years and was fluent in English. "It's hard to be sure, because the message doesn't say who it's from or who it's for, but it speaks of a certain hill where American soldiers are located and says there is a Japanese troop build-up in front of that hill. It orders other American soldiers to proceed to that hill and be wary of the Japanese troop concentration."

Colonel Shibata thought for a few moments. As far as he knew, the only Japanese troop build-up on Guadalcanal consisted of his regiment moving up on the line. "Hand me my pants."

"Yes, sir."

Lieutenant Isangi lifted Colonel Shibata's pants off a chair and gave them to him. Colonel Shibata got out of bed and put on his pants while Lieutenant Isangi looked the other way. Colonel Shibata walked three steps to his map table and lit the kerosene lamp with a match. The wick glowed and brightened, illuminating the map laid out on the table.

Colonel Shibata bent over the table and looked at the hills in front of his regiment's position. "Lieutenant Isangi, do you see these hills here?" He pointed at them with his finger.

"Yes, sir."

"The Americans referred to in the message must be in these hills someplace. Send out patrols immediately to find out where they are."

"Yes, sir."

"And alert all units that other American troops may be moving into our zone of operations."

"Yes, sir."

"Hurry!"

Lieutenant Isangi dashed out of the tent, and Colonel Shibata sat on his cot, putting on his socks. He was glad there were Americans in front of him. Maybe he could strike quickly and draw the first blood. That would knock the Americans off balance and really slow them down. Besides, he'd much rather attack than defend. It was always the best way to win battles.

• • •

Samuel Ching stood at the window in the attic of his hotel in Rabaul and watched activity in the harbor through a pair of binoculars. Ships had been arriving all day and night, with dock crews running up and down the gangplanks, and he couldn't figure out what they were doing, but he knew something big was taking place.

Rabaul was the headquarters of the Japanese army and navy in the southwest Pacific, and Samuel Ching was a spy for the Americans. He was a wizened seventy-eight-year-old Chinese man with teeth stained brown because of too many cigarettes and not enough dentistry. He owned the Shining Moon Hotel, which overlooked the harbor, and his wife ran the hotel while he engaged in his undercover activities.

He lowered his binoculars and moved away from the window. Pulling down the shade, he sat on the chair and took out a Japanese cigarette, lighting it with a match. *What's going on down there?* he wondered. He'd been holding off sending his report to the Americans until he had a more definite idea of what the Japanese were up to, but now decided he'd better report the activity anyway and let the Americans try to interpret it. They might have other information, and this additional material might help them put together a puzzle they were trying to figure out.

On the table in front of him was a shortwave radio. He clicked it on and the tubes glowed orange. Waiting a few minutes for it to heat up properly, he began to tap out the message on the key in the special code the Americans had given him.

MUCH ACTIVITY IN RABAUL HARBOR. MANY TRANSPORT SHIPS ARRIVING AND LEAVING PAST 24 HOURS. HAVEN'T BEEN ABLE TO FIND OUT WHAT'S GOING ON.

The signal beamed out over the vast reaches of the Pacific Ocean to the American receiving station in Australia, where it was decoded, stamped, and passed along through channels to the intelligence section.

TEN . . .

Butsko woke up at daybreak, rinsed out his mouth with fresh water from his canteen, and lit a cigarette. His men were snoring all around him in the hut, and he got dressed silently as rain fell in torrents on the hut. He put on his helmet and went outside, the rain wetting him thoroughly after he'd taken only three steps.

He ran through the cluster of huts to the one occupied by the chief and saw two guards sitting in front of it under a thatched shelter. Butsko dove underneath it.

"The chief up yet?" Butsko asked.

The guards shook their heads.

"Has the messenger come back yet?"

They shook their heads again.

"He should have been back by now, right?"

They nodded.

The door to the tent was pushed aside and the chief appeared, bleary-eyed with sleep, wearing his lavalava.

"Sorry to wake you up," Butsko said.

"What is wrong?"

"I was wondering if the messenger came back yet."

"No," said the chief, "not yet. The weather is bad. Maybe later."

"Okay. I'll try to be patient."

"It is always good to be patient."

Butsko turned and ran back to his hut. He figured if the messenger wasn't back by noon, he'd assume the Japs had gotten him. Butsko would leave with his men and try to work their way back to the American lines without the benefit of instructions from Colonel Stockton.

On the top of Hill Eighty-three, Nutsy Gafooley was totally miserable. He was sitting in a foxhole half full of water and there was nothing he could do about it. Rain pinged on his helmet and splattered on his uniform. It was difficult to light cigarettes, but he had one going and shielded it with his hand so the rain wouldn't fall on it.

Around him across the top of the hill were other foxholes containing the men from George Company. Even Captain Orr was in a foxhole, but he had his pup tent pitched over it because he had to study maps and keep his walkie-talkie dry. Everybody else had to sit and soak. Nutsy reflected on his past and realized he'd never been so unhappy in his entire life.

The only bright spot was that some of the men in the recon platoon still were alive. The message had come in last night from regiment and traveled on the grapevine. It said a dozen of the recon platoon men had been taken prisoner by the Japs and then escaped. George Company was supposed to be on the lookout for them. The names of the recon platoon men who'd survived hadn't been provided. Nutsy wondered which ones they were.

Whenever Nutsy was unhappy, he tried to think of happier days. He recalled when he was a hobo, living by his wits, riding the rails. How nice it was to jump off a freight train on the edge of a town and find a Hooverville full of people who had become homeless due to the Depression. If there was any stew in a pot, they gave you some. If there was tobacco, you got a share. And often there were pretty young girls around, too, because many women had been forced into the hobo life by the economic hard times.

A shot was fired from his front, and he instinctively ducked his head. It was followed by a flurry of fire in the woods at the bottom of the hill. Captain Orr's listening post was down there, and evidently some Japs had shown up. Nutsy had been in combat enough to be able to measure the size of the fight. It sounded to him as if no more than a Japanese patrol had wandered into the defense perimeter.

After a few minutes the firing stopped; Nutsy knew what was happening then too. The Jap patrol was withdrawing so that it could report the contact.

In other words Company G could expect problems pretty soon.

Fuck 'em all, Nutsy thought, puffing the stub of his cigarette. *Let the brass worry about it. I got my own problems.*

Colonel Stockton was in his operations tent, planning the day's advance, when the call came in on the radio. Lieutenant Harper got the message from the radio operator and handed it to Colonel Stockton, but Colonel Stockton was in the midst of some intricate planning and waved the sheet of paper away.

"What does it say?" he mumbled out the corner of his mouth.

"It's from Captain Orr on Hill Eighty-three, sir. A Japanese patrol has found them."

Colonel Stockton turned around and the operations room became still. Colonel Stockton had to make a tough decision: whether to leave G Company where it was and send help, or pull them out of there. He weighed the pros and cons quickly. His Second Battalion was closest to Hill Eighty-three but couldn't get there sooner than two hours, maybe three, and the Japanese main force might be closer than that. But on the other hand, he'd told Butsko to link up with Company G on Hill Eighty-three. Colonel Stockton didn't know that the messenger hadn't gotten through.

If he had to choose between saving twelve men or saving a company, he'd have to save the company. "Tell Captain Orr to get the hell out of there," he told Lieutenant Harper.

"Yes, sir."

Lieutenant Harper returned to the radio, and Colonel Stockton looked down at the map. He wasn't worried about Company G, because they'd have plenty of time to get away, but the survivors of the recon platoon were another story. *Butsko knows how to handle himself,* Colonel Stockton thought. He should be okay.

"Sir," said Major Cobb, pointing to the map, "I think we should advance part of the Second Battalion along the beach here."

"I agree," replied Colonel Stockton, "and I want you to tell Colonel Smith to move his men west as quickly as he can, because we expect Japs to arrive in that sector soon. Also tell him to be on the lookout for George Company and the recon platoon."

"Yes, sir."

Major Cobb walked to the telephone operator. Colonel Stockton scratched his chin and thought about the Japanese patrol. If the Japs were retreating, as he'd been led to believe, they wouldn't be sending out patrols. Maybe the Japs weren't as weak as had been thought. Maybe they were planning a counteroffensive.

Colonel Stockton turned around and shouted to Major Cobb, "When you finish with Colonel Smith, call General Patch's headquarters and tell him about the Japanese activity around Hill Eighty-three!"

"Yes, sir!"

In the pouring rain Colonel Shibata was inspecting the fortifications on his front line, congratulating the soldiers who'd dug good holes, shouting at those who'd done a lousy job. With Colonel Shibata were members of his staff, plus his radio operator, and when the message from the patrol came in, it was handed to Lieutenant Isangi immediately. Lieutenant Isangi read it, his eyes widening with every word, and then he approached Colonel Shibata.

"Sir," he said, "one of our patrols has made contact with the Americans."

"Where?"

Lieutenant Isangi showed him on the map. Colonel Shibata set his lips in a thin line and thought for a few moments. "Which battalion is facing that hill?"

"Battalion A, sir."

"Send them forward to occupy it and the territory nearby."

"Yes, sir."

"And have the other battalions prepare to follow at a moment's notice."

"Yes, sir."

Lieutenant Isangi dropped to one knee so he could write out the orders. Colonel Shibata gazed east through the pouring rain. He felt enlivened for the first time since he came to Guadalcanal, because a battle was in the offing. His troops were fresher and better equipped than the Americans, because the Americans had been fighting on Guadalcanal longer. *I have a good chance to set the Americans back on their heels*, he thought. *How wonderful that would be if I can do it*.

At Henderson Field, General Patch sat at his desk, thinking about the dispatch that had arrived from Australia an hour before. It was the one that reported the activity in the port of Rabaul.

The intelligence section hadn't known what to make of the activity and suggested it might be the prelude to a major Japanese reinforcement of Guadalcanal. General Patch was advised to take the appropriate precautions, but he didn't know how far to go.

He could play it safe and move all his forces back to Henderson Field, the principal strategic objective on Guadalcanal, so that his defense would be at full strength if the Japanese invasion came. But what if it didn't come? What if that shipping activity was geared toward something else entirely? Then he'd look like a fool, and he'd throw away all the ground he'd taken west of the Matanikau River. That would give the Japs time to regroup, and they'd descend on Henderson Field like gnats. He couldn't give them that opportunity.

The only thing to do was move the bulk of his forces back to Henderson Field and leave only sufficient units in the field to make the Japs think he was still pressing his offensive. In a week or two he'd know whether the situation in Rabaul meant an invasion of Gudalcanal, and if it wasn't, he'd switch his main forces back to the west and really get after the Japs.

There was a knock on his door.

"Come in!"

A young lieutenant entered the office, a dispatch in his hand. He saluted and laid the dispatch on General Patch's desk. "This just came in for you, sir."

General Patch looked at the dispatch; it was the message from Colonel Stockton about the trouble on Hill Eighty-three. The lieutenant saluted again and marched out of the office while General Patch reread the dispatch. It gave him something new to worry about. It appeared that the Japs might try to break out in the west, so he'd have to leave more troops there than he wanted. But maybe not. Maybe he should wait and see what developed. The Twenty-third Infantry was moving toward Hill Eighty-three, and maybe they could handle whatever the Japs tried. If they needed help, they could ask for it.

General Patch cursed the generals in Washington for not giving him what he needed to win on Guadalcanal. Then he wouldn't have to make such an agonizing decision. But the bulk of the US war effort was aimed at North Africa and Europe, and the war in the Pacific was just a sideshow. The Guadalcanal campaign had been nicknamed "the Shoestring War."

He decided to leave the Twenty-third Infantry in the west and pull everyone else back to Henderson Field. He'd tell Colonel Stockton to call for reinforcements if things ever got too hot out there. General Patch felt relieved now that the decision had been made. He picked up his phone to call for an aide who would write the orders down.

He had no way of knowing that the shipping activity in Rabaul was preparation for the evacuation of all Japanese soldiers on Gudalcanal, not their reinforcement. In years to come General Patch would be harshly criticized for his decision to break off his campaign in the west.

The rain was falling in torrents on the little village in the jungle, and the paths between huts had become rivers. Butsko ran toward the chief's hut, holding his collar up around his ears, his feet soaking wet. It was noon and he figured it was time to move out if the messenger hadn't returned yet. He'd already told his men to get ready to leave the village. The only person he hadn't told yet was Bannon, but he wanted to give him as much time with his new wife as possible.

Butsko lowered his head and entered the chief's hut. The chief and a few of the village elders sat around a fire pit that had no fire in it, because the smoke would give their village away to the Japs. They were talking in their native language and stopped suddenly at the sight of Butsko, who removed his helmet.

"Sorry to bother you sir," he said to the chief, "but I was wondering if your messenger came back yet."

The chief shook his head. "If he had, I would have told you. He should have been back by now. We're afraid that something has happened to him."

Butsko crouched down near the firepit. "Well, I've got to get our men back to our lines."

"Why not stay here for a while?"

"I don't think my commanding officer would like it if I took a vacation right now."

"But some of your men are injured."

"They can all travel. One of the reasons I want to leave is so I can get them medical attention."

The old chief sighed. "If that's your decision, so be it."

"I'll have to take your new son-in-law with me."

"So be it."

"I'll stop by before I leave," Butsko said.

Butsko passed through the door of the hut into the rain again and headed for the hut where Bannon was laid up with his new wife. He jumped over puddles and saw trees swaying in the wind. It looked to Butsko like the beginning of a hurricane. Running up the corridor between two rows of huts, he finally came to the one Bannon was in.

"Hey, Bannon!" he said, banging on a wall.

"Come on in!"

Butsko ducked into the doorway and saw Bannon and his new wife underneath blankets, a candle burning nearby. Bannon lay on his back and the girl was on her side next to him. Butsko wondered what naughty thing she'd been doing when he knocked on the wall.

"We're moving out in about an hour," Butsko said. "Report

to my hut as soon as you get ready."

"Okay," Bannon replied.

Butsko smiled at the girl. "Sorry to take your old man away, kid, but there's a war on out there."

Before she could say anything, Butsko was out the door again, running through the water and mud. The girl looked at Bannon and began to cry.

He hugged her tightly. "Don't cry. Everything will be all right."

"I not want you to go."

"But I've got to go. I'm a soldier."

"Stay just another day."

"You know I can't."

She hung her head. "I know."

Bannon crawled out from underneath the blanket and got dressed while the girl watched him, tears dripping down her cheeks. Bannon lit a cigarette and was afraid he'd start crying too. He didn't want to leave her, but the war was still going on.

"C'mon, now," he said to her as he pulled on his boots. "Knock it off."

"I can't help it," she said, sniffling.

"I'll be back someday."

"You promise?"

"I promise."

"Soon?"

"As soon as I can."

He tied up his bootlaces and put his pack of cigarettes in his shirt pocket. His helmet and other gear were with the guys in their huts on the other side of the village. There was nothing to do now except say good-bye, and he'd rather face the whole Jap Army.

He knelt beside her and held her shoulders in his hands, looking into her big, wet eyes. "I gotta go," he said.

"Go," she said petulantly, like a child.

"Now, don't be mad."

"I not mad."

"Yes, you are."

"No, I not."

He kissed the tears on her cheeks. "I'll come back to you again as soon as I can. I swear it."

"I be an old lady then."

"But you knew I couldn't stay here."

She nodded sadly. "Yes, I knew."

"You know I'd stay if I could."

She nodded again.

"I'll love you forever."

"Me too."

Bannon kissed her lips, which tasted of salt tears. He smelled the tropical fragrance of her hair, and her smooth shoulders were quaking. He knew he had to get out of there before he broke down completely, so he turned suddenly and dived out the front door of the hut.

He was in the drenching, ferocious rain, and it lashed his face and body as he ran toward the huts where the recon platoon was staying. His feet splashing through puddles and mud, he felt as though his heart were torn apart. The girl was so lovely, so innocent, the exact opposite of the war. Now he had to go back to the war, the killing and misery, the fear that he'd be dead in an hour.

He came to Butsko's hut, pushed the hanging door aside, and ducked inside. The soldiers were stuffing their belongings into their packs or checking the carbines the natives had given them. Everybody looked up at him, their hearts filled with envy.

"Your stuff's over there," Butsko said, pointing.

Bannon knelt next to his pack and picked up his carbine. It would be his wife from now on. He worked the bolt and heard its harsh metallic sound. The metal was cold and the stock hard. What a wife.

"How're you doing, Bannon?" Frankie La Barbara asked.

"Okay."

Frankie opened his mouth to say something lewd, but thought better of it. Even Frankie La Barbara could sense that a lewd remark would be inappropriate just then.

"Fall out," Butsko growled.

The men frowned and grumbled as they crowded around the door and went outside into the rain one by one. They looked

149

around at the wet gloomy day and became even more disheartened.

"Gimme a column of twos right here," Butsko said.

The men lined up and Butsko went into the next hut to get the others. They, too, came outside and got into the formation. Homer Gladley and the Reverend Billie Jones carried young Private Hilliard on a makeshift stretcher. The men were bandaged and some limped from wounds sustained in the fight with the Japs.

"Right *face!*" said Butsko. "Forward *march!*"

The recon platoon plodded through the mud as the rain soaked through their uniforms. They passed rows of huts and saw murky faces in the doorways, looking at them. Bannon inclined his head toward the ground and watched the mud pass underneath his feet. He was afraid if he looked up and saw Mary he'd break formation and run to her arms.

"Platoon—*halt!* Left Face!"

The platoon turned around. Butsko entered the chief's tent and saw him still sitting with his elders. Butsko took off his helmet. "So long," he said, "Thanks for everything."

The chief and some of his men came outside. The chief was shorter than the men, with brown wrinkled skin and graying hair. Silently and with great dignity he walked up to each man, placed his hands on the man's shoulders, looked into his eyes for a few seconds, and then passed to the next man. When he came to Bannon he did the same thing and touched his cheek to Bannon's. After finishing with the last man, he shook Butsko's hand, then turned to face the men.

"Be brave soldiers!" he said. "Win great battles!"

The old weird-looking medicine man came out of the hut, the strand of crocodile teeth hanging around his neck. He stood still as a statue, looking up at the heavens, as the rain washed his face. Then he let out a shriek, jumped into the air, and began to dance, hopping twice on one foot and then the other. He danced in a circle in front of the men, danced around them, and touched each of them on the head with a stick wrapped with leather. Stopping in front of them again, he looked at the sky, let out another shriek, then retreated back into the hut.

The chief and his elders followed him inside, leaving the recon platoon outside all alone.

"Left *face!*" said Butsko. "Forward march!"

The recon platoon turned and marched out of the village. In minutes they were swallowed up by the jungle.

ELEVEN . . .

Advance units of the Sixty-sixth Regiment of the Imperial Army reached the top of Hill Eighty-three at ten o'clock that morning. They saw the abandoned American foxholes and reported back to Colonel Shibata that the Americans had fled. Colonel Shibata ordered a pursuit of the Americans, and the Japanese soldiers descended the eastern side of the hill, their scouts having no difficulty following the American trail.

The Japanese soldiers were angry about the suffering they'd seen among the cadaverous troops of General Hyakutake's Seventeenth Army and thirsted for revenge. They could see the American footprints in the mud and knew the Americans weren't far away. Although the rain caused their wet garments and boots to chafe their skin, they pressed forward, anxious to engage the Americans. They shouted encouragement to each other and brandished their weapons in the air. They were well equipped, had plenty of ammunition, and were confident of inflicting heavy losses on the Americans. Their officers had told them the Americans were exhausted and wouldn't be able to stand up to them.

The Japanese soldiers streamed through the jungle at a rapid pace, certain they'd find the Americans soon.

• • •

A mile ahead of them, George Company was in the middle of an especially thick patch of jungle. Soldiers at the front of the column hacked through the jungle with machetes, but their progress was slow. Captain Orr pushed them hard, replacing machete bearers as soon as they got tired. His worst fear was that somehow the Japs would work around him and cut off his retreat.

Nutsy Gafooley slipped on a patch of mud and fell on his ass. Somebody grabbed his pack and helped him to his feet. He saw that his rifle was covered with mud, and took his handkerchief out of his back pocket, wiping it clean as he trudged along. He felt strange being with so many soldiers he didn't know. If there was a fight, he wanted to be with the recon platoon, not with strangers.

"Gafooley!" shouted Sergeant Kemp. "Go up there and relieve Shroeder!"

Nutsy moved to the side of the trail and double-timed past the column to get to its head. Private Shroeder, a blond young man with a baby face, was in front with a machete, and he looked like he didn't have any strength left in his body. Nutsy drew close to him and held out his hand. Schroeder passed him the machete handle first. Schroeder's eyes were bloodshot and at half-mast. The young soldier looked like he was ill.

Pow!

Shroeder's shirt exploded, and an expression of shock came onto his face. Another shot was fired, and it whistled past Nutsy's ear, but he was already on his way down to the mud. He landed and the mud covered his wrists. A volley of gunfire opened up in front of George Company and all its men dived for shelter.

Farther back, Captain Orr believed that his worst fears had been realized; he had been cut off. He had no idea of how many Japs were in front of him, and there was only one way to find out. He had to try and break through.

"Skirmish line!" he yelled.

George Company spread out through the jungle, forming a ragged line. The soldiers slithered through the mud and looked ahead through the rain and thick foliage for signs of the Japs, but they couldn't see anything. Leeches dropped from branches onto their skin and sucked their blood, but there was no time to burn them off. Captain Orr cocked his ears and tried to discern from the gunfire how many Japs were in front of him. It didn't sound as if there were many.

"Advance!" he shouted.

George Company crawled forward through the mud. The Japanese fire, which hadn't been very intense to begin with, slackened off to an occasional shot. Nutsy pushed with his feet and elbows as low-hanging branches scraped across his back and down his legs. His eyes searched the jungle ahead for Japs, but the rainfall made all the leaves and branches dance around, and he didn't know which of those motions had Japs behind them.

A bullet zipped into the mud a few inches from his face, and he knew that a Jap had spotted him. Rolling to the side, he got behind the trunk of a tree and peered around it. Another bullet slammed into the tree, and bits of wet wood flew past his face.

"There's a Jap up there!" he screamed.

"Where?" asked Sergeant Kemp, who was to his right.

"Somewheres in front of me! I can't see him, but the fucker can see me!"

"Where's my BAR?" shouted Sergeant Kemp.

"Over here!" replied a voice in the jungle.

"Gimme some fire over this way! Everybody else move out!"

Nutsy didn't feel like moving out, but an order was an order. He flattened himself on the ground and inched with little motions of his toes and fingers. He heard sporadic shots up and down the line and couldn't be sure whether they were coming from the Japs or George Company. Out in the open again, he could hear the rattle of a BAR close by, and in front of him the spray of bullets ripped up the leaves and vines. Then a bullet landed a few feet away and he realized that the Jap hadn't forgotten about him.

"The son of a bitch is still after me!" shouted Nutsy.

"Keep your head down!"

Nutsy imagined the Jap zeroing in on him and felt paranoid. Out of all the men in George Company, the Jap was trying to kill *him*. "You fucking cocksucker!" Nutsy muttered. "If I ever find you, I'm gonna cut you up into little pieces."

Pow!

A bullet whistled over his left shoulder, but this time Nutsy was looking straight ahead and saw the faint puff of smoke in the foliage.

"There he is!" Nutsy cried.

"Where?"

"Over there!" Nutsy pointed with his rifle.

"Throw a fuckin' grenade at him!"

Nutsy pulled a grenade out of the big side pocket on his pants. It was cool and heavy in his hand, and he yanked out the pin. Drawing his arm back, he let it fly; it landed in the midst of the puff of smoke he'd seen. The grenade exploded, brightening the dark jungle for an instant, blowing leaves and vines everywhere, leaving a cloud of smoke behind.

"Forward!" yelled Sergeant Kemp.

Kemp's squad crawled toward the spot where the grenade had exploded, and Nutsy lagged behind because he knew he'd been the Jap's main target. He pasted his eyes on the spot and strained his eyes, trying to see movement that would indicate whether the Jap still was alive, but nothing happened. Bodies in Army green appeared in his field of vision, and he recognized Sergeant Kemp leading the way. Kemp disappeared into the grenade crater and poked up his head a few seconds later.

"You got him!"

Nutsy felt grim satisfaction as he crawled forward. *That'll teach you to fuck with old Nutsy Gafooley,* he thought. Sergeant Kemp was crouching in the grenade crater, which had caved in the side of a foxhole. Inside the foxhole was a skinny Jap minus his head. The Jap's arms looked like toothpicks and he had nothing in the foxhole except his rifle and a few clips of ammo. His skin was covered with sores and he had no shoes.

"Let's move it out," said Kemp. "Keep your fucking heads down."

Gradually George Company moved through the jungle and

overwhelmed more solitary foxholes manned by Japs who looked nearly starved to death. Captain Orr realized that no major Jap unit had worked its way around him, and the resistance consisted only of scattered foxholes containing sick Japs who'd been left behind to slow down the American advance. But although there weren't many Japs, you couldn't stand up and walk through them. Each foxhole had to be knocked out and it was time-consuming. Captain Orr sat in one of the captured foxholes next to a Jap who'd been riddled with BAR bullets. He took out his map to see if he could circumvent the Japs in front of him, wondering whether to head for the sea or go through the jungle to the south. He figured there'd probably be more Japs toward the sea, so he decided to veer toward the jungle to the south.

As he was folding his map to put it away a fusillade of rifle fire erupted behind him, and he dropped low in the foxhole. A thick hail of bullets ripped through the jungle, and he heard the shouts of Japanese soldiers. A sizable Jap unit had snuck up to his rear!

"Lieutenant Holt!"

"Yes, sir!"

"Get over here!"

Lieutenant Holt was ten yards away, crouching behind the tree, and he dropped to the ground, crawling toward Captain Orr. Lieutenant Holt believed George Company had been surrounded and was scared shitless. He rolled down into the foxhole with Captain Orr, blanched at the sight of the Japanese corpse, and said, "Yes, sir?"

Captain Orr had drawn three curved lines on the mud in the bottom of the hole; they formed a semicircle. Behind the three lines was a small circle. "Holt, deploy the company like this, with platoons One, Two, and Three in front and the weapons platoon in back here. Station machine guns between each of the platoons. Got it?"

"What about the Japs in back of us?"

"Forget about 'em. They're not going anywhere. The problem is that way." He pointed west. "Get going."

"Yes, sir!"

157

Lieutenant Holt crawled away to get the company organized, and Captain Orr called for Pfc. Nordell, who was lying on the ground a few feet away. "Gimme the walkie-talkie!"

"Yes, sir!"

Nordell handed it over and Captain Orr held it against his face. "Mission Bell calling Cathedral Ace! Mission Bell calling Cathedral Ace! Over!"

He let the button go and heard crackling and hissing sounds. He spoke the call letters again, but there was still no response. He tried a third time but still couldn't get through. He was in a poor transmission zone.

He handed the radio back to Pfc. Nordell. Machine-gun bullets ripped across the ground a few feet in front of his foxhole, and Captain Orr ducked his head.

Nearby, the soldiers from G Company moved into position to meet the Japanese threat from the west. The Japs were firing steadily as they probed for the Americans. It was only a matter of time before they found what they were looking for.

A few miles away, on the beach facing Ironbottom Sound, the Second Battalion was marching west toward Cape Esperance. The lead units heard firing in the distance and passed the word back to Lieutenant Colonel Joseph William Smith, the commanding officer of the battalion.

Smith was a potbellied no-nonsense officer with a flask of jungle juice in his back pocket. His drinking was a scandal in the twenty-third Infantry Regiment, but he was a solid, aggressive frontline commander and happy only when he was moving forward. He was riding behind the main column in his jeep, watching the waves crashing on the beach, when Captain Watford approached, holding his hand in the air. The driver braked and the jeep coasted to a stop.

Captain Watford approached the side of the jeep. "Sir," he said, "Easy Company is hearing a battle going on to the southwest of its position."

Major Cobb realized it must be George Company because they were the only unit in that direction. "Okay," he said, "send Easy Company directly in to the sound of the fighting, and have Fox Company try to get behind it if they can. The rest of the battalion will go in behind Easy Company. George Company might be in trouble, so have everybody make the best time that they can."

"Yes, sir."

Captain Watford ran forward to his jeep to pass the orders to all the companies, and Colonel Smith reached for his radio so he could report to Colonel Stockton what he was doing.

His radio transmission went through, but he found out that Colonel Stockton was at a meeting with General Patch back at Henderson Field. He had to speak with Major Cobb and told him the information.

"As soon as you can assess the situation there," Major Cobb said, "let us know. You might need some help."

"If I do, you can be sure I'll ask for it," Colonel Smith said.

Colonel Smith handed the headset back to Sergeant Shirley, who was perched in the backseat of the jeep. Colonel Smith tapped his driver on the shoulder. "Move it out," he said.

The driver shifted into gear and the jeep rolled over the wet sand on the beach. Colonel Smith pulled the collar of his poncho tighter and wondered what Captain Orr had run into in the jungle up ahead.

The recon platoon was moving along past a swollen stream when the shots began in the distance. Butsko held up his hand and listened as the GIs stopped behind him.

"Sounds like fighting," said Bannon, standing nearby.

Butsko knew that if there was fighting in that direction, there would have to be Americans in the vicinity. It was tempting for him to continue in that direction and try to link up with them, because they didn't sound very far away, but he was afraid he might stumble into Japs, and his platoon was in no condition for a fight. He decided to continue in a southeasterly direction and avoid the fight. It might take longer to make contact with Americans, but it'd be safer. He looked at his watch; it was ten-thirty in the morning.

"Okay, let's take a break," he said. "Smoke 'em if you got 'em."

The men collapsed onto the ground, took out their cigarettes, and passed them to those who didn't have any. Bannon, soaked to his skin, puffed his cigarette and felt miserable. He missed Mary in every cell of his body, and his wounded leg was bothering him. It had been all right when they'd begun to march, but had slowly worsened as the hours passed.

He thought of Mary crying in her hut, and the vision of her devastated him. He wished now that he'd never grabbed her behind that bush, because if he hadn't he wouldn't be so unhappy now and neither would she.

He wondered why he missed her so, because he'd slept with other women and felt very little when he left them the next morning. What was so great about her? Why did he love her so?

He thought he'd better do something to take his mind off her. He arose, limped a few steps, and knelt beside Private Hilliard, whose chest was one big bandage. Hilliard was conscious but woozy, shot full of morphine. He was the youngest man in the platoon, having lied about his age to join the Army and fight for his country.

"How're you doing?" Bannon asked, looking down into Hilliard's pale face.

Hilliard turned his head to look at Bannon and opened his mouth to speak, but no words came out.

"How is he?" Bannon asked Blum, the medic.

"Piss poor. He's lost a lot of blood."

"Will he make it?"

"I don't know."

Bannon looked down at Hilliard again. "Sure you'll make it," Bannon said, touching his hand to Hilliard's shoulder. "We'll have you to a hospital before you know it."

Hilliard stared at Bannon but didn't see him and didn't understand what he was saying. He was from the Florida panhandle and hallucinated about the Gulf of Mexico, about the girls in their bathing suits swimming in the warm azure water, and about eating a peanut-butter-and-jelly sandwich that his mother had made for him when he'd left home earlier in the day.

In another part of the jungle Colonel Shibata stood under a tarpaulin held by four posts; he was looking down at his portable map table. His aides surrounded the table, and he'd just received word that his forward elements had made contact with the US Army. He pointed to his present position on the map and traced a curving line through the jungle.

"While Battalion A holds the Americans in front," he said, "Battalion B will move around them to the left and Battalion C will do the same on the right. We will catch them in a pincer and squeeze the life out of them. Battalion D will be kept in reserve. I want the pincers to swing out quite far on the flanks so that none of the Americans will get away. Then we will dig in on a broad front and respond to whatever moves the Americans make next. Does anyone see any flaws in this plan?"

Nobody said anything.

"Carry the plan out," Colonel Shibata said.

The officers moved away from the map table to transmit the orders down to the line units. Colonel Shibata held his hands behind his back and continued looking at the map. His blood was stirring in his veins; he smelled victory. In the history of the Imperial Army, small numbers of troops had often won major battles against superior enemy forces, and he thought that perhaps, with his fresh troops and intelligent strategy, he might be able to win a decisive contest against the Americans.

"Sir," said Lieutenant Isangi, holding out the field telephone, "General Miyazaki is on the telephone."

Colonel Shibata narrowed his eyes and reached for the telephone. "This is Colonel Shibata," he said calmly.

"Colonel Shibata!" shouted General Miyazaki on the other end. "I understand you've left the positions you have been ordered to hold!"

"I am attacking the enemy in front of me," Colonel Shibata explained.

"Attacking the enemy in front of you! What enemy in front of you? Have you gone mad!"

"There are American soldiers in front of me, and I am attacking them before they attack me. What is so mad about that?"

"Colonel Shibata," General Miyazaki said firmly, "your orders are to protect the Seventeenth Army's retreat."

"That's what I'm doing, sir. I am following orders to the letter."

"But you're not where you're supposed to be."

"I am fighting the Americans and keeping them away from you so you can run away."

"What!"

Colonel Shibata bit his lip. He knew he shouldn't have said that, but the words were out of his mouth before he could stop himself. "I am doing everything I can to make your evacuation possible, sir."

"Listen to me, Colonel Shibata," the general said. "We are following orders and so must you. You are not in the position you should be in right now."

"That is correct, sir. I am in a better position. I saw an opportunity and I took it. And I shall continue to take advantage of opportunities because that is the way to win victories."

"Win victories?" General Miyazaki asked incredulously. "You think you can win a victory?"

"That is correct."

"One regiment against the American army?"

"Anything is possible."

"Colonel Shibata, I believe you've taken leave of your senses."

"The Imperial Army has fallen to a sorry state if officers who try to win victories are accused of being insane."

"You're not being realistic," General Miyazaki said. "You're moving too far away from Cape Esperance. When the time comes for the Sixty-sixth Regiment to evacuate, you may not return in time."

Colonel Shibata set his feet firmly on the ground and gripped the telephone tightly. "The Sixty-sixth Regiment is not eager to evacuate. The Sixty-sixth Regiment desires only to die on the field of battle for the Emperor."

There was silence on the other end for a few moments.

"Colonel Shibata, you are disobeying orders. I am instructing you to return to the line you are supposed to hold."

"It's too late for that, sir."

Colonel Shibata held the phone in one hand and wrapped the wire around his other hand as General Miyazaki's voice squawked at the rain. Colonel Shibata pulled with all his strength and the wire snapped loose. General Miyazaki's voice was cut off.

The Sixty-sixth Regiment was on its own.

TWELVE . . .

A bullet whapped into the mud three inches in front of Nutsy Gafooley's face. Another whistled past his ear. A third hit a branch over his head, water spilling onto him from the wide leaves. He lay on his stomach behind the tree and fired at figures moving in the rain. The Japs were advancing steadily, utilizing the principles of fire and maneuver. And Captain Orr's men were retreating before their onslaught, leaving casualties behind.

Captain Orr's mortars were blowing up the jungle in front of him, but there were too many Japs and they kept on coming. His mortar rounds were rapidly diminishing and his machine guns were running out of ammunition. He lay in a shell crater, firing his carbine and trying to think at the same time. He knew that he was greatly outnumbered and he'd have to do something fast.

"Platoon sergeants assemble on me!" he shouted. *"Lieutenant Holt too!"*

He continued firing his carbine, gritting his teeth, trying to make every shot count. The Japs were converging on his platoon from three directions and the only thing to do was make a run for it before they got too close. Next to him, Private Nordell was firing his carbine, cursing, his teeth chattering; then suddenly he went flying backward, a bullet hole in the center of his forehead. Captain Orr pulled the walkie-talkie from Private Nordell's shoulder as the platoon sergeants leaped into the shell crater. Lieutenant Holt was the last one to arrive.

"We're pulling out," Captain Orr said in his slow Texas drawl, "and we're gonna split up so it'll be harder for the Japs to get us. Each platoon will be on its own. I'll go with the First Platoon and Lieutenant Holt with the Second. We'll cut through whatever's in back of us, so don't stop for anything. Just run like bastards. Any questions?"

"What about the Japs back there?" Lieutenant Holt asked.

"Go right over them. Got it?"

The sergeants nodded grimly.

"Let's go!" Captain Orr said.

The sergeants jumped out of the shell crater and ran to their platoons, shouting orders. Captain Orr followed Sergeant Kaczmarczyk as bullets flew around them like bees.

"Pull back!" shouted Sergeant Kaczmarczyk.

That was the order Nutsy Gafooley was praying for, and he turned around, stretching out his long, sinewy legs. He dodged around a tree, jumped over a foxhole containing a dead Jap, bulled through a bush, and saw men from the weapon platoon breaking down their mortars. Nutsy ran in a zigzag right through them, jumped over a log, and plunged into the jungle.

"Stay together!" yelled Sergeant Kaczmarczyk.

Stay together my ass, thought Nutsy Gafooley. He elbowed a branch out of the way, ducked underneath another one, and kept going. He saw a muzzle blast in front of him and simultaneously a bullet banged into a tree three feet away. Pulling his last hand grenade from his pocket, he yanked the pin on the run, threw it toward the spot where he'd seen the muzzle blast, and dived to the ground. The grenade exploded and the ground rumbled beneath Nutsy's body. Nutsy leaped to his feet and charged the spot where he'd seen the muzzle blast, firing his M 1 from the hip as fast as he could pull the trigger. He saw movement in the hole—the Jap was struggling to raise his rifle—and one of Nutsy's bullets richocheted off the top of the hole, making the Jap flinch.

Nutsy bounded forward and jumped into the air, landing on the Jap with both feet. The Jap was weak and frail, and he

166

crumpled under the weight of Nutsy, who lost his balance and fell to the side. The Jap moved slowly, trying to pull his bayonet out of his sheath, but Nutsy was like greased lightning. He lunged at the Jap and grabbed him by the throat, squeezing with all his might.

The Jap coughed and clawed at Nutsy's wrists, but Nutsy hung on and kept squeezing. Drool appeared on the Jap's lips and his eyes bulged out of his head. Nutsy was amazed at the weakness of the Jap; he was as spindly as a newborn kitten. The Jap made a horrible gagging sound and then something cracked in his throat. He went limp and Nutsy let him fall into the mud.

Nutsy grabbed his rifle and climbed out of the foxhole, running east toward Henderson Field. Bullets were fired in the jungle all around him, and he heard men shouting in English and Japanese. Nutsy came to a stream and waded across it, holding his rifle high. When he was halfway across he heard a rifle shot and saw a splash as a bullet zipped into the water next to his knee.

"Son of a bitch!" said Nutsy, plowing through the water and diving onto the mud on the other side. Another bullet was fired at him, ricocheting off a rock in the mud a few feet away. Nutsy looked around but couldn't see the Jap and didn't feel like searching for him. Veering to the left, Nutsy crawled along the riverbank to get away. A bullet whizzed over his back and he cursed again, trying to reach a cluster of boulders just ahead. He was so low to the ground that his chin dragged in the mud and he could smell fermenting vegetation. Grenades and mortar shells exploded not far away, and machine guns chattered throughout the jungle. Nutsy made it behind the pile of boulders and looked through the cracks. He couldn't see anything except jungle, the leaves and vines and gray mist rising from the ground. Catching his breath, he leaned his back against the boulders, glad to be alive. He thought that maybe he should try to get away silently, instead of running through the jungle like a maniac. If he had to travel all the way to Henderson Field on his belly, that was okay with him, just as long as he was alive when he got there.

Nutsy got low to the ground and crawled into the densest

part of the jungle, cradling his rifle in his arms, determined to get away alive, even if it took two weeks to get back to Henderson Field.

The heavens blanketed Guadalcanal with rain, and the recon platoon was making slow progress through the jungle. Shaw could no longer walk on his left foot and had to be helped by Frankie La Barbara, whose nose was covered by a huge bandage. Bannon's leg had become numb, but he could still walk unassisted. Butsko had difficulty moving his left arm, due to the bullet in his shoulder. Homer Gladley and the Reverend Billie Jones were getting tired of carrying Private Hilliard. Jimmy O'Rourke had periodic attacks of dysentery and was suffering from double vision. On the point, Corporal Gomez had a cramp in his stomach. Craig Delane was sure he had a broken rib. The cut on Morris Shilansky's scalp was stinging as if someone had poured salt into it.

It was nearly high noon and they were passing a section of thick jungle. Whenever they took a step, they sank ankle-deep into the muck. Insects buzzed around them and bit their exposed skin. They all thought they couldn't go on, but they kept putting one foot in front of the other anyway.

The heavy rain made a constant roaring sound in their ears, and it was difficult to hear danger. Visibility was terrible in the mist and rain. They didn't have the energy to talk, and Bustko thought if he let the men take a break, they'd never get up again.

Corporal Gomez clicked his teeth and slapped his face to keep himself awake. He hallucinated Japs in the jungle ahead of him and thought he was hearing tanks and Japanese soldiers talking. He shook his head and tried to clear out his mind. *I think maybe I got some malaria*, he thought. *I should tell Butsko I can't handle the point no more.*

He realized everybody else was in bad shape, too, so he kept going, holding his carbine in both hands, his eyes sweeping from left to right, his helmet straps dangling back and forth.

Suddenly he heard a loud clanking sound to his front and then heard shouting in Japanese. This time he knew he wasn't dreaming and dropped to the ground. Looking behind him, the others had sought cover too. Gomez crawled underneath a thick bush and peered through its branches. He couldn't see anything or hear anything unusual. But something was there; he knew that now.

Butsko had heard it, too, and crawled forward to see what was going on. He'd noticed where Gomez had gone and joined him in the bush.

"See anything?" Butsko asked, his voice weary.

"Not yet."

They waited side by side, smelling each other's stinking bodies, searching the jungle for Japs. Butsko had a hole in his shirt, and a swarm of flies dived inside to eat up his skin. He reached back and slapped them, crushing a few, but the moment he removed his hand they returned.

"Look!" whispered Gomez.

A column of Japs appeared in the jungle ahead of them. Their pale-green uniforms were drenched, but they looked healthy and full of energy, unlike most of the Japs Butsko had seen recently. Some carried machine guns or mortars on their shoulders, and Butsko guessed the noise he'd heard had been one of them dropping a piece of heavy equipment, and then getting chewed out by his sergeant. The Japs were traveling in a column of twos and moving rapidly through the jungle, as if they were on their way to an objective and had to reach it by a certain time. Sergeants and officers exhorted the men to move faster. Butsko saw one sergeant kick a man in the ass, and Butsko couldn't help smiling because that's what he often did.

The smile vanished from his face when he heard a new sound to his right. He sucked wind when he saw another column of twos emerge from the jungle and head straight for the bush he and Gomez were hiding in.

"Santa Maria!" whispered Gomez.

"Ssshhhh."

Butsko silently dipped his hand into the mud and covered his face with it. Gomez did the same. The Japs were drawing closer, carrying their rifles, mortars, and machine guns. Butsko could see their faces and insignia—even which ones were wearing mustaches. He thought for sure the Japs would see him and Gomez.

The Japs approached and walked in front of the bush. Butsko looked at the leggings of the enlisted men and the soiled boots of the officers. If he held out his rifle, he could trip one of them up. They were so close, he was afraid they'd hear his heart beating. Butsko looked at Gomez, who was lying on the ground, still as a dead salamander, his mouth hanging open, his eyeballs wiggling as the Japs passed by.

The procession seemed to go on forever, and Butsko realized it was a sizable troop movement. The Japs were up to something big, and Butsko wished he could warn Colonel Stockton, but all he could do was lie still on the ground and hope no Jap saw him or Gomez.

Suddenly a pair of officer's boots stopped in front of the bush, and Butsko thought his luck had run out. His grip tightened around the carbine, because he wanted to take as many with him as he could. Then the Japanese officer bent over to tighten his bootlaces. Butsko looked straight ahead at the side of the officer's face and could see that he was a young man, probably around Bannon's age. Butsko's heart beat like a tom-tom: If the officer glanced to the side he'd see him and Gomez. Butsko swallowed hard. He thought of a hundred Japs swarming over him, stabbing him with their bayonets.

The officer fixed his bootlaces, then straightened up and walked off. Butsko took a deep breath. He looked at Gomez, who was as white as a sheet. The Jap columns continued to pass by. Butsko relaxed and breathed normally again, watching Japanese boots trudge through the mud. He thought there couldn't be many more of them, but they kept on coming. After a while he realized it was a major troop movement and that a big battle was shaping up somewhere.

Nutsy Gafooley had crawled away from the main fighting and now was on his feet, moving quickly across a field of kunai grass as tall as he was. Far behind him he could hear sporadic firing and figured some of the men in George Company still were in trouble. He had no compass and couldn't orient himself with the sun, but thought he was moving in an easterly direction toward Henderson Field.

He came to the edge of the field and entered the jungle. After a few steps he heard the sound of a machete striking wood and dived behind a tree. He looked around for someplace better to hide and then saw movement in the jungle again. An American GI pushed through the foliage, and behind him came another GI.

"Hey, there!" said Nutsy. *"Hello!"*

The GIs dropped to the ground and pointed their rifles toward Nutsy. *"Who's there?"* one of them shouted.

"Private Marion Gafooley, recon platoon, Twenty-third Infantry Regiment!"

"Stand up so we can see you!"

Nutsy showed his face and part of his body. *"Don't shoot!"*

"Come on out of there!"

Nutsy walked into the open, holding his rifle at port arms.

"Drop your rifle!"

"I ain't droppin' my fuckin' rifle!"

"I said drop your rifle!"

"Fuck you!"

"Drop your rifle or I'll plug ya!"

Nutsy dropped his rifle. The GIs stood up and approached him, and behind them more GIs appeared.

"He looks like an American to me," said one of the GIs.

"Of course I'm an American!" Nutsy replied angrily.

"What're you doing here?"

"I was with George Company and we got swamped by Japs back there." Nutsy picked up his rifle.

"We'd better take him to Captain Kallas," said one of the GIs.

"Let's go," said the other GI to Nutsy.

They escorted him back past the column of soldiers coming through the jungle, and Nutsy felt safe at last. He'd made it. He figured he was due for a two-week furlough in Hawaii.

Captain Kallas was short and swarthy-faced, with a lantern jaw covered with thick stubble. He looked at Nutsy with fierce intensity as the GIs told him about Nutsy.

"How far back are the Japs?" Captain Kallas asked Nutsy.

"About a mile, maybe more."

"How many of them?"

"I don't know. A company at least."

Captain Kallas held out his hand. "Gimme my walkie-talkie."

Colonel Smith had been forced to leave his jeep behind and was trudging through the jungle with his headquarters, bringing up the rear of the battalion, when the call came through on the radio. His brow became furrowed when Captain Kallas told him about George Company being overrun by the Japanese.

"Continue your advance," Colonel Smith told Captain Kallas. "If you run into any Japs, deploy for attack immediately."

Then Colonel Smith called Colonel Stockton and was able to reach him this time. He told him the news about George Company and explained that he moving forward to rescue any survivors.

"I don't have any idea of how many Japs are ahead of me," Colonel Smith said, "and I don't have time for a reconnaissance. I think you'd better move up the rest of the regiment as fast as you can, sir, in case we get in over our heads."

"The rest of the regiment is on its way. All I can do is tell them to double-time, and I'll be coming in with them. We'll be there in about two hours."

"Thank you, sir."

Colonel Smith handed his headset to Sergeant Shirley and hiked up his pants. "Okay," Colonel Smith said. "Let's go save George Company."

Captain Kallas posted Nutsy Gafooley at the front of Easy Company with the point man, Pfc. Harry Chambers from Wilkes-Barre, Pennsylvania. Nutsy led the company across the field of kunai grass into the jungle behind it, retracing his footsteps, heading toward the sound of firing in the distance. He had a good sense of direction and remembered landmarks he'd passed as he'd escaped from the Japs. Anxious to pay back the Japs for what they did to George Company and the recon platoon, he didn't know that an entire full-strength Japanese regiment was deploying across a broad front in front of him. If he had known, he might have turned around and run, because a battalion is only one-quarter the size of a regiment, and Colonel Smith's battalion wasn't even at full strength. On top of that Colonel Smith had made the mistake of splitting his battalion up; Fox Company had been ordered to attempt the cutoff of the Japanese rear.

The Second Battalion surged through the jungle behind Nutsy and Pfc. Chambers, eager to save George Company—or what was left of it. Before they got close to the spot where George Company had been attacked, machine guns opened fire in front of them, followed by volleys of rifle fire.

Easy Company hit the dirt and spread out into a skirmish line. They'd bumped into the left flank of Colonel Shibata's regiment, but Captain Kallas suspected he was facing no more than a company or two. He radioed this information back to Colonel Smith, who ordered H Company, his heavy-weapons company, to set up their mortars behind East Company and begin a bombardment of the Japanese force ahead of him.

Before he could get all the words out of his mouth, Japanese mortars began lobbing shells at the Second Battalion. Colonel Smith dropped to the ground, finished relaying orders to H Company, and then called Captain Kallas and told him to attack.

Colonel Shibata heard the mortars and knew his regiment had finally made firm contact with the US Army. Almost simultaneously a radio message came back to confirm that the battle was joined. Colonel Shibata looked down at his map and noted the position of the Americans. He figured they were trying to roll up his left flank, but instead he'd deliver a blow that would rock them back on their heels.

His Battalion A was holding down his left flank, and he transmitted an order to its commander that consisted only of one word: *Attack!*

The mortar rounds fell with the rain on Company E, and almost as heavily. Nutsy hugged the ground, which trembled beneath him. He'd been on Guadalcanal long enough to know that when you are hit by a mortar barrage, you either advance or retreat, because to stay in the same place is murder.

Behind him Captain Kallas hollered: *"Fix bayonets!"*

Nutsy reached to his side and drew his bayonet, snapping it on the end of his M 1. Now he knew what was going to happen. They were going to advance through the barrage.

Captain Kallas jumped to his feet. He raised his rifle and bayonet high over his head and pumped his arm up and down. *"Charge!"* he screamed. *"Follow me!"*

Captain Kallas ran to the front of his company, mortar rounds blasting all around him, his head hunkered down, heading for the Japs in the jungle ahead. Nutsy scrambled to his feet and ran after Captain Kallas, and so did the rest of the men in Company E. They sped through the jungle—which was exploding like the bowels of hell all around them—trying to get out of the barrage, looking for Japs to stick on the ends of their bayonets.

Nutsy made no effort to come abreast of Captain Kallas because Nutsy had no desire to win medals. If Butsko was around, he'd kick Nutsy in the ass, but Butsko wasn't around and Nutsy could lay back a little.

Then suddenly the mortar barrage stopped. Nutsy's ears rang with the silence.

"Banzai!" came the cry to the front of Company E.

The GIs saw Japs swarming through the jungle toward them, their bayonets fixed, screaming and hollering, bearing their teeth.

"Attack!" yelled Captain Kallas.

The GIs and Japs closed the distance between them and came together in the pouring rain. Bayonets clashed in the air and rifle stocks jammed against each other. Sporadic shots were fired and the soldiers on both sides grunted and heaved, trying to kill each other.

Nutsy thought he saw Captain Kallas go down, but he didn't have time to think about it because a Jap with fixed bayonet was running straight for him, shrieking at the top of his lungs. Nutsy didn't like his attitude and just waited for him, planting his left foot behind him so that he wouldn't be bowled over.

"Banzai!" screamed the Jap, lunging for Nutsy.

Nutsy parried him out of the way and the Jap went flying

174

past him, losing his balance and falling to the ground. Nutsy was on him in an instant and rammed his bayonet into the Jap's left kidney. The jap hollered even louder and Nutsy gave it to him again, this time through the center of his back. Blood oozed out around Nutsy's bayonet and the Jap continued to scream. Nutsy would have stabbed him again but heard footsteps behind him. He spun around and saw another Jap charging him, hollering like a lunatic; Nutsy didn't like his attitude either.

The Jap pushed his rifle and bayonet forward and Nutsy danced to the side, swinging around his rifle butt, connecting with the rifle on the Jap's face. He broke the Jap's cheekbone and knocked the Jap unconscious. The Jap fell at Nutsy's feet and Nutsy harpooned him through the back, pulled out his bayonet, and looked around.

Two Japs were running toward him, but before they came close they split up, one heading for Nutsy and the other for another GI. Nutsy charged his Jap and lunged first. The Jap parried his blow and tried to bash him in the head with his rifle butt, but Nutsy dodged backward and the Jap butted rain and thin air.

The Jap gritted his teeth and jabbed forward with his bayonet. Nutsy parried the blow and kicked the Jap in the balls. The Jap grunted and bent over. Nutsy delivered an uppercut with his rifle butt, connecting with the Jap's nose, smashing it flat and straightening the Jap out, sending him sprawling backwards. The Jap fell on his back and Nutsy buried his bayonet in the Jap's stomach, then pulled it out, looked up, and saw another Jap coming at him.

"Banzai!" screamed the Jap.

He lunged at Nutsy with his rifle and bayonet and Nutsy lunged at him at the same time. Their rifles smashed together and they got all tangled up with each other. The Jap tried to kick Nutsy in the balls, but Nutsy turned his hip in time and caught the blow harmlessly. Nutsy shot his elbow forward to the Jap's face, but the Jap lowered his head and Nutsy bruised his elbow on the Jap's helmet.

Nutsy and the Jap pulled away from each other and started all over again. The Jap feinted with his bayonet but didn't

175

sucker Nutsy out of position. He feinted again and Nutsy shot his rifle and bayonet forward, his bayonet cracking through the Jap's ribs. The Jap vomited blood and his knees collapsed. Nutsy tried to pull his bayonet out, but it was stuck. He tugged with all his strength and glanced up to see the Japanese officer aiming a pistol at him.

Pow!

Nutsy dived to the ground and the bullet sizzled over his head. He picked up the dead Jap's rifle and hid behind his bleeding torso.

Pow!

A bullet slammed into the dead Jap. Nutsy felt trapped like a rat. He couldn't run and there wasn't much room to hide. He waited for the next bullet, squinching his eyes shut, but it didn't come. Finally he had the nerve to peek over the dead Jap. The officer was lying in a clump on the ground: Somebody had done him in. Nutsy picked up the dead Jap's rifle and bayonet and got to his feet. Japanese and American soldiers were grappling all around him, and there were many more Japanese soldiers. They were swarming over the GIs like maggots, cutting them down, and many of the GIs were turning and running, although no one had ordered them to retreat. Nutsy thought Captain Kallas was dead. He couldn't see anybody else who had any authority.

Should I give the order? Nutsy thought. Before he could answer his own question, three Japanese soldiers charged him through the drenching rain. Nutsy dropped to one knee, steadied the rifle against his shoulder, and pulled the trigger—*Blam*—the Japanese soldier on the left tripped and fell down. Nutsy worked the bolt quickly, aimed at the next Japanese soldier—*blam*—and he, too, went down for the long count. Then the third Japanese soldier was on top of Nutsy, aiming his bayonet down. Nutsy didn't have time to work the bolt. He sprang forward and tackled the Jap as the Jap was moving forward. The Jap fell over Nutsy and landed on his hands. Nutsy twisted around and jumped on the Jap's back, reaching his right forearm around the Jap's neck, locking his right hand in the crook of his left arm, and placing his left hand on the back of the Jap's head.

Nutsy pushed the Jap's head with his left hand, and the Jap's throat pressed against Nutsy's right forearm. It was an old juijitsu trick taught to Nutsy in basic training, but this was the first time he'd used it. He was surprised and pleased that it was working so well. Just like the sergeant said, it was the easiest way to break a man's neck. Nutsy pushed with all his strength and heard the Jap's neck go *snap!*

Nutsy picked up a rifle and looked around. Five Japs were charging toward him, and beside them were three more Japs. A few GIs tried to stop them, but the Japs ran right through them. Nutsy said to himself, *Fuck this!*

He turned around and ran away. *"Retreat!"* he shouted. *"Pull back!"*

The GIs who were still alive heard his voice and reacted like robots, because that's the way they were trained to react. They didn't know who Nutsy was, but they figured he must know what he was doing, and who had time to think about it anyway? The GIs disengaged and retreated into the jungle, firing their rifles wildly behind them as they tried to get away. Fortunately the jungle was thick and provided a lot of cover, but the Japs came after them all the same. Nutsy fired his Japanese rifle until it was out of bullets, then threw it away and ran like hell. He zigzagged through the jungle and soon came to Easy Company's weapons platoon, with their machine guns and mortars. They looked up at Nutsy and the other GIs speeding through the jungle.

"Get ready with those guns!" Nutsy said. "The Japs are coming!"

The GIs manning the machine guns got into position. Nutsy saw a BAR lying on the ground next to a dead GI and dropped down. He pulled the BAR to his shoulder, checked the clip, and watched GIs fleeting through the jungle toward him in a wild rout.

"Wait for the Japs!" Nutsy shouted to the machine gunners. "They'll be coming through any minute now!"

The machine gunners were scared shitless, but they gritted their teeth and waited for the Japs to appear. They didn't have to wait long. The Japs came through the jungle like a hurricane, trying to shoot the retreating GIs in the back. They appeared in hordes in front of the machine guns.

"Open fire!" yelled Nutsy Gafooley.

Nutsy pulled the trigger of his BAR and swung it from side to side, spraying hot lead at the Japs. The two machine gunners did the same thing, and the front wave of Japs went down like wheat before a threshing machine. The next wave of Japs also were taken by surprise and bit the dust. The third wave took cover and tried to see what was going on.

"Let's get out of here!" Nutsy bellowed.

He picked up the BAR and ran back into the jungle before the Japs figured out what to do. The machine gunners broke down their weapons and fled also, while the Japanese officer in front of them was trying to assess the strength of the Americans he'd run into.

It wouldn't take him much time to figure out that there were no Americans in front of him anymore, but by that time Nutsy and the other survivors from Easy Company would be long gone.

Meanwhile, far to the south, the recon platoon was passing through a wooded valley. They were dragging ass because they were all tired and the rain was making the ground difficult to walk over. Shilansky had replaced Gomez on the point because Gomez had come down with the chills, and it was Shilansky's first time on point. He was afraid to alert the platoon to something that wasn't there, or not alert them to something that was there.

The wooded area wasn't as thick as the terrain they'd passed over previously, and Shilansky's field of vision was relatively clear. The tree trunks were thick and a fog hung over the ground, giving the forest a sinister atmosphere.

Then, out of the fog, Shilansky saw the figures of men. At first he thought he was seeing things, so he blinked, but they were still there. It was no hallucination and he dropped to his belly. Those behind him took cover also.

Butsko crawled forward to see what was happening. There wasn't as much protection in the forest as there was in the jungle, and if Japs were coming, they'd see the recon platoon without much difficulty. Butsko didn't think the recon platoon could handle a battle with a superior number of Japs and hoped it was only a patrol. Maybe he could set up an ambush if he could see where the Japs were headed before the Japs got too close.

He came abreast of Shilansky and peered ahead. The figures were coming closer, and there was something about their gait and posture that made Butsko think they were GIs. He wished he had his binoculars, but he'd lost them when he was captured by the Japs.

"They're ours!" Shilansky said.

"You sure?"

"Yeah!"

Shilansky started to get up, but Butsko pulled him back down. "Not yet."

"But they're ours!"

"Shaddup!"

Butsko looked at the advancing soldiers, and as they drew closer, he realized that Shilansky was right. They were GIs!

"Hey, there!" Butsko cried out. *"Hello!"*

The GIs dropped to the ground and looked around. *"Who's there?"* one of them shouted.

"The recon platoon from the Twenty-third!"

"That you, Butsko?"

"Yeah!"

Butsko stood up and so did the GIs. Behind Butsko, the men of the recon platoon got to their feet, big grins on their faces. Their ordeal was over at last! They were home!

Butsko walked toward the GIs and recognized Master Sergeant Fargo Raines from J Company, an old drinking buddy of Butsko's.

"Hey," said Raines, "what you doing out here?"

"Trying to get back to Henderson Field."

"That's a long ways off."

"Where you going?"

"That way!" Raines pointed to the sound of the fighting in the distance.

"What's over there?" Butsko asked.

"A lot of Japs."

"We passed a bunch of them a couple of hours ago."

J Company kept moving forward, and soon there was a big crowd around Butsko and the recon platoon. Lieutenant Jason Wright, the CO of J Company, pushed his way through. "What's going on up here?"

"We just found the recon platoon," Raines told him.

Wright looked at Butsko. "What're you doing here?"

Butsko gave him a quick rundown on their capture, rescue, and effort to get back to Henderson Field.

"I think you'd better come with us," Wright said. "Japs are moving into this sector in force."

"We saw about a battalion of them a ways back."

Wright took out his map. "Where?"

Wright's runner held his poncho over the map and Butsko pointed. "Around here, and they were headed into this direction."

Wright could see that the Japs were going to the same general section of the jungle in which he was aimed.

"I'd better report this to battalion," Lieutenant Wright said. "The rest of you, move out. I'll catch up later."

Third Battalion headquarters relayed the message to Colonel Stockton, who was moving up to the line with his headquarters, the First Battalion, the Sixty-eighth Field Artillery Battalion, and the Fifteenth Combat Engineer Battalion.

Colonel Stockton was on foot, surrounded by aides, runners, signalmen, and his staff. The road had petered out a short way back, and now the regiment was advancing toward the sound of fighting on fairly decent jungle trails cut a month earlier for another offensive. If Colonel Shibata had stayed on the line he'd been ordered to hold, the Americans would not have been able to get to him so easily.

Colonel Stockton stopped beneath a taro tree, and aides held up ponchos to keep him dry as he examined his maps. By then he had a fairly clear picture of how many Japs were in front of him and what they were up to. He decided he'd better call General Patch and ask for help, just in case.

His radio transmission got through, but General Patch wasn't in his office. Instead Colonel Stockton spoke with Brigadier

General Edmund B. Sebree, General Patch's chief of staff, who had been nicknamed "John the Baptist" because of his ascetic appearance and habits.

"General," said Colonel Stockton into his headset, "it looks like the Japs are trying to do something significant out here, and I think I'd better have some help, because there are more of them than us. My Second Battalion has already taken a licking, and I'm not sure I can hold the Japs back with the remainder of my regiment."

"I'll have to take it up with General Patch when he gets back," General Sebree said. "His main concern right now is the security of Henderson Field."

"If the Japs break through the regiment, there won't be anything between them and Henderson Field. I think it'd be best if we stopped them out here instead of back there, and there isn't much time."

"Do you think you can hold them with another regiment?"

"Another regiment ought to do it."

"Okay," said General Sebree, "I'll release the Eighteenth as soon as I get off the radio. Anything else?"

"Thanks, General."

"Over and out."

Nutsy Gafooley and the survivors of Easy Company were running through the jungle, with the Japs close on their heels. Fortunately the jungle was thick and the Japs had poor visibility. Bullets whistled around Nutsy and banged into trees, but he kept on running, dodging trees, leaping over logs.

A distance was widening between the Easy Company GIs and the Japs, because the Japs had to be somewhat cautious; they didn't know what was in front of them. The GIs, on the other hand, knew that the rest of the battalion was behind them and that they'd have to bump into it sooner or later—and sooner if they moved quickly. Moreover, the men from Easy Company had spread out, so the Japs didn't know exactly where to place their main effort.

"Halt—who goes there?" shouted a voice in front of Nutsy Gafooley.

Nutsy stopped and ducked down. *"Private Marion Gafooley from the recon platoon, and the Japs are right behind me, so here I come!"*

Nutsy jumped up and ran into the front elements of H Company, who held him in their sights all the way to make sure he wasn't a sneaky Jap who spoke English. Behind Nutsy and on both sides of him came the other men from E Company who were still on their feet.

"The Japs are right behind us!" Nutsy said. *"Give 'em hell!"*

The men from H Company dropped to the ground and got their rifles, BARs, and machine guns ready. The mortars were set up at the rear. Word was passed to Colonel Smith, who was traveling at the rear of H Company, that Japs were on the way, and he pulled his Colt .45, checked the clip, and spat on the ground.

"Let 'em come," he said.

The Japs screamed and hollered as they sped through the jungle, shaking their rifles and bayonets, flushed with victory. Their officers waved their samurai swords in the air and urged them on. The Japs poured around the trees and bushes—and in their eagerness couldn't see that the GIs from H Company and Colonel Smith's headquarters were right in front of them, on their bellies, their weapons ready to fire.

The GIs pulled their triggers and a tremendous roar filled the jungle. The air filled with hot lead, and the first wave of Japs collapsed under its fury. The second wave was ripped to shreds and the third wave kept charging, followed by hordes of other Japanese soldiers. The GIs kept firing and the Japs kept coming, screaming at the tops of their lungs, jumping over their fallen comrades, pushing forward in one of the wild banzai charges that was the mainstay of Japanese army tactics.

Nutsy Gafooley saw them charging forward and kept the trigger of his BAR pulled back, shifting his weight from side to side, cutting them down. But there were too many of them and he couldn't stop them all. The Japs kept bursting out of the jungle and finally were so close the GIs had to stand up and fight them hand-to-hand.

Nutsy jumped to his feet, adjusted the BAR strap over his

shoulder so that it wouldn't be so heavy, and cradled it in his arms. A bunch of Japs were bearing down on him and he pulled the trigger, swinging the BAR from side to side. His bullets tore into the Japs' bodies and they lost their footing, tumbling to the ground. Three more Japs appeared and Nutsy shot them to pieces. Then the battle became too close, as Japs and GIs grappled with each other face-to-face and hand-to-hand.

Nutsy felt weird with the BAR. He should have had a rifle and bayonet, but instead he had the heavy BAR, with its massive firepower, and he had to be careful that he didn't kill any GIs. A Jap with a rifle and bayonet charged him, and Nutsy waited until he was three feet away before pulling the trigger. The BAR barked viciously and the Jap's chest was crumpled by three bullets landing almost simultaneously. Nutsy swung around and saw another Jap bending over a GI lying on the ground, about to run him through, and Nutsy ran toward the Jap, pulling the trigger of his BAR. His bullets hit the Jap in the arm and ribs, knocking him over.

"Banzai!"

Nutsy looked up and saw three Japs charging toward him. He pulled the trigger of the BAR and blew them totally away. Nutsy couldn't believe how easy it was. He felt invincible with the BAR. He saw a Jap break loose from the tangle of fighting men all around him, and the Jap fired his rifle from his waist. The bullet whizzed past Nutsy's ear, and Nutsy dropped to one knee, aiming up at the Jap, waiting for him to come closer so that he could shoot him dead.

The Jap advanced toward Nutsy, holding his rifle and bayonet low. Evidently he didn't want to take the chance of shooting any of his comrades—just like Nutsy, who sprang to his feet and charged, pulling the trigger on his BAR.

Clank!

The chamber was empty and Nutsy was almost right on top of the Jap. He didn't have time to reload, and the Jap shouted a battle cry as he lunged with his rifle and bayonet. Nutsy managed to parry the thrust with the heavy BAR, and he lashed out with his foot, hoping to kick the Jap in the balls. The Jap darted backward just in time and prepared to charge Nutsy again.

Nutsy grabbed the barrel of his BAR, hoping to swing it like a baseball bat, but the barrel was hot from all the firing he'd done and he burned both his hands. Screaming, he dropped the BAR, and at that moment the Jap thrust his rifle and bayonet toward Nutsy's heart.

Ka-pow!

The Jap faltered and fell over Nutsy, a bullet hole in his chest. Nutsy pushed the Jap off him and was astonished to see Lieutenant Colonel Joseph William Smith, his big belly hanging over his belt, his flask of jungle juice in his back pocket, a Colt .45 service pistol in his right hand and an entrenching tool in his left. Colonel Smith had shot the Jap and saved Nutsy's life.

Colonel Smith moved forward, breathing heavily, his nostrils flared. Two Japs ran toward him, their rifles and bayonets angled toward his potbelly, and Colonel Smith fired his Colt .45, picking off the one on his left. The Jap on the right pushed his rifle and bayonet forward, and Colonel Smith shot him in the face at point-blank range. The Jap's head exploded and covered Colonel Smith with blood and brains.

Another Jap came at Colonel Smith from the side, and Colonel Smith clobbered him with the entrenching tool. The Japs in the vicinity could see the little silver leaf on Colonel Smith's collar and knew he was a high-ranking officer. They turned and converged on him, but he stood his ground, firing his pistol as fast as he could pull the trigger and swinging ferociously with the entrenching tool. A Japanese bayonet pierced his left arm in the center of his biceps, and the Jap shouted for joy, but Colonel Smith shot him in the throat and the Jap collapsed onto the ground.

Colonel Smith's biceps were sliced badly and he couldn't hold the entrenching tool anymore. Letting it fall to the ground, he shot a Jap in the chest and another one in the stomach.

Click!

His Colt .45 was out of ammo, and a big Jap with his rifle and bayonet aimed forward like a lance came at him.

Blam!

The Jap collapsed onto the ground, and Colonel Smith looked

up to see a scrawny American soldier with an M 1 rifle and bayonet in his hands.

"Load up, sir!" said Nutsy Gafooley. "I'll keep the Japs away!"

Colonel Smith reached into his ammo pouch and pulled out a fresh clip of bullets. He ejected the empty clip just as three Japs emerged from the tussle all around him, charging like bulls. Nutsy hollered and jumped in front of them, swinging his rifle butt around, cracking one in the head, slashing another across the throat with his bayonet. The third ran toward Colonel Smith, who slapped the fresh clip into his Colt .45. Nutsy threw his rifle and bayonet like a spear and it thunked into the Jap's back. The Jap sagged to the ground in front of Colonel Smith.

Nutsy rushed back and yanked the rifle and bayonet out of the Jap's back. Colonel Smith stood, blood dripping down his left arm, and looked around. His men appeared to be holding the Japs.

"Stand fast!" he yelled. *"Don't let any of the bastards through!"*

He raised his pistol and shot a charging Jap between the eyes. The Jap crashed to the ground and Nutsy jumped over his body, impaling the next Jap on the end of his bayonet. A Jap bashed a GI in the head, fracturing his skull, and Colonel Smith shot the Jap in the side. Nutsy parried a thrust and kicked a Jap in the balls as the battle continued to rage all around him.

Colonel Shibata was pacing back and forth behind his map table. He knew his regiment had attacked the Americans and wondered how the battle was progressing.

Lieutenant Isangi held up the field radio. "Sir!" he said. "Captain Otsuki!"

Colonel Shibata reached for the radio eagerly because Captain Otsuki commanded the battalion on the Sixty-sixth's left flank, where the fighting had broken out.

"What is it?" Colonel Shibata said.

"The Americans have stopped my attack, but give me another company and I can break through!"

"You're sure of that?"

"Yes, sir! The fight can go either way right now, but with another company we'll win!"

"I'll send it to you as soon as I can!"

Colonel Shibata handed the radio to Lieutenant Isangi and looked down at the map to see what company he should send to Captain Otsuki. Should he take one from his reserve or switch a company already nearby on the line?

"Sir!" said Lieutenant Isangi, holding out the field radio again. "Colonel Seki!"

Colonel Seki commanded the battalion in the middle of the Sixty-sixth's line, and Lieutenant Isangi grabbed the radio. "Yes?"

"Sir, we've just been hit by a major American counterattack!"

Colonel Shibata was stunned. It was Colonel Smith and the First Battalion coming up on the line. "Can you hold?"

"I believe we can, sir!"

"Make sure that you do! Report to me any change in your situation!"

Colonel Shibata looked down at the map and pulled out his pack of cigarettes. He lit one up and tried to figure out what to do. He realized he couldn't switch any units from his line to his left flank, and he didn't dare release anything from his reserve. All he could do was hope that everybody could hold the initial American onslaught and then push the Americans back.

He puffed his cigarette nervously. He hadn't expected the Americans to fight with such determination.

New trouble was looming on the right flank of Major Shibata's line, because the Third Battalion of the Twenty-third Infantry Regiment, commanded by Lieutenant Colonel Vincent McGough, had reached the Japanese outposts and gone through them like shit through a tin horn.

Ahead was the main body of Japanese soldiers, still digging in for the battle they expected, a battle that was descending on them with sudden fierceness. J Company was in front of the

Third Battalion, and in their forward rank was the recon platoon, lusting for revenge.

Butsko jogged forward, holding his carbine with fixed bayonet in his hands, barely feeling the wound in his shoulder; he couldn't wait to kill a Jap. Next to him was Bannon, limping on his left leg, also raring to go. They were advancing behind a creeping mortar barrage that was making the Japs scurry for cover, and Lieutenant Jason Wright had posted his machine guns to support the advance.

The mortars blew apart the jungle in front of the charging GIs, who were shouting and screaming rebel yells, Bronx cheers, cattle calls, and anything else that came to mind. The machine guns ripped up the Japs in converging fields of fire. The Japs hadn't completed their fortifications and were out in the open. Bravely they tried to man their guns, but hell was breaking loose all around them.

Suddenly the mortar barrage stopped and the GIs came charging through the smoke, leaping over shell craters, aiming their bayonets at the Japs who were getting to their feet to meet the onslaught.

Butsko's carbine was set in its automatic mode, and he opened fire on the first Jap he saw, a sergeant—like himself—crawling out of a ditch. The burst of bullets hit the Jap on the chest, mangling his heart, lungs, and ribs, and flinging him onto his back. Butsko jumped on the Jap's face with both feet and fired a burst at a Japanese officer running toward him with his samurai sword high in the air. The officer's shirt became splattered with blood as he tumbled to the ground. Butsko stepped over him and saw a platoon of Japs running toward him and the GIs nearby. Butsko pulled the trigger of his carbine and the bullets spat out in a swirling spray, cutting into the Japs and knocking some of them down, but the rest kept coming, firing their weapons, and GIs went down dead and wounded.

The bullets flew wild and fast for a few moments, and then the Japs and Americans were face-to-face. Butsko was a powerful man and put all his weight behind a solid thrust with his rifle and bayonet. The Japanese soldier in front of him tried to parry Butsko's bayonet away, but he simply didn't have the strength. Butsko's bayonet buried itself to the hilt in the Jap's chest, and the Jap died instantly, hanging on the bayonet like a rag doll.

Butsko flung the Jap away, slammed another Jap in the mouth with the carbine butt, and slashed another Jap with his bayonet. Butsko charged forward, saw another Jap in front of him, and parried the Jap's lunge easily, whacking the Jap in the face with his carbine butt, hitting him again in the face and then kicking him in the balls. The Jap dropped to the ground and Butsko stomped his mouth twice, recalling the beating he'd taken when he'd been captured by the Japs and becoming even more furious.

He saw another Jap and feinted with his bayonet and carbine. The Jap raised his rifle to block the thrust that never came, and Butsko brought his carbine butt around, striking the Jap in the stomach. The Jap said "Oof!" and keeled over, and Butsko kicked him in the face, nearly knocking his head off his shoulders.

The Jap went flying backward and Butsko turned to see two Japs charging Bannon from both sides. Bannon faced one of the Japs, thrust first, and buried his bayonet in the Jap's stomach. Bannon didn't even see the other Jap, and Butsko stuck the Jap in the back. The Jap, taken by surprise, shrieked and threw his rifle into the air, and Butsko pulled his bayonet out, spun around, and cracked a Japanese corporal in the jaw with his carbine butt.

Bannon limped as he charged forward, feeling a tremendous surge of energy at the vengeance he was wreaking on the Japs. A Jap jumped in front of Bannon and feinted with his rifle and bayonet, but Bannon didn't fall for it. The Jap feinted again, and Bannon saw an opening to kick him in the balls, but he couldn't do that with his wounded leg. The Jap decided to go all the way this time and shot his rifle and bayonet forward. Bannon parried it and brought his carbine butt up, breaking the Jap's jaw. The Jap went sprawling backward and Bannon followed him, poking his bayonet into the Jap's intestines. The Jap collapsed onto his back, and Bannon looked up to see another Jap in front of him.

Bannon let loose a Texas cattle call and leaped unsteadily

at the Jap, thrusting forward with his carbine and bayonet. The Jap parried the blow and Bannon lost his balance, falling to the side, landing on the body of a dead American soldier. The Jap tried to harpoon Bannon, but Bannon spun away and the Jap's bayonet buried itself in the dead GI's ribs. The Jap tugged on his rifle but couldn't pull the bayonet loose.

Bannon jumped to his feet, picked a big rock up from the ground, and cracked the Jap on the head with it. Blood appeared instantly on the Jap's khaki cap, and the Jap's eyes rolled up into his head.

"Banzai!"

Another Jap ran at Bannon and Bannon threw the rock at him, hitting the Jap on the chest, making him falter. Bannon picked up the other Jap's rifle and bayonet, aimed at the faltering Jap, and pulled the trigger, but the bolt went *click;* the rifle was empty.

"Banzai!" cried the Jap, charging again.

Bannon was ready for him, feinted, and pushed his rifle and bayonet forward. The Jap saw it coming at the last moment and tried to get out of the way, and Bannon's bayonet stuck into the Jap's shoulder. The Jap was stunned by the sudden pain and Bannon pulled the bayonet out, took aim again, and this time plunged it in all the way into the Jap's stomach, then ripped up and pulled out. Disemboweled, blood foaming from his mouth, the Jap collapsed at Bannon's feet.

Bannon looked around and saw men tussling everywhere. Frankie La Barbara was being rushed by three Japs, and Bannon charged to his rescue. The Japs saw him coming and one peeled off the group and turned toward Bannon, who lunged with his rifle and bayonet. The Jap parried the thrust and smacked Bannon on the helmet with his rifle butt. Bannon saw stars and fell on his back. The Jap tried to spear him, and Bannon rolled out of the way. The Jap tried again and suddenly realized a mountain was in front of him. It was Homer Gladley, swinging his rifle like a baseball bat. He hit the Jap alongside his head. Blood squirted out of the Jap's nose, mouth, and ears, and he was thrown to the ground by the force of the blow.

Frankie La Barbara was in a terrible, fearsome rage and was barely aware of the battle all around him. All he knew was he wanted to pay the Japs back for ruining his beautiful nose. The two Japs in front of him lunged at the same moment, and he leaped like a rabbit to his right, then shot his rifle and bayonet forward into the ribs of the closest Jap. He pulled back, but his bayonet wouldn't come loose, so he let his rifle go and jumped on the other Jap, sticking out his thumbs. They sank deeply into each of the Jap's eyes, and the Jap screamed horribly. Frankie held the Jap's head tightly, his thumbs still in the Jap's eye sockets, and pounded the Jap's head against the trunk of the nearest tree. He heard a sickening crunching sound, and the Jap went limp. Frankie let him fall to the ground, kicked him in the face, and picked up the Jap's rifle.

He turned around. A Jap officer was in front of him, and the Jap swung his samurai sword from the side, knocking the rifle out of Frankie's hands. Frankie leaped at the Jap and punched him with all his strength, connecting with the Jap's nose, flattening it on his face. The Japanese officer was stunned and dropped his samurai sword. Frankie picked it up, raised it high in the air, and brought it down, connecting with the top of the Japanese officer's head and cutting it in two like a melon.

The sword was dripping blood and Frankie raised it over his head again, running toward a bunch of Japs surrounding the Reverend Billie Jones. He swung down, hitting a Jap on the shoulder and cutting off his arm. The other Japs turned toward Frankie, who swung the samurai sword from the side, hacking into a Jap's ribs. Billie Jones stabbed a third Jap in the back with his bayonet, and Frankie pulled his sword loose.

A fourth Jap lunged at Frankie, aiming his rifle and bayonet toward Frankie's heart, and Frankie batted the bayonet out of the way with his elbow, then brought the samurai sword down diagonally, catching the Jap on the neck and slicing down to his lungs.

"Yeah!" said Frankie. *"Yeah!"*

Another Jap ran at Frankie, and Frankie swung the sword from the side, but the Jap jumped backward and the sword sailed harmlessly through the air. Frankie was off balance, his arms nearly wrapped around his back, like Joe DiMaggio after hitting a home run. The Jap thrust his rifle and bayonet forward and Frankie dropped the samurai sword, catching the Jap's rifle in his hands and bringing up his knee, connecting with the Jap's testicles. The Jap lurched to the ground and Frankie pulled the rifle and bayonet out of the Jap's hands, pounding him in the head with the rifle butt.

The Jap went limp on the ground and Frankie stood over him, bashing his head with the rifle butt again and again, making it look like a plate of lasagne, because nobody was going to fuck up Frankie La Barbara's face and get away with it.

THIRTEEN . . .

The Twenty-third Infantry Regiment and the Japanese Sixty-sixth Regiment were locked in combat for the rest of the day, neither side giving ground, and as night fell the fighting became so confused that both sides disengaged to lick their wounds.

Colonel Shibata was dismayed that his regiment hadn't broken through, but consoled himself with the thought that at least they'd withstood the shock of the American attack and his lines hadn't broken seriously anywhere. Throughout the night he planned an attack for the morning, with a feint at the center of his line and the main effort coming on his left flank, where he thought the Americans were weakest.

Colonel Stockton, on the other hand, realized he'd just about exhausted his resources on the first day, and he'd even committed his reserves. Everything would depend on the arrival of the Eighteenth Regiment the next day. He called Henderson Field and spoke directly with General Patch, who told him that the Eighteenth was expected to reach the line around noon.

"I hope I can hold out that long," Colonel Stockton told him.

"You'd damn well better!" General Patch replied.

Throughout the night there was patrolling and sporadic fighting as each side tried to get a better picture of what it was facing, but by morning neither side was wiser because of the darkness and entangled lines.

Colonel Shibata launched his attack in the morning. At first it appeared to be going well. He thought he could deliver a knockout punch if he sent his reserves to his left flank and barreled through the America positions there. He thought he could roll up the American flank, shift all his forces to the left, and make a wild charge toward Henderson Field.

"Lieutenant Isangi!" he said. "Give me the radio!"

"A message is coming in, sir," Lieutenant Isangi replied excitedly.

Lieutenant Isangi listened to the headset and wrote the message down as Colonel Shibata waited impatiently. Writing the last words, Lieutenant Isangi stood and handed Colonel Shibata the message.

Colonel Shibata read it and his hair stood on end. A quartermaster unit in his rear was being attacked by a huge American force! The paper trembled in Major Shibata's hand. For the first time since the battle began, he became afraid.

He didn't know that his rear echelon was being attacked only by Fox Company, which Colonel Smith had sent behind the Japanese line the day before to cut off its retreat. That was before Colonel Smith knew the size of the Japanese force in the jungle. After that everybody forgot about Fox Company, because it dropped out of radio contact.

Fox Company, under Captain Leach, had gotten itself lost, wandered around in the jungle all day and night, and finally blundered onto the Japanese quartermaster unit. The Japanese quartermasters weren't frontline soldiers and panicked immediately, thinking they were being attacked by at least a battalion. The quartermasters ran away and Fox Company set to work blowing up all the ammunition dumps and supplies.

Colonel Shibata thought his rear was in danger of collapse and ordered the immediate turnaround of his reserves to meet the new threat. Lieutenant Isangi transmitted the order to the reserves, and as soon as he finished, a new transmission came over the airwaves. Lieutenant Isangi nearly fainted on the spot.

"Sir," he shouted, spit flying out of his mouth, "Americans

in the center of our line have been reinforced and they're breaking through!"

"*What!*" Colonel Shibata grabbed the headset out of his hand. "*Who's there?*"

"Major Toriumi, sir!" said the voice on the other end.

"What's happened?"

"A massive counterattack by the Americans!"

"*Stop them!*"

"We can't! There are too many of them! My line is cracked apart!"

"Pull back your flanks to stop the counterattack!"

"My flanks are under attack too!"

It was the American Eighteenth Regiment hitting the line in full force, and Colonel Shibata tried to calm himself. His reserves were on the way to the rear and he could expect no help from General Hyakutake. "Very well," he said. "Pull back all your men."

"To where?"

"I'll tell you later. Just pull back as quickly as you can and try to keep your men together."

"Yes, sir."

Colonel Shibata wiped his face with his hand and handed the headset back. He looked down at the map and looked for a spot to make his last stand. His eyes fell on a mountain range to the southeast. "Lieutenant Isangi!"

"Yes, sir!"

Colonel Shibata pointed to the map. "Direct all units to retreat here. I'll give them precise locations as soon as I have them worked out."

"Yes, sir!"

Lieutenant Isangi put on the headset and made the first call to a frontline commander while Colonel Shibata bent over the map. The sound of fighting was furious at his front, and he heard the whistle of an incoming artillery shell.

"*Get down!*"

He dived underneath his map table, and the shell landed a few hundred yards away, blowing a hole in the jungle. Colonel Shibata got to his feet, brushed some mud off his pants, and looked at the map again, but heard the whistles of more shells and had to get down again.

"Captain Nakao!" he yelled.

"Yes, sir!"

"Break camp! Prepare to move out!"

"Yes, sir!"

The soldiers scurried around as shells dropped into the jungle around them. Colonel Shibata looked at the map, trying to figure out the direction of the mountain range.

"That way!" Colonel Shibata shouted, pointing toward the mountains.

Colonel Shibata gathered up his maps and folded them as neatly as he could as Lieutenant Isangi relayed his retreat order to the front and men picked up equipment, hoisting it onto their backs.

Colonel Shibata knew he'd lost his big gamble, and Guadalcanal now belonged to the US Army.

FOURTEEN . . .

The Twenty-third Infantry Regiment and the Eighteenth Regiment pursued Major Shibata's regiment across the jungle and into the mountains, where the Japanese soldiers took shelter in caves, and the last bloody act was played out in the battle for Guadalcanal.

While that grim struggle was taking place, the Japanese Seventeenth Army began its evacuation from Guadalcanal. Transport ships arrived from Rabaul and the loading began on the night of February 1, 1943, amid constant fear that the US Navy would attack from the sea and American soldiers would attack on land. The evacuation continued unhindered for five nights, and Genera Hyakutake couldn't understand why the US Army didn't attack Cape Esperance.

General Hyakutake and his staff departed on the last ship, leaving behind over 23,800 Japanese soldiers dead or missing in action, plus the remnants of Colonel Shibata's regiment fighting their desperate last stand in the mountains. Thirteen thousand Japanese soldiers made it to safety on the transport ships, to fight another day.

General Hyakutake stood on the deck of his transport ship and looked back at Guadalcanal, his eyes filled with tears. Rain continued to fall on the sad little island as it receded into the distance. He knew that Japanese dreams of an empire stretching across the southern seas had been shattered by the Americans on Guadalcanal, but there would be other islands and other battles. It was a long way from Guadalcanal to Tokyo, and the Imperial Army had many thousands of soldiers left. It still was strong and one day would rebound, pushing the Americans back and reoccupying Guadalcanal, or so he hoped.

General Hyakutake gripped the rail tightly as tears streamed down his face. Jagged lightning bolts tore apart the sky, followed by reverberations of thunder. He thought of his soldiers, so strong and brave when they'd first come to Guadalcanal. Now they were emaciated and ill belowdecks, their eyes glazed with sorrow, their spirits broken. "Oh, you island, " General Hyakutake whispered, "What have you done to my army?"

On the ninth of February, General Patch transmitted the following message to Admiral Bull Halsey:

TOTAL AND COMPLETE DEFEAT OF JAPANESE FORCES
ON GUADALCANAL EFFECTED 1625 TODAY. AM
HAPPY TO REPORT COMPLIANCE WITH YOUR
ORDERS. THE TOKYO EXPRESS NO LONGER HAS A
TERMINUS ON GUADALCANAL.

Within the hour Bull Halsey's reply was received and decoded at Henderson Field:

WHEN I SENT A PATCH TO ACT AS TAILOR FOR
GUADALCANAL, I DID NOT EXPECT HIM TO REMOVE
THE ENEMY'S PANTS AND SEW IT ON SO QUICKLY.
MY THANKS AND CONGRATULATIONS TO YOU AND YOUR
MEN FOR WINNING THIS FINE VICTORY.

The news spread like wildfire across Guadalcanal. The recon platoon was bivouacked in the mountains, and the caves around them were littered with dead soldiers from Colonel Shibata's Sixty-sixth Regiment, and even Colonel Shibata himself was rotting behind a pile of rocks. Butsko heard screaming and shouting from the direction of Captain Orr's headquarters and poked his head out of his pup tent to see what was going on.

Nutsy Gafooley ran toward him, both his hands high in the air. *"It's over!"* he hollered. *"We won!"*

Butsko crawled out of the tent and put on his helmet. Nutsy leaped into the air and hugged Butsko with his arms and legs. *"It's over!"*

Butsko pried Nutsy loose. "What's over?"

Nutsy was about to say *"The war"* but knew the war wasn't over. Butsko pushed Nutsy away, and Nutsy tried to get it together in his mind.

"There ain't no more Japs on Guadalcanal, Sarge! We won!"

"Who told you that?"

"The message just came down from regiment! We beat the Nips!"

"No shit?"

"No shit!"

Butsko took off his helmet and flung it into the air. *"We won!"*

The men from the recon platoon surged out of their tents, knocking over tent poles, ripping up tent pegs, tearing canvas.

"We won!" shouted Butsko, jumping up and down.

"It's all over!" yelled Nutsy Gafooley.

The GIs went totally out of their minds. They hugged and kissed each other and danced around. The Reverend Billie Jones dropped to his knees and gave thanks to the Lord. Homer Gladley was thrilled because he thought they might start getting more chow.

Morris Shilansky ran off to buy some jungle juice for the celebration. He obtained two jugs from the mess sergeant in Fox Company and returned on the run, a jug in each hand. Everybody proceeded to get rip-roaring drunk. As night fell on Guadalcanal, the men were carousing, singing around campfires, shooting their rifles into the air. Frankie La Barbara looked into a mirror and hoped the Army nurses would still fuck him despite his broken nose. Jimmy O'Rourke wondered if the regiment would be sent to Hawaii for R&R.

All quarrels and former fistfights were forgotten. Craig Delane sat down with Corporal Gomez, whom he'd never liked, and they got wrecked together. Nutsy Gafooley and Hotshot

Stevenson wondered if Betty Grable would come to Guadalcanal with a USO show and display her famous gorgeous legs. Shaw shadowboxed in the bushes, hoping Special Services would set up a program of fights so he could get back in shape. Shilansky bought more jungle juice from a group of Louisiana moonshiners in Company M.

As the night grew older, the men became subdued. They lay around in drunken stupors, thinking of the battles they'd been through on Guadalcanal, their scrapes with death, their buddies who'd been shipped back to the States in boxes.

Bannon wanted a pass so he could go to the interior of the island and see his wife. Staggering around rocks and bushes, he looked for Butsko. Gunshots resounded across the island, and for the first time since he'd hit the Guadalcanal Beach, Bannon felt no apprehension.

He saw Butsko sitting with his back against a tree, staring off into the distance. Butsko had a jug in his hand; the features of his face were slack from so much drinking.

"How ya doing, Sarge?" Bannon asked, kneeling beside Butsko.

Butsko turned and looked at him, appearing not to recognize him for a few moments. "Not bad, kid. How're you doing?"

"Okay." Bannon wiped his mouth with the back of his hand. "Listen, I was wondering if I could get a pass to see my wife."

Butsko's answer was slurred. "I'll talk to Colonel Stockton about it tomorrow."

"Think it'll be okay?"

"How the fuck should I know?"

Bannon dropped into a sitting position on the ground and played with the dirt. It was still moist from the rain, which stopped three days earlier, and clouds in the sky obscured the moon and stars.

"Gee," said Bannon. "I can't believe it's over."

"It ain't over yet," Butsko said. "Won't be over for a long time."

"I meant here on Guadalcanal. It's over here at least."

"This is only the first round," Butsko said, and then he burped. "There's gonna be a lot more rounds."

"Where do you think we'll go now?"

Butsko tightened his grip on the jug and raised it to his lips. "How the fuck should I know?"

Butsko gulped some jungle juice, then passed the jug to Bannon, who took a swig. It was awful, like fermented garbage juice, but it burned all the way down and made Bannon feel cozy.

"Nice night, huh, Sarge?" Bannon asked, looking at the treetops.

"Real nice, kid," Butsko replied, reaching for the jug. "The very best."

Watch for

GREEN HELL

next novel in the new RAT BASTARDS series from Jove
coming in May!